Tin House
MAGAZINE

Volume 13, Number 3

The "scientific" life itself has much to do with maybes, and human life at large has everything to do with them.

—WILLIAM JAMES

From Tin House Books

NO ONE

a novel by Gwenaëlle Aubry
Translated by Trista Selous

No One is the portrait of a man without a true self, a one-time distinguished lawyer and member of the Paris bar who became a drifter and frequent visitor to mental institutions. This beautifully written novel is a vivid exploration of a particular experience of mental illness and what it can reveal more generally about human experience.

"A bright gem . . . *No One* rises up out of a field of European contemporary writing with an uncanny clarity."

—from the introduction by Rick Moody

Available Now :: Trade Paper :: $12.95

HOT ART: CHASING THIEVES AND DETECTIVES THROUGH THE SECRET WORLD OF STOLEN ART

by Joshua Knelman

Sweeping and fast-paced, *Hot Art* is a major work of investigative journalism and a thrilling joyride into a mysterious criminal world. The book traces Joshua Knelman's five-year immersion in the shadowy world of art theft, where he uncovers a devious game that takes him from Egypt to Los Angeles, New York to London, and back again, through a web of deceit, violence, and corruption.

"Joshua Knelman has painted a luminous portrait of the interconnected world of thieves, cops, and lawyers obsessed with stolen art . . . Knelman's gifts as an investigator and storyteller drip from every page. Hot Art? Hot book."

—Jeremy Keehn,
Associate Editor at *Harper's Magazine*

Available Now :: Trade Paper :: $16.95

For more information or to order, please go to www.tinhouse.com

THE SICKNESS

a novel by Alberto Barrera Tyszka
Translated by Margaret Jull Costa
Introduction by Chris Adrian

Dr. Miranda is faced with a tragedy: his father has been diagnosed with terminal cancer and has only a few weeks to live. He is also faced with a dilemma: How does one tell one's father he is dying? Alberto Barrera Tyszka's tender, refined novel interweaves the stories of four individuals as they try, in their own way, to come to terms with sickness in all its ubiquity.

"With riveting specificity and haunting insight, *The Sickness* probes the most vulnerable territories of the human spirit. Within them, it offers the tender illumination of a sure-handed masterful writer."

—Dr. Vincent Lam, author of *Bloodletting* and *Miraculous Cures*, winner of the Giller Prize

Available Now :: Trade Paper :: $14.95

WELCOME TO PARADISE

a novel by Mahi Binebine
Translated by Lulu Norman
Introduction by Anderson Tepper

Mahi Binebine's courageous novel takes place in Morocco, where seven would-be immigrants, pulled by the dream of a better life, gather one night near the Strait of Gibraltar to wait for a signal from traffickers that it is time to cross. *Welcome to Paradise* delivers a compassionate glimpse into the difficulties facing asylum seekers and a striking portrait of human desperation.

"At once sympathetic to a people's plight and angry with its self-delusions, this is a brave book to have written and a rich, unsettling one to read."

—*Literary Review*

Available April :: Trade Paper :: $14.95

Perfect for any writer.

September · 9781931520270 · Spiral bound · 6 x 9 · 160 pp · $13.95
full color · class/group discounts available. Distributed to the trade by Consortium.

smallbeerpress.com · facebook.com/smallbeerpress · weightlessbooks.com

SUBSCRIBE TO THE BELIEVER

AND RECEIVE, FOR FREE: A POSTER FEATURING CHARLES BURNS COVER SUBJECTS FROM THE PAST FIVE YEARS OF THE BELIEVER

To receive your bonus item, go to the website and enter the promo code "BP04" with your subscription or renewal at checkout.

BELIEVERMAG.COM/SUBSCRIBE

Tin House MAGAZINE

EDITOR IN CHIEF / PUBLISHER
Win McCormack

EDITOR	Rob Spillman
ART DIRECTOR	Janet Parker
MANAGING EDITOR	Cheston Knapp
EXECUTIVE EDITOR	Michelle Wildgen
POETRY EDITOR	Matthew Dickman
EDITOR-AT-LARGE	Elissa Schappell
POETRY EDITOR-AT-LARGE	Brenda Shaughnessy
PARIS EDITOR	Heather Hartley
EDITORIAL ASSISTANTS	Desiree Andrews, Lance Cleland, Emma Komlos-Hrobsky

CONTRIBUTING EDITORS: Dorothy Allison, Steve Almond, Aimee Bender, Charles D'Ambrosio, Brian DeLeeuw, Anthony Doerr, CJ Evans, Nick Flynn, Matthea Harvey, Jeanne McCulloch, Christopher Merrill, Rick Moody, Whitney Otto, D. A. Powell, Jon Raymond, Rachel Resnick, Peter Rock, Helen Schulman, Jim Shepard, Karen Shepard, Bill Wadsworth

DESIGNER: Diane Chonette

INTERNS: David McFarlane, Catherine Polityllo, Elizabeth Pusack, Emily Sproch, Jakob Vala

READERS: Shomit Barua, Kylie Byrd, David Cameron, Polly Dugan, Erin Gravley, Mark Hammond, Stacy Heiney, Laura Horley, Chris Keady, Emily Kiddell, Jake Kinstler, Christin Lee, Chris Leslie-Hynan, Shannon McDonald, Heidi McKye, Rachel Medrano, Amy Myer, Lindsey O'Brien, Sara Phinney, Annie Rose Shapero, Jennifer Taylor, Linda Wooly

DEPUTY PUBLISHER	Holly MacArthur
CIRCULATION DIRECTOR	Laura Howard
DIRECTOR OF PUBLICITY	Nanci McCloskey
COMPTROLLER	Janice Carter

Tin House Books

EDITORIAL ADVISOR Rob Spillman
EDITORS Meg Storey, Tony Perez, Nanci McCloskey
EDITORIAL AND PUBLICITY ASSISTANT Desiree Andrews

Tin House Magazine (ISSN 1541-521X) is published quarterly by McCormack Communications LLC, 2601 Northwest Thurman Street, Portland, OR 97210. Vol. 13, No. 3, Spring 2012. Printed by R. R. Donnelley. Send submissions (with SASE) to Tin House, P.O. Box 10500, Portland, OR 97296-0500. ©2012 McCormack Communications LLC. All rights reserved. No part of this publication may be reproduced, stored in a retrieval system, or transmitted in any form or by any means, electronic, mechanical, photocopying, recording, or otherwise, without the prior written permission of McCormack Communications LLC. Visit our Web site at www.tinhouse.com.

Basic subscription price: one year, $50.00. For subscription requests, write to P.O. Box 469049, Escondido, CA 92046-9049, or e-mail tinhouse@pcspublink.com, or call 1-800-786-3424. Additional questions, e-mail laura@tinhouse.com

Periodicals postage paid at Portland, OR 97210 and additional mailing offices.

Postmaster: Send address changes to Tin House Magazine, P.O. Box 469049, Escondido, CA 92046-9049.

Newsstand distribution through Disticor Magazine Distribution Services (disticor.com). If you are a retailer and would like to order Tin House, call Dave Kasza at 905-619-6565, fax 905-619-2903, or e-mail dkasza@disticor.com. For trade copies, contact Publisher's Group West at 800-788-3123, or e-mail orderentry@perseusbooks.com.

EDITOR'S NOTE

"Imagination is more important than knowledge," Einstein once said. On the surface, this might seem surprising coming from one of the greatest modern scientists, but Einstein didn't speak until he was four, and later in life said perhaps he should have been a locksmith. There was a universe forming inside the young Einstein's head. His desire to open doors, to chart the world, dissect it, understand it, and make order out of chaos, echoes the experience of creation found in writing.

Writers, too, work in solitude, inside their heads, solving problems and stitching together worlds. They calculate the geometry of human relationships, the velocity of a falling expectation, the force of a breaking heart. And yet, despite similarities, scientists and writers often find themselves grappling not only with the world but also with one another.

Given the overlap of literary and scientific worlds, we at Tin House asked ourselves, why are they at odds? And could we, as a literary magazine, do anything to clear the air?

Writers from both camps excitedly took up our challenge and, we think, succeeded in bridging the supposed divide. Andrea Barrett, who has been twining fiction and science for more than twenty years, braids the narrative of one man's single-minded pursuit of genetic coding during the onset of World War II. Synethesia, the curious condition of overlapping senses that causes people to hear colors, or see tastes, seems like the stuff of fiction, but Rachel Riederer's investigation proves it is in fact a very real, and very odd, medical condition. Karl Iagnemma, a novelist who also works as a professor of robotics at MIT, emerged from his lab with a whimsical look at how to build a robot that also tells us something about making art. And the poets wrote about everything from nanobots to body doubles.

As with writing and science, the act of reading, at bottom, is about exploration, looking at the world through a new lens, be it a microscope or a point of view, and being open to discovery. So join us. Turn the page and unlock something inside you.

CONTENTS

ISSUE #51 / SCIENCE FAIR

Fiction

Julia Elliott
LIMBS ← *For the past few months, nanobots have been rebuilding Elise's degenerating neural structures.* 12

Andrea Barrett
THE PARTICLES ← *Not long after midnight, a faraway gleam, which may have been a periscope caught by the light of the moon, caused two women to shriek.* 52

Etgar Keret
PARALLEL UNIVERSES, TRANSLATED BY MIRIAM SHLESINGER ← *There are some parallel universes where I'm having sex with a horse, and ones where I've won the lottery.* 128

Namwali Serpell
BOTTOMS UP ← *This would never have happened if it weren't for herpes.* 177

Poetry

Jessica Johnson
Tonight's Anatomy 30

Megan Levad
Nanobots 39
Why We Live in the Dark Ages 40

Patricia Lockwood
An Animorph Enters the Doggie-Dog World 94
The Computer Plays a Game of Chess 96

Jared Harel
My Body Double Goes to the Home Depot 130
My Body Double Tells Me I'm Away on Business 131

Dara Weir
When I Stared Down into an Empty Ballistic Missile Silo One Day in Nebraska 163

Kiki Petrosino
I Love You, No Discussion 184
Moon-Wrapped Fragrant Spareribs 185

Donna Hunt
Dimension 5 205
Dimension 0 206

NEW VOICE ~ POETRY

Katy Chrisler
Ness 51

Interviews

Robert Krulwich and Jad Abumrad

The hosts of the hit show Radiolab *talked with Tony Perez, of Tin House Books, about sound effects, stories, science, and that warm thing that glows a little—a friendship.* 132

Features

Alan Lightman

THE TEMPORARY UNIVERSE ✦ *The novelist yearns for the eternal; the physicist knows better.* 31

Rebecca Newberger Goldstein

THE HARD PROBLEM OF CONSCIOUSNESS AND THE SOLITUDE OF THE POET ✦ *There's more to the mind's eye than meets, well, the eye.* 42

Amy Leach

THE WILD WHAT ✦ *An amateur astronomer daydreams about constellations and lets her imagination run rampant.* 98

Justin Nobel

ATOMIC CITY ✦ *The secret, sordid history of America's forgotten nuclear disaster, and the lovers who caused it.* 120

Jesse Lichtenstein

THE SYNTHESIZERS ✦ *The revolutionary science being done in the beginning of this, the biological century, will make your head spin.* 147

Karl Iagnemma

HOW TO BUILD A ROBOT ✦ *Domo arigato for the guide that explores the similarities between scientific and artistic inspiration.* 166

Rachel Riederer

UNCOMMON SENSE ✦ *Sorting out the mixed-up signals of synesthesia, the sensitive soul's disease of choice.* 186

Clancy Martin
BOYHOOD ADVENTURES IN THE MAGICAL SCIENCE OF ASTRAL PROJECTION ⁃ *Plus nitrous oxide.* 198

Lost & Found

Gabriel Blackwell
ON LAWRENCE WESCHLER'S *Mr. Wilson's Cabinet of Wonder* ⁃ *A tour of the Museum of Jurassic Technology's assortment of curios entraps you in a web of dubious references.* 104

Alexandra Kleeman
ON RACTER'S *The Policeman's Beard is Half Constructed: Computer Prose and Poetry* ⁃ *Has a computer attained Eliot's ideal of a poet without a personality.* 107

Cheston Knapp
ON C. P. SNOW'S *The Two Cultures and the Scientific Revolution* and *The Third Culture: Beyond the Scientific Revolution*, ED. JOHN BROCKMAN ⁃ *Attempting to bridge the dizzying divide between science and art.* 110

Michelle Legro
ON AMBROISE PARÉ'S *On Monsters and Marvels* ⁃ *From the tame to the tetratoid, a compendium of sixteenth-century birth defects.* 114

Jessica Handler
ON LULU HURST'S *Lulu Hurst (The Georgia Wonder) Writes Her Autobiography, and for the First Time Explains and Demonstrates the Great Secret of Her Marvelous Power* ⁃ *The magnetic girl's mysterious aura attracts attention. And more!* 117

Readable Feast

Deborah Blum
THE FLAVOR OF BLUE
The ailing business of dying food. 207

Julia Elliott

FICTION

LIMBs

On a gauzy day in early autumn, senior citizens stroll around the pear orchard on robot legs. Developed by the Japanese, manufactured by Boeing, one of the latest installments in the mechanization of geriatric care, Leg Intuitive Motion Bionics (LIMBs) have made it all the way to Gable, South Carolina, to this little patch of green behind Eden Village Nursing Home. And Elise Mood is getting the hang of them. Every time her brain sends a signal to her actual legs, the exoskeletal LIMBs respond, marching her along in the gold light.

A beautiful day—even though Elise can smell chickens from the poultry complex down the road and exhaust from the interstate, even though the pear trees in this so-called orchard bear no fruit. The mums are in bloom. Bees glitter above the beds. And a skinny man comes toward her, showing off his mastery of the strap-on LIMBs.

"Elise." He squints at her. "You still got it. Prettiest girl at Eden Village."

She flashes her dentures but says nothing.

"You remember me. Ulysses Stukes, aka Pip. We went to the BBQ place that time."

Elise nods, but she doesn't remember. And she's relieved to see a tech nurse headed her way, the one with the platinum hair.

"Come on, Miss Elise," she says. "You got Memories at three."

Elise points at the plastic Power Units strapped to her lower limbs.

"You're gonna walk it today," says the nurse. "I think you got it down."

Elise grins. Only three people from the Dementia Ward were chosen for the test group. So far, she's the only one with nerve signals strong enough to stimulate the sensors. As she strides along amid flowers and bees, she rolls the name around on her tongue—Pip Stukes—recalling something familiar in the wry twist of his mouth.

For the past few months, nanobots have been rebuilding Elise's degenerative neural structures, refortifying the cell production of her microglia in an experimental medical procedure. Now she sits in the Memory Lane Neurotherapy lounge, strapped into a magnetoencephalographic (MEG) scanner that looks like a 1950s beauty parlor hair-drying unit. As a young female therapist monitors a glowing map of Elise's brain, a male spits streams of nonsense at her.

"Corn bread," he says. "Corn-fed coon. Corny old colonel with corns on his feet."

Elise sniggers. Who was that colonel she knew? Not a colonel, but a corporal. She once kissed him during a thunderstorm. But she was all of sixteen and he was fresh from Korea, drenched in mystique and skinny from starving in a bamboo cage. Elise vaguely recollects his inflation into a three-hundred-pounder who worked the register at Stukes Feed and Seed. Pip Stukes.

In a flash, she remembers the night they ate barbecue together, back when the world was still green, back when Hog Heaven hung paper lanterns over the picnic tables and Black River Road was dirt. After wiping his lips with a paper napkin, he'd said, *You ought to be my wife,* in his half-joking way—and she'd dropped her fork.

"Look," says the female therapist. "We've got action between the inferior temporal and the frontal."

"Let's try another round," says the male, the one with the ponytail so little and scraggly that Elise wants to snip it off with a pair of scissors.

"One unit of BDNF," says the female. "And self-integration image therapy with random auditory sequencing and a jolt of EphB2."

The boy clamps Elise's head into the padded dome, and the room goes dark. She hears birdsong and distant traffic as a screen lights up to display a photo of a couple, the girl decked out in a wiggle dress and heels, the man slouching beside her in baggy tweed, his face obscured by a straw hat. At first Elise thinks they're walking on water, but then she realizes they're standing at the edge of a pier, a lake glinting all around them.

> **She was all of sixteen and he was fresh from Korea, drenched in mystique and skinny from starving in a bamboo cage.**

Something about the lake makes her gasp, and Elise wonders if the young woman in the photograph is her daughter—though she's pretty sure she never had a daughter—so maybe it's her mother's daughter, which means she and the girl are the same person.

"We've got action all over," says the female therapist, "mostly in the temporal and right parietal lobes."

"Emotional memory and spatial identity," says the male, tapping a rhythm on the desk with his fingertips.

Elise glares at him for breaking her stream of thought, then looks back up at the image, noting a streak of silver in the upper right corner.

"Boat," she whispers.

And then she sees him clear as day: Pip Stukes at the wheel of the boat, his hair swept into a ducktail by the wind.

In the pear orchard, Elise takes long strides, easy as thought, around the bed of mums. Scanning the lawn for Pip Stukes, she notes a cluster of wheelchair-bound patients idling at the edge of the flower bed, two women and a sleeping man, his shoulders slumped forward, his chin resting on his chest.

"Hey, good-lookin', what you got cookin'?" Pip Stukes struts toward her on cyborg legs. His eye sockets look delicate, parchment skin shrunk down to the bone. While one of his eyes shines as blue as a tropical sea, the other is frosted with glaucoma. But Pip still flirts like a demon, sadness nestled under the happy talk.

Elise blushes and Pip laughs, stands with his hip cocked.

"Pretty day for a walk." He holds out his arm and she takes it.

> Elise sits by the lake on a towel in early spring, delighted to see that she's young again.

He leads her into a stand of planted pine. Interstate 95 drones, but Elise thinks she hears a river. Looking for a thread of blue, she gazes through the trees, but all she sees is the blurry outline of a brick building. A crow flutters down in a shaft of green light.

And Pip turns to her with an aching look from long ago.

"Elise."

She studies him, mentally peeling back layers of wrinkled skin to glimpse the shining young man inside. She thinks he may have been *the one*, the dark shape in the bed beside her when she came gasping from the depths of a bad dream.

She practices the phrase in her head first—*Are you my husband?*—but her lips twitch when she tries to say it.

"What?" says Pip.

And then a male tech nurse, alerted by their RFID alarms, rushes into the patch of woods to retrieve them.

Elise sits by the lake on a towel in early spring, delighted to see that she's young again. As the sun sinks behind the tree line, she shivers, waiting for someone. She sees a wet glimmer of motion out past the end of the pier, a lithe young man doing tricks in the water. He crawls dripping from the lake, a merman with seal black hair and familiar green eyes. As he inches toward her, his tail, a long fishy appendage glistening with aqua scales, swishes behind him in the sand.

Elise wakes, panting, in her semi-electric bed. She reaches into the dark, claws at the aluminum railing. She's cold, her blanket wadded beneath her feet. And her roommate moans, a steady animal keening. The night nurse drifts in with pills in tiny cups. Though Elise can't see her, she knows her voice, low and soothing like a sheep's. The night nurse fixes her blanket, checks her diaper, gives her a drink of water, and then slips out of the room. Now her roommate's snoring. The air conditioner hums. And Elise lies awake, thinking about the beautiful swimmer from her dream.

Elise can smell the stuffiness of Eden Village Nursing Home only when she returns from being outside for a while. It's like they've shellacked the floors with urine and Lysol. And in the cafeteria, some gravy is always boiling, spiked with the sweat and waste and blood of the dying, all the juices that leak from withering people—huge cauldrons of gravy that emit a meaty, medicinal steam.

Now that Elise can walk, now that she's thinking a little faster, she feels up to exploring. She wants to find the room where Pip Stukes lives, ask him point-blank if he's the man she married.

Someone's approaching down the endless hallway, a speck swelling bigger and bigger until it transforms into a nurse, a boy with a golden dab of beard.

"Looking for the Dogwood Library?" he says. "Elvis and the Chipmunks?" He points toward a small corridor, then shuffles off into nonexistence.

Peering down the passageway, Elise sees a parlor: wingback chairs, sofas, a crowd of patients in wheelchairs. She wills her strap-on LIMBs to move and, after a heartbeat pause, lurches down the hall. Over by a makeshift stage, a group of wheelchair-bound patients watches some middle-aged men set up equipment. A few people with LIMBs weave amid the furnishings. Elise recognizes a tall woman with bald spots and a stubby old man with big ears. She creeps behind a potted palm to watch Elvis and the Chipmunks take the stage. Three large plush rodents sporting high pompadours, they jump into a brisk, twittering version of "Jailhouse Rock." Elise is about to leave in disgust when she spots a man slumped in a wheelchair, dozing, his face so familiar that the shock of it interrupts the signals pulsing from her legs into the sensors of her Power Units. She collapses onto a brocade couch. Sits there panting in the blotchy light. Then she calms herself and looks the man over. She remembers the hawk nose, the big, creased forehead.

The Chipmunks croon "Love Me Tender" in their earsplitting rodent way, and Elise snorts. The man in the wheelchair had a great voice, could play guitar by ear. All those summer evenings they spent on the porch have been streamlined into archetypes and filed away in different sections of her cerebral cortex. And now the memories come trickling out. She remembers the sound of the porch fan and the smell of the lake and the feel of his hand on the back of her neck. She recalls swimming under stars and singing folk songs and drinking wine until their heads floated off their necks.

Elise steps around a coffee table heaped with *Reader's Digests*. She studies the pink bulges of the man's closed eyes, the blanket draped over his legs, the big, fleshy head, humming with mysterious thoughts. The mouth is what strikes her hardest, the lips full, just a quirk feminine. When he opens his eyes and she sees the strange green, she knows it's him, the man who once kissed her in a birch canoe, moonlight twitching on the water.

"Who are you?" she says, the words pouring miraculously from her tongue.

He studies her, and she fears he's been drained dry, all of his memories siphoned by therapists into that electric box, where they bump around like trapped moths.

He makes a gurgling sound, small and goatish. His left eye is blighted with red veins. His hands rest on his knees, and she wonders if he can move them at all.

"Are you my husband?" she says.

The man's tongue pokes out and then retreats back into the cave of his mouth. He grunts. His left hand closes into a fist.

"I thought you were dead," she says.

"Bwa," he says, but then a nurse seizes his wheelchair, jerks him around, and trundles him off toward the corridor. Elise staggers in a panic and her LIMBs malfunction, leaving her crumpled on the carpet as the chipmunks mock her with "Heartbreak Hotel."

She pulls herself up, squats, then stands, wills her legs to move fast, and they do, speeding her along like a power-walker, but then a CNA with dyed black hair stops her. Scans her tag, beeps the Dementia Ward, and shuffles her back to the place she's supposed to be.

Hands folded in her lap, Elise slumps in the MEG scanner. Groggy from an antipsychotic called Vivaquel, she's having a hard time concentrating on what the therapists are saying.

"Barbecue bubba," says the boy. "Magnolia, moonshine, Maw and Paw."

"Very original," says the girl. "How about some limbic work? Aural olfactory?"

"Whatever," says the boy.

"Doo-wop and gardenias." The girl giggles. "Who the hell makes this shit up?"

Elise wishes they'd quit flirting and get on with it. She has half a mind to tell the boy that he'd be attractive with a decent haircut, but she doesn't. She sits with her arms crossed until the boy slips in her ear buds and clamps a plastic cup over her nose. In minutes Elise smells sickly sweet aerosol air freshener. She coughs, and they lower her olfactory levels. As the Everly Brothers croon "Dream" in their wistful Appalachian twang, she can't help but sway to the music, breathing in a whiff of synthetic cherry, the exact scent of a Lysol spray that was marketed in the 1980s.

She fears he's been drained dry, all of his memories siphoned by therapists into that electric box.

"She doesn't like it," says the boy.

"She's responding," says the girl. "Look at her amygdala. It's glowing."

Elise recalls a cramped hospital room that smelled of cherry Lysol, the green-eyed man hunched in a bed, looking at the wall. He dove into the lake one summer night and bashed his head against a rock. Now his legs wouldn't work right and he refused to look her in the eye. She held his balled fist in both hands and squeezed. The doctor said his motor neurons were damaged, compromising his leg muscles. The doctor went on and on about *partial recovery* and *physical therapy*, but the man didn't seem to be listening.

Elise remembers the smell of the man and the way he cleared his throat when he got nervous. She remembers how his silence filled the room every time he heard a motor boat fly by on the water. Stiffly, they'd wait for the sound to fade, and then pretend they hadn't heard it.

She wakes up with his name on her tongue: Robert Graham Mood, otherwise known as Bob. In the depths of her Vivaquel nap she saw him, swimming in the lake's brown murk, down near the silty bottom. Enormous primordial catfish flickered through the hydrilla, and Bob fed them night crawlers with his hands. Right where his sick legs used to be, Bob was growing flippers, two stunted incipient fins sprouting from his knees.

This merman *was* her husband, Elise realized, and he was swimming away from her, down toward the deepest part of the lake, where the

Morrison family's pontoon had sunk during a severe thunderstorm. The whole family had drowned: mother, father, three sons. And scuba divers swore they'd seen ghosts slithering near the wreck, glowing like electric eels.

Elise rolls onto her side. Her room has a window, but an air-conditioning unit blocks the view. And now a tech nurse is here to attach LIMBs to her scrawny legs. As he hooks up her sensors, he doesn't say one word, doesn't make eye contact: he might as well be tinkering with an old lawn mower.

Out in the pear orchard, Pip Stukes comes strutting, does a little turn around a park bench, and stoops to pluck a fistful of chrysanthemums, which he presents with a debonair smirk.

"Thank you," says Elise, shocked when the words pop out of her mouth.

"So you *can* talk!" says Pip. "I knew it. I could tell by the look in your eyes. I knew Elise Boykin was in there somewhere."

Elise Mood she wants to say, but keeps her lips zipped. Elise Boykin married Bob Mood, but Pip Stukes had refused to honor her changed name.

"Have you seen the goldfish pond?" Pip extends his arm, and she takes it in spite of herself. Curls her fingers around his bicep and gives it a squeeze, surprised by the wobble of muscle encased in the sagging skin. They amble over to the pond, which is tucked behind a stand of Canna lilies.

"Watch this," says Pip. He pulls a plastic bag from his pocket, shakes a mound of crumbs into his hand, and flings them into the water.

Elise concentrates on the oblong circle of liquid, eyeing it like an old queen gazing into a magic mirror. She sees a glimmer of orange, and then another, and another: six fish flickering up from the black depths. Lovely, greedy, they pucker their lips to suck up bits of bread.

Pip laughs and slips his arm around her, a gesture so familiar that she mechanically follows suit, twining her arm around his waist. She ought to pull away, but she doesn't.

She studies his profile and sees him as a younger man, after his grandfather died and left him the money, after the Feed and Seed shut down and he took up jogging. He'd run by her house at dawn, handsomeness emerging from his body in the form of cheekbones and muscle tone. Meanwhile, Bob slumped, staring at the TV—a man who used to hate the tube. Called it the idiot box, the shit pump, opiate of the masses. But now he said nothing, just eyeballed the screen, silence filling the house like swamp gas.

She took up smoking again, would slip down to the dock and sit with her feet in the water. She's the one who checked the catfish traps. She's the one who picked the vegetables that summer and trucked them to the market. She still sold her chowchow and blueberry jam and eggs from the chickens whose house needed a new roof. She sold azalea seedlings to the Yankees who were buying up every last waterfront lot on the lake. After Bob's accident, they'd sold fifty acres of their land, the woods shrinking around them, big houses popping up in every bay.

One day in July she took a break to go swimming. Just before Bob's accident, she'd bought a French-cut one-piece that now seemed shameless—too young for forty-three—but she was alone in the cove. She dove into the water and swam out to the floating dock. Let the sun dry her hair, which had darkened to auburn over the years. And then Pip Stukes whisked by in his new motorboat, a dolphin blue Savage Electra. He looked sharp in aviator sunglasses, slender and tan, a cigarette clenched in his teeth.

Elise eats every bit of her supper, fast, even the creamed corn. Remembering the ears of sweet corn Bob used to roast on the grill, she swallows the filthy goop. Smiles at the CNA when he sweeps up her tray. Sits waiting in bed, listening to her roommate smack up her gruel. Then she gets up and teeters toward her LIMBs, which rest against a Lazy-Boy. Panting, she sits in the chair and grapples for one of the units, grabs it by the upper thigh and drags it to her, shocked by how light it is. She's been watching the tech nurse, knows exactly how to strap the contraptions onto her legs, fastens the Velcro and then a hundred little metal snaps. She stands up. Takes a test run around the room. Pokes her head out into the hall, looks both ways, and then lurches into the white light.

Since most of the Dementia Ward nurses are in the dining room with patients, Elise has a clear shot down the hall. She makes it all the way to the main desk without incident, then stands, baffled, trying to remember which passage she took the time she came upon Robert Graham Mood. She recalls a different kind of fluorescent light, bluer than usual, a lower ceiling. That's the one, she thinks, the one with the green wall. Elise ambles down the hall, finds the library. Over by the front desk, a solitary CNA reads a magazine.

Elise recognizes the corridor down which that bitch of a nurse took her husband, a man she thought was dead. She strides down the hallway, peeks into dim rooms, sees lumps curled on beds, aged figures zoned out before televisions. When a wheelchair emerges from one of the doorways, her heart catches, but it's not Robert Graham Mood. She keeps walking like she knows where she's going, nods whenever she passes a nurse. The hallway narrows. At the end of the hall, she spots a nurse's station around the corner, the CNA at the desk bent over a gadget.

Elise squats, scampers like a crab around the desk, almost laughing at the ease of it, and enters the little hall where the severely disabled are stashed away. She sniffs, the burn of disinfectant stronger here. And then she peers into each room until she finds him, three doors down on the left, her husband, Bob, drooping in his wheelchair before a muted TV.

She remembers that summer—when the stubble on his face grew into a dirty beard and his sideburns fanned into wild whiskers. Jimmy Carter was floundering, the oil running out, those hostages still rotting in Iran. And Bob, TV-obsessed, sat wordless as a bear. Soviets in Afghanistan and J.R. Ewing shot and Bob's legs as weak as they were the day before. She couldn't keep up with the okra picking. Blight had taken the tomatoes. One of their hens had an abscess that needed to be lanced. It wasn't Bob's sick legs that had pushed her over the edge, but his refusal to talk about the details of their shared life.

Elise steps between Bob and the TV, just like she did that day in July when she'd had enough of his silence.

His eyes stray from the screen—still the strange green, steeped in obscure feelings.

"Robert Graham Mood," she says. And he blinks.

"Elise." His voice rattles like a rusty cotton gin, but to her the word sounds exquisitely feminine, the name of some flower that blooms for just half a day, almost too small to see but insanely perfumed in the noon heat.

"How long have you been here?" she asks.

He looks her up and down.

"You're my husband?" she says.

"Yes," Bob rasps. The air conditioner drones and they stare at each other.

Elise is about to touch his arm when a CNA rushes in, smiles, speaks softly as to a cornered kitten, and takes her firmly by the arm.

When Elise wakes up from her Vivaquel nap, a boy looms over her—Robert Graham Mood, a sleek young stunner with red hair. She frowns, for Bob's hair had been black, his lips plump and just a tad crooked. She thinks she may be dead at last, Bob's golden spirit hovering to welcome her to the next phase.

"Mom," says the boy.

When her eyes adjust, she notes lines around his eyes, the bulge of a budding gut. Not the father but the son.

"Just give her a few minutes," says the nurse. "According to the neurotherapists, she's made enormous strides. Her roaming incident shows some planning, thinking ahead, which indicates enhanced semantic memory."

> She thinks she may be dead at last, Bob's golden spirit hovering to welcome her to the next phase.

"And you think she knows he's my father?"

"She knows he's somebody. Found him halfway across the complex. I had no idea they'd even been married."

"They still are, technically, you know."

Elise snorts at this, but nobody pays one bit of attention.

"Of course. Very odd, though it happens from time to time. Married people in different wings. We don't do couples at Eden Village."

"It really didn't matter until now," says the boy, sinking into the chair by the bed. "I didn't think the therapies would lead to anything, with her so far gone. But still, I figured *why not?*"

Elise claws at her throat, her tongue as dead as a slab of pickled beef. She knows the boy is her son, but she can't remember when he was born or how he got to be grown so fast.

"Mom," says the boy, that familiar tinge of whininess in his voice, and it comes to her: her son home from college for a few days, pacing from window to window, restless as a cooped rooster. He said the house felt smaller than he remembered. Stayed out on the boat all day with the spoiled-rotten Morrison boys. Acted skittish when he came in from the water, pained eyes hiding behind the soft flounce of his bangs. He'd gone vegetarian, looked as skinny as Gandhi, and she fed him fried okra and butter beans.

As the two of them sat at the kitchen table making conversation, Bob's silence leaked from the boy's old bedroom like nuclear radiation from a triple-sealed vault—the kind of poison you can't smell but that sinks into your cells, making you mutant from the inside out.

LIMBs

"Bye, Mom." The boy pats her crimped hand. "I'll be back soon." And they leave her in the semidarkness, window shades down, unable to tell if it's night or day.

The therapists have strapped her into the MEG scanner and popped in a retro-TV sense-enhanced module. As the therapists play footsy under the desk, Elise turns her attention to a montage of *The Incredible Hulk* episodes, breathing in smells of Hamburger Helper and Bounce fabric-softening sheets. She never cooked Hamburger Helper; she never wasted money on fabric softeners. She never sat through a complete episode of *The Incredible Hulk*, but the seething mute giant reminds her of Bob. Of course, Bob watched it religiously after his accident, and she remembers peering into his room, standing there in the hallway for just one minute to watch the green monster rage. Then she'd close the door, drift out into the night with her pack of cigarettes.

> The first time Pip took her to his secret island she drank until her head thrummed.

Now the screen goes dim and Elise hears crickets, smells cigarette smoke and a hint of gas. Pip's boat had a leak that summer, and everything they did was enveloped in the haze of gasoline. What did they do? Zigzagged over the lake. Dropped the anchor and sat rocking in the waves, drinking wine coolers and watching for herons. Then they'd drift up to this island he knew. The first time Pip took her to his secret island—the one with the feral goats and rotting shed—she drank until her head thrummed. Bob had not said one word for sixty-two days. Each night before bed she'd stick her head into the toxic glow of his room to say good night, and he'd grunt. She kept track of the days. Ticked them off with a pencil on a yellow legal pad.

He sat there glued to the TV, waiting for news on the hostages, wondering if Afghanistan had turned Communist yet, trying to figure out who shot J.R. She even caught him watching soaps in the middle of the day—*Like sands through the hourglass, so are the days of our lives*—foolishness he used to laugh at. Now he sat grimly as Marlena mourned the death of her premature son and her marriage to a two-timing lawyer fell apart. The dismal music, the tedious melodrama, and the flimsy yet opulent interiors sank Elise into a malaise. And she'd leave Bob in the eternal twilight of the TV.

Out in the humming afternoon heat, Elise had started talking to herself. *Goddamn grass*, she'd hiss. *Bastard ants*. One day, in the itchy okra patch, where unpicked pods had swollen into eight-inch monsters, where fire ants marched up and down the sticky stalks, crawling onto her hands and stinging her in the tender places between her fingers, Elise ripped off her sun hat and shrieked. Then she stormed inside and changed into her swimsuit. Without looking in on Bob, she grabbed her smokes and jogged out to the cove, walked waist-deep into the water while taking deep drags. *Fuck*, she hissed—a trashy cuss she never indulged in. And then she felt drained of wrath.

She tossed her cigarette butt and swam out to the floating dock, where the water was cooler. Pip Stukes came knifing through the waves, skinny again, his sunglasses two mirrors that hid his sad eyes, and Elise crawled up into his glittery boat. She swigged wine coolers like they were Cokes and laughed a high, dry laugh that was half cough. She lost track of herself: let another man kiss her on an island where shadowy goats watched from the woods. She stayed out past dusk and got a sunburn, a bright red affliction that she didn't feel until the next day.

When she came in that night, Bob didn't ask where she'd been. Didn't say one word. Just kept clearing his throat over and over, like he had something stuck in it—a bit of gristle in his windpipe, a dry spot on his glottis, acid gushing up from his bad stomach. He cleared his throat when she served him supper (one hour later than usual). Cleared his throat when she changed his sheets and punched his pillow with her small fist. Cleared his throat when she quietly shut his door, and kept on clearing his throat as she brushed her teeth and crawled into the bed they'd shared for twenty years.

Elise's skin blistered and peeled. For several nights she lay in bed rolling it into little balls that she'd flick into the darkness. And then, one week later, her skin tender, the pale pink of a seashell's interior, she went off with Pip Stukes again.

"I figured out how they catch us," whispers Pip.

Elise widens her eyes. As they take a little turn around the birdbath, Elise scans the crowd for wheelchairs. They sit down on a concrete bench.

"Feel that bump on your arm?" Pip slides the tip of his index finger over her forearm, stops when he reaches that hard little pimple that won't go away. Maybe it's a wart. Maybe it's a mole. Elise doesn't know what it is, but she blushes when he touches the spot.

"Microchip," he says. "My son put one in his dog's ear. A good idea. Except we're not dogs."

Pip laughs, the old, dark laugh that lingers in the air like a gas you can almost see. Elise can't remember Pip's children. And what about his wife? He must have had one. But now she's unsettled by his eyes, the clear one at least, which drills her with a secret force while the other stares at nothing.

Something about his laugh and fading smile, something about the slant of light and the wash of distant traffic remind her—of what, she's not sure, not until a blush spreads from her hairline to her chest, not until she sees Pip walking naked from the lake, sees the scar on his chest, the sad apron of belly skin, relic of his previous life as a fat man. And then she remembers. He did have a wife, a girl named Emmy from Silver. They'd had two boys and divorced. Emmy had kept the house in Manning and Pip moved out to the lake house, free to whip around on the empty water.

For two months they boated out to the little island almost every afternoon. Got sucked into the oblivion of the dog days: shrieking cicadas and heat like a blanket of wet velvet that made you feel half asleep. It was easy to sip wine coolers until you couldn't think. Easy to swim naked in water warm as spit. In September they finally went to his lake house, a fancy place with lots of gleaming brass, the TV built into a clever cabinet, a stash of top-notch liquor behind the wet bar. Showing her around, Pip pointed out every last effect, all bought with his grandfather's money. Something bothered her: the way he smoked afterward in the air-conditioned bedroom, the way he slapped her rear like a rake on *Dallas*. Hiding his saggy gut under the sheet, he kept checking himself out in the mirror. He ran his fingers through his gelled hair.

As Pip went on about the Corvette he wanted to buy, she thought about Bob, how, in the past, he was always quietly tinkering with something. And then poor Pip started up on Korea, told her about coming back home after starving in that bamboo cage, eating for a solid year in a trance, waking up one day to the shock of three hundred pounds. He'd lost the weight and gotten married. But then he gained it back, got divorced, lost it again—his whole life staked to that tedious fluctuation.

That night when she got home, Bob turned from the television and spoke to her.

"Look at this joker," he said, pointing at Ronald Reagan, the movie star who was running for president, the one who looked like a handsome lizard.

The next day Bob bathed himself and rolled out onto the screened porch. Watching the lake, they shelled field peas all morning. She knew that Pip would come flying out of the blue in his boat, and when he did, Bob cleared his throat and said nothing.

Pip's boat appeared every afternoon for the next week. They'd hold their breath and wait for the high whine of his motor to fade.

Bob started doing his leg exercises, made an appointment with the hot-shot therapist in Columbia. In two years he could get around the house with a walker. By Reagan's second term he was ambling with a cane. He took care of the chickens, started dabbling with quail. And every year they sold more land, acre by acre, until all they had was their cottage—mansions towering on every side, the lake a circus of Jet Skis, houseboats so big they blotted out the sun.

Bob and Elise got old on the lake, their son breezing in twice a year to say hello. And they planned to die there, right on the water, even though the place was turning to shit.

> **They planned to die there, right on the water, even though the place was turning to shit.**

Elise fingers the scab on her arm. It's been a week since she gouged the microchip out with the sharp scissors she nabbed from the Dementia Ward desk. All this time she's kept the fleck of metal in her locket and nobody's said one word. The nurses know better than to touch her locket, thirtieth-anniversary gift from Bob—not a heart, like you'd expect, just a circle of gold that opens via a hinge, a clip of Bob's gray hair stuffed inside as a sweet joke. *To thirty more years of glorious monotony*, Bob had said, and they'd laughed, opened another jar of mulberry wine.

A tech nurse escorts Elise out to the pear orchard. Just as soon as she's released into the flock of seniors, Pip Stukes comes swaggering across the grass.

"Hey, good lookin', what you got cookin'?"

Elise takes his arm as usual and they promenade across stepping-stones, over to their favorite bench. Pip talks about his son, who dropped by this morning with Pip's grandbaby, now a grown girl. He talks about the artificial bacon he had for breakfast and the blue jay that perched on his windowsill. Then he goes quiet and just stares at her, filling the space between them with sighs. It's warm for November. The mums have dried up and the pear trees drop their last red leaves. When Pip leans in to kiss her, Elise embraces him, keeping her lips off limits while hugging him close enough to slip the microchip into his shirt pocket.

She leans back and smiles. It feels good to be invisible.

"You remember that island?" says Pip.

Elise nods, touches his cheek, stands upon her robot legs, and then walks off into the Canna lilies. Behind the dead flowers are two big dumpsters, and, if she's calculated correctly, a door leading into the Dogwood Library.

When Bob wakes up, she's standing there in a shaft of late-morning light, a small-boned woman wearing strap-on plastic Power Units like something from the Sci-fi Channel, her gray hair cropped into an elfin cap.

"Elise," he rasps.

"Bob," she says.

His thick lids slide down over watery eyes.

"Bob?" she says. He shifts in his chair but won't wake up.

She checks his pulse, grabs his blanket from the bed, and tucks it around him. Makes sure he's got on proper socks under his corduroy slippers. And then she rolls him toward the door.

Though Elise has spent many an afternoon wrinkling her nose at the smell of chickens, she isn't prepared for the endless stream of barracks southwest on Highway 301: three giant buildings as long as trains and leaking a stench so shocking she can't believe it doesn't jolt Bob from his nap. Mouth-breathing, she hustles to get past the nastiness, fingering the button that operates his chair, kicking it into high gear, the one the nurses use when they're in a tizzy.

She's been walking for an hour, on a strip of highway shoulder that comes and goes, smooth sailing for a mile and then she'll hit a patch of bumpy asphalt and veer onto the road. A number of motorists have passed—mostly big trucks, pickups, the occasional SUV—and she worries that some upstanding citizen has already called Eden Village. She expects a cop car to roll up any minute. Expects to see the officer put on his gentle smile, the one he uses with feeble-minded people and lunatics, geezers and little children. She would prefer a back road, some decent air and greenery, but she knows she wouldn't remember the way.

If she recalls correctly, 301 is almost a straight shot to the water. Though her legs don't hurt, her shoulders do, an ache that dips into her bones. Her fingers cramp as they grip the handles of Bob's chair. And she's too thirsty to spit. She imagines sweating glasses of sweet tea, cold Coca-Cola in little bottles, lemonade with hunks of fruit floating in the pitcher. She remembers the time she took Bob to meet her grandmother. They drank from a pump on the old wraparound porch, drawing cool spring water up from the earth. She recalls sipping from the garden hose and tasting rubber. Remembers the special flavor of Bob's musty canteen, the one they always took camping. She and Bob once hiked up Looking Glass Rock, crouched under a waterfall with their mouths open, taking giant gulps, the whole mountain wet with dew. Hosts of tiny frogs had clung to the stone, suckers on their toes.

When they get to the lake Elise wants to roll Bob to the end of their old pier. It'll be dusk by then, she thinks, catfish crowding in the shallows. When Bob wakes up she wants him to see water on every side, vast and black with the sky in pink turmoil, as though it's just the two of them, out there floating in a little boat.

Jessica Johnson

TONIGHT'S ANATOMY

The ruffled heart: a sea
The iris-flinch: anemone
Counterbalanced ribs: give way
Between the hips: the drifted snow
The thumbnail: dawn
The neck: bastille
Fingertips: foment unrest
The risen vein: a rope across
An awkward load: the fist

ESSAY

THE TEMPORARY UNIVERSE

Alan Lightman

At odds with our nature

Last August my oldest daughter got married. The ceremony took place at a farm in the little town of Wells, Maine, against the backdrop of rolling green meadows, a white wooden barn, and the sounds of a classical guitar. Each member of the wedding party stepped down a sloping hill toward the chuppah, while the guests sat in simple white chairs bordered by rows of sunflowers. The air was redolent with the smells of maples and grasses and other growing things. It was a marriage we had all hoped for. The two families had known each other with affection for years. Radiant in her white dress, a white dahlia in her hair, my daughter asked to hold my hand as we walked down the aisle.

It was a perfect picture of utter joy, and utter tragedy. Because I wanted my daughter back as she was at age ten, or twenty. As we moved together toward that lovely arch that would swallow us all, other scenes flashed through my mind: my daughter in first grade holding a starfish as big as herself, her smile missing a tooth; my daughter on the back of my bicycle as we rode to a river to drop stones in the water; my daughter telling me that she'd started her

first period. Now, she was thirty. I could see lines in her face.

I don't know why we long so for permanence, why the fleeting nature of things so disturbs. With futility, we cling to the old wallet long after it has fallen apart. We visit and revisit the old neighborhood where we grew up, searching for the remembered grove of trees and the little fence. We clutch our old photographs. In our churches and synagogues and mosques, we pray to the everlasting and eternal. Yet, in every nook and cranny, nature screams at the top of her lungs that nothing lasts, that it is all passing away. All that we see around us, including our own bodies, is shifting and evaporating and one day will be gone. Where are the one billion people who lived and breathed in the year 1800, only two short centuries ago?

The evidence seems overly clear. In the summer months, mayflies drop by the billions within twenty-four hours of birth. Drone ants perish in two weeks. Daylilies bloom and then wilt, leaving dead, papery stalks. Forests burn down, replenish themselves, then disappear again. Ancient stone temples and spires flake in the salty air, fracture and fragment, dwindle to spindly nubs, and eventually dissolve into nothing. Coastlines erode and crumble. Glaciers slowly but surely grind down the land. Once, the continents were joined. Once, the air was ammonia and methane.

> I don't know why we long so for permanence, why the fleeting nature of things so disturbs.

Now it is oxygen and nitrogen. In the future, it will be something else. The sun is depleting its nuclear fuel. And just look at our own bodies. In the middle years and beyond, skin sags and cracks. Eyesight fades. Hearing diminishes. Bones shrink and turn brittle.

Just the other day, I had to retire my favorite shoes, a pair of copper-colored wingtips that I purchased thirty years ago to wear at a friend's graduation. For the first few years, all I had to do to keep the shoes looking spiffy was polish them. Then, the soles began to wear down. Every couple of years, I would take my wingtips to a small shoe repair shop I knew to have new soles installed. The shop was run by three generations of an Italian family. In the early years, the grandfather worked on my shoes. Then he died and his son took over the job. The resoling kept my shoes going another twenty years. My wife begged me to surrender. But I loved those shoes. They reminded me of me in my salad days. Eventually, the upper leather of the shoes became so thin that it cracked and split. I took the shoes back to the shop. The cobbler looked at them, shook his head, and smiled.

Physicists call it the second law of thermodynamics. It is also called the arrow of time. Oblivious to our human yearnings for permanence, the universe is relentlessly wearing down, falling apart, driving

The Temporary Universe | 33

itself towards a condition of maximum disorder. It is a question of probabilities. You start from a situation of improbable order, like a deck of cards all arranged according to number and suit, or like a solar system with several planets orbiting nicely about a central star. Then you drop the deck of cards on the floor over and over again. You let other stars randomly whiz by your solar system, jostling it with their gravity. The cards become jumbled. The planets get picked off and go aimlessly wandering through space. Order has yielded to disorder. Repeated patterns to change. In the end, you cannot defeat the odds. You might beat the house for a while, but the universe has an infinite supply of time and can outlast any player.

Consider the world of living things. Why can't we live forever? The life cycles of amoebas and humans are, as everyone knows, controlled by the genes in each cell. While the raison d'etre of the majority of genes is to pass on the instructions for how to build a new amoeba or human being, an important fraction of genes concerns itself with supervising cellular operations and replacing worn-out parts. Some of these genes must be copied thousands of times; others are constantly subjected to random chemical storms and electrically unbalanced atoms, called free radicals, that disrupt other atoms. Disrupted atoms, with their electrons misplaced, cannot properly pull and tug on nearby atoms to form the intended bonds and architectural forms. In short, with time, the genes get degraded. They become forks with missing tines. They cannot quite do their job. Muscles, for example. With age, muscles slacken and grow loose, lose mass and strength, can barely support our weight as we toddle across the room. And why must we suffer such indignities? Because our muscles, like all living tissue, must be repaired from time to time due to normal wear and tear. These repairs are made by the mechano growth factor hormone, which in turn is regulated by the IGF1 gene. When that gene inevitably loses some tines . . . Muscle to flab. Vigor to decrepitude. Dust to dust.

> Every civilization has sought the "elixir of life"—the magical potion that would grant youth and immortality.

In fact, most of our body cells are constantly being sloughed off, rebuilt, and replaced to postpone the inevitable. As one might imagine, the inner surface of the gut comes into contact with a lot of nasty stuff that damages tissue. To stay healthy, the cells that line this organ are constantly being renewed. Cells just below the intestine's surface divide every twelve to sixteen hours, and the whole intestine is refurbished every few days. I figure that by the time an unsuspecting person reaches forty years old, the entire lining of her large intestine has been replaced several thousand times. Billions of cells have been shuffled each go-round. That makes trillions of cell divisions and whispered messages in the DNA to pass along to the next fellow in the chain. With such numbers, it would be nothing short of a miracle if no copying errors were made, no messages misheard, no foul-ups, and no instructions gone awry. Perhaps it would be better just to remain sitting down and wait for the end. No, thank you.

Despite all the evidence, we continue to strive for youth and immortality; we continue to cling to the old photographs; we continue to wish that our grown daughters were children again. Every civilization has sought the "elixir of life"—the magical potion that would grant youth and immortality. In China alone, the substance has one thousand names. It is also known in Persia, in Tibet, in Iraq, in the aging nations of Europe. Some call it Amrita. Or Aab-i-Hayat. Or Maha Ras. Mansarover. Chasma-i-Kausar. Soma Ras. Dancing Water. Pool of Nectar. In the ancient Sumerian epic *Gilgamesh*, one of the earliest known works of literature, the warrior king Gilgamesh goes on a difficult and dangerous journey in search of the secret of eternal life. At the end of the journey, the flood god, Utnapishtim, suggests that the warrior king try out a taste of immortality by staying awake for six days and seven nights. Before Utnapishtim can finish the sentence, Gilgamesh has fallen asleep. In his old age, Qin Shi Huangdi, the first emperor of China, sent hundreds of minions in search of the elixir of life. When they returned empty-handed, his court doctors prescribed mercury pills to make him immortal, and he soon died of mercury poisoning.

But he would have eventually died anyway.

We pay good money for toupees and tummy tucks, face-lifts and breast lifts, hair dyes, skin softeners, penile implants, laser surgeries, Botox treatments, injections for varicose veins. We ingest vitamins and pills and antiaging potions and who knows what else. I recently did a Google search for "products to stay young" and found 37,200,000 Web sites.

But it is not only our physical bodies that we want frozen in time. Most of us struggle against change of all kinds, both big and small. Companies dread structural reorganization, even when it may be for the best, and have instituted whole departments and directives devoted to "change management" and the coddling of employees through tempestuous times. Stock markets plunge during periods of flux and uncertainty. "Better the devil you know than the devil you don't." Who among us clamors to replace the familiar and comfortable incandescent light bulbs with the new, odd-looking "energy efficient" compact fluorescent lamps and light emitting diodes? We resist throwing out our worn loafers, our thinning pullover sweaters, our childhood baseball gloves. A plumber friend of mine will not replace his twenty-year-old water pump pliers, even though they have been banged up and worn down over the years. Outdated monarchies are preserved all over the world. In the Catholic Church, the law of priestly celibacy has remained essentially unchanged since the Council of Trent ended in 1563.

I have a photograph of the coast near Pacifica, California. Due to irrevocable erosion, California has been losing its coastline at the rate of eight inches per year. Not much, you say. But it adds up over time. Fifty years ago, a young woman in Pacifica could build her house a safe thirty feet from the edge of the bluff overlooking the ocean, with a beautiful maritime view. Five years went by. Ten years. No cause for concern. The edge of the bluff was still twenty-three feet away. And she loved her house. She couldn't bear moving. Twenty years. Thirty. Forty. Now the bluff was only seven feet away. Still, she hoped that somehow, someway, the erosion would cease and she could remain in her home. She hoped that things would stay the same. In actual fact, she hoped for a repeal of the second law of thermodynamics, although she may not have described her desires that way. In the photograph, a dozen houses on the coast of Pacifica perch right on the very edge of the cliff, like fragile matchboxes, with their undersides hanging over the precipice. In some, awnings and porches have already slid over the side and into the sea.

Over its 4.5-billion-year history, our own planet has gone through continuous upheavals and change. The primitive earth had no oxygen in its atmosphere. Due to its molten interior, our planet was much hotter than it is now, and volcanoes spewed forth in large numbers. Driven by heat flow from the core of the earth, the terrestrial crust shifted and moved. Huge landmasses splintered and glided about on deep tectonic plates. Then plants and photosynthesis leaked oxygen into the atmosphere. At certain periods, the changing gases in the air caused the planet to cool; ice covered the earth; entire oceans may have frozen. Today, the earth continues to change. Something like ten billion tons of carbon are cycled through plants and the atmosphere every few years—first absorbed by plants from the air in the form of carbon dioxide, then converted into sugars by photosynthesis, then released again into soil or air when the plant dies or is eaten. Wait around a hundred million years or so, and carbon atoms are recycled through rocks, soil, and oceans, as well as plants.

What about our sun and other stars? Shakespeare's Caesar says to Cassius: "But I am constant as the northern star, of whose true-fix'd and resting quality there is no fellow in the firmament." But Caesar was not up on modern astrophysics or the second law of thermodynamics. The North Star and all stars, including our sun, are consuming their nuclear fuel, after which they will fade into cold embers floating in space or, if massive enough, bow out in a final explosion. Our sun, for example, will last another five billion years before spending its fuel. Then it will expand enormously into a red gaseous sphere, enveloping the earth, go through a series of convulsions, and finally settle down to a cold ball made largely of carbon and oxygen. In past eons, new stars have replaced the dying stars by the action of gravity pulling together cosmic clouds of gas. But the universe has been expanding and thinning out since its big bang beginning; large concentrations of gas are gradually being disrupted, and, in the future, the density of gas will not be sufficient for new-star formation. In addition, the lighter chemical elements that fuel most stars, such as hydrogen and helium, will have been used up in previous generations of stars. At some point in the future, new stars will cease being born. Slowly but surely, the stars of our universe are winking out. A day will come when the night sky will be totally black, and the day sky will be totally black as well. Solar systems will become planets orbiting dead stars. According to astrophysical calculations, in about a million billion years, plus or minus, even those dead solar systems will be disrupted from chance gravitational encounters with other stars. In about ten billion billion years, even galaxies will be disrupted, the cold spheres that were once stars flung out to coast solo through empty space.

Buddhists have long been aware of the evanescent nature of the world. *Annica*, or impermanence, they call it. In Buddhism, annica is one of the three signs of existence, the others being *dukkha*, or suffering, and *anatta*, or nonselfhood. According to the *Maha-parinibbana Sutta*, when the Buddha passed away, the king deity Sakka uttered the following: "Impermanent are all component things, They arise and cease, that is their nature: They come into being and pass away." We should not "attach" to things in this world, say the Buddhists, because all things are temporary and will soon pass away. All suffering, say the Buddhists, arises from attachment.

If I could only detach from my daughter, perhaps I would feel better.

But even Buddhists believe in something akin to immortality. It is called Nirvana. A person reaches Nirvana after he or she has managed to leave behind all attachments and cravings, endured countless trials and reincarnations, and finally achieved total enlightenment. The ultimate state of Nirvana is described by the Buddha as *am ravati*, meaning deathlessness. After a being has attained Nirvana, its reincarnations cease. Indeed, nearly every religion on earth has celebrated the ideal of immortality. God is immortal. Our souls might be immortal.

To my mind, it is one of the profound contradictions of human existence that we long for immortality, indeed fervently believe that something must be unchanging and permanent, when all of the evidence in nature argues against us. Either I am delusional or nature is incomplete. Either I am being emotional and vain in my wish for eternal life for myself and my daughter (and my wingtips), or there is some realm of immortality that exists outside nature.

If the first alternative is right, then I need to have a talk with myself and get over it. After all, there are other things I yearn for that are neither true nor good for my health. The human mind has a famous ability to create its own reality. "The mind is its own place," wrote Milton, "and can create a heaven of hell or a hell of heaven." If the second alternative is right, then it is nature that has been found wanting. Despite all the richness of the physical world—the majestic architecture of atoms, the rhythm of the tides, the luminescence of the galaxies—nature is missing something even more exquisite and grand: some immortal substance, which lies hidden from view. Such exquisite stuff could not be made from matter, because all matter is slave to the second law of thermodynamics. Perhaps this immortal thing that we wish for exists beyond time and space. Perhaps it is God. Perhaps it is what made the universe.

Of these two alternatives, I am inclined to the first. I cannot believe that nature could be so amiss. Although there is much that we do not understand about nature, the possibility that it is hiding a condition or substance so magnificent and utterly unlike everything else seems too preposterous for me to believe. So, I am delusional. In my continual cravings for eternal youth and constancy, I am being sentimental. Perhaps with the proper training of my unruly mind and emotions, I could refrain from wanting things that cannot be. Perhaps I could accept the fact that in a few short years, my atoms will be scattered in wind and soil, my mind and thoughts gone, my pleasures and joys vanished, my I-ness dissolved in an infinite cavern of nothingness. But I cannot accept that fate, even though I believe it to be true. I cannot force my mind to go to that dark place. "A man can do what he wants," said Schopenhauer, "but not want what he wants."

Suppose I ask a different kind of question: if against our wishes and hopes, we are stuck with mortality, does mortality grant a beauty and grandeur all its own? Even though we struggle and howl against the brief flash of our lives, might we find something majestic in that brevity? Could there be a preciousness and value to existence stemming from the very fact of its temporary duration? And I think of the night-blooming cereus, a plant that looks like a leathery weed most of the year. But for one night each summer, its flower opens to reveal silky white petals that encircle yellow lacelike threads, and another whole flower like a tiny sea anemone lies within the outer flower. By morning, the flower has shriveled. One night of the year, as delicate and fleeting as a life in the universe.

Megan Levad

NANOBOTS

All of the nanobots? Or just the nanobots in the bloodstream? You know, the new immune system. Nanobots are really small tiny robots and, and um basically if you were to get cancer or something where your body doesn't naturally respond to it they would inject the nanobots oh they're self-replicating of course so the nanobots are self-replicating so when they're in your bloodstream say you'd only have to inject like two, I guess only one it's not like they're mating or anything. So the one would be in the bloodstream and it just starts reproducing itself and it's programmed to attack the cancer or other ailment. Also if your limb gets cut off or something it will rebuild your bones using your body's tissue or whatever. It will rebuild. They don't exist yet. They're working on it.

WHY WE LIVE IN THE DARK AGES

Oh the dark ages. Let me tell you about the Dark Ages. Okay. Oh. I was reading this lecture by Jacques Barzun. B-a-r-z-u-n. B-a-r-z-u-n. Who is a great culture historian. Art historian. Anyway the lecture was called uh, The Use and Abuse of Art. And there's a section in this lecture where he talks about the Dark Ages. And how it relates to our own time. A very popular subject. And he made a very interesting point. That the reason why no, no a very interesting point that in the Dark Ages the people of this time period were, were smart people essentially. They had art they had uh you know I don't know interesting conversation I don't know they were they were consumers they were functioning people but the reason why we refer to it as the Dark Ages is because not much is basically because the populace of we view them as being sort of dumb and uh from our standpoint because they weren't literate in the Latin which was the language where everything was being written in for like "the intellectuals" and uh all this intellectual thought was going on and was controlled largely by the Church. And he makes a comparison to our own time where our populace is you know we may be literate and um producing art and doing all these sorts of things but the power within our society is in science and that most of us sort of everyday people don't really understand science very well and uh, like Latin to the Church sort of like abstract or, or any sort of scientific thought isn't common isn't common language among our society at all and all the power is held with scientists or this very select group of people in the scientific community.

ESSAY

THE HARD PROBLEM OF CONSCIOUSNESS AND THE SOLITUDE OF THE POET

Rebecca Newberger Goldstein

Being between mind and body

I was on a near-empty subway train heading downtown from 181st Street, where I lived, to my late-morning class at Barnard College. I was twenty and love had gone wrong. At the edge of consciousness, which is where I tried to keep it, was the sickening smell of singed trust. There was a host of other unpleasant feelings pushing to break through, if I let them. I was determined not to let them. On my lap was the Haldane and Ross edition of *The Philosophical Works of Descartes*. I hadn't completed the reading assignment for that day's class on the seventeenth-century rationalists. Whenever I glanced up from my book, I met the urgent eyes of the man sitting directly opposite me, his legs sprawled wide, his lips making wet kissy-kissy sounds. His attentions were not having a positive effect on my state of mind.

The second volume of the Haldane and Ross collection consists of a set of seven objections to Descartes's *Meditations on First Philosophy* from prominent contemporaries, along with his replies to them. I was reading, or trying to read, the objections of Thomas Hobbes, the most prominent of Descartes's respondents. Hobbes rejected

Cartesian dualism—that is, the thesis that each person is a composite of two things, a material body and an immaterial mind, intimately entangled with each other in a dense thicket of two-way causal connections and yet existentially distinct. I was on Hobbes's side. My downtown-train-riding philosophical position: we are our bodies, one functionally integrated, though extraordinarily complicated, material thing, a thing whose functioning, including mental functioning, is ultimately to be explained by the laws of physics, which means the laws describing matter in motion. Hobbes seemed, roughly speaking, to grasp the gist of the modern scientific view, emphasizing that all the contents of the mind—its "phantasms," as he put it—are ultimately the products of matter in motion, our material sense organs colliding with other material objects.

Primitive, yes, but also prescient. The scientists and philosophers of the seventeenth-century were only just beginning to get an inkling in the mid-seventeenth-century that all laws of physics ultimately reduce to descriptions of matter in motion and were still lacking such fundamental concepts as that of a force field. Descartes and Hobbes were pre-Newtonian; they both thought that matter could be completely described using only geometrical properties, and therefore they both identified extension as the essential property of matter. (As a result, Descartes hypothesized an excruciatingly complex system of vortices to move matter around.) They had no concept yet of those nongeometrical dynamical, properties of matter—force, inertia—that would allow Newton to state his laws of motion with such economy, accuracy, and generality.

But Hobbes's intuition of the explanatory power to be unleashed by the new science of matter led him to chastise Descartes for being overly hasty in drawing a distinction between mind and body, since, according to Hobbes, it might well be the case that all those complexities of reasoning and phantasm formation—which is what Hobbes saw as the two basic functions of mind—were not external to the powers of material bodies. Hobbes writes, "If this is the case, as it may well be, then reasoning will depend upon names, names upon imagination [i.e., forming images], and imagination perhaps, as I see it, upon the motions of the corporeal organs. And thus the mind will be nothing but movements in parts of an organic body." He doesn't bother to point out the fact that the part of the body most centrally implicated is, of course, the brain.

On the other side of the argument was Descartes, who had a more robust notion of the mind than Hobbes, extending its contents to what it's given by way of sensing and perceiving, feeling pains and pleasures, remembering, imagining, dreaming, willing, hallucinating, having moods and emotions, as well as reasoning. The whole inner landscape is covered in his notion of the mind, though he doesn't use the word *consciousness*, or a French or Latin equivalent, for this landscape, as we would, but rather forms of the verb "to think,"

penser, cogitare.[1] The English word *consciousness* was in use in his time, but its meaning closely followed its Latin etymology: *con*, which means "together," plus *scire*, which means "to know" (from which we eventually got the word *science*; up until the nineteenth century, the term *natural philosophy*, or sometimes just *philosophy*, did the trick). "Consciousness" was used to mean a kind of intersubjective shared knowledge. So, for example, Hobbes writes in *Leviathan*, "Where two, or more, men know of one and the same fact, they are said to be Conscious of it to one another." It was John Locke, in his *An Essay Concerning Human Understanding*, who transformed the word *consciousness* so that it could do all the work that Descartes's "thinking" had done. The Lockean transformation of the word *consciousness* was officially ratified when it was included in Samuel Johnson's celebrated *A Dictionary of the English Language* in 1755.

In any case, putting semantics aside, according to Descartes, there was my living, breathing body, parked on a hard bench of a downtown-bound IRT train, which was now stalled in the tunnel between 125th Street and my 116th Street stop.[2] And then there was my mind, hovering in the same general vicinity and causally intertwined with my body, but distinct from it. My perceptual perspective of the world widened out from where my material eyes were situated, but the content of my perceptions was all in my mind. Putting Cartesian dualism in post-Cartesian scientific terms: the apparatus of my material eyes was affected by the photons of the light waves, and the apparatus of my material ears was affected by the molecules of the airwaves, but it was my mind—composed of entirely immaterial stuff—that experienced my fellow traveler's obscene attentions to me, that felt the mixture of annoyance and disgust as a result, though, really, it couldn't have cared less, not while it was simultaneously permeated by a sense of desolation that it was trying to pretend wasn't there, and was being bombarded by memory images of what had transpired between me and the man it thought it loved, and was hearing echoes of words that had been spoken that devastated it, which would have activated my tear glands had it not forcefully opposed such activation, and was trying to imagine what should be done as a result of what it categorized as a betrayal, what decisions should be made, including, possibly, pretending that what had happened hadn't happened, because all the other options it was imagining terrified it, so that, no matter what it actually felt, it could quite possibly decide on actions that belied its feelings, could direct my mouth to say placating falsehoods—or perhaps it would eventually find it within itself to forgive—and was still, in all this swill of roiling subjectivity, willing itself to read the words of Hobbes's objections to Descartes's *Meditations on First Philosophy*, so that my eyes conscientiously followed along the lines of the book, and my hands dutifully turned the pages, even though the sense of the words didn't quite make it into it, that is, my mind. All this clamoring interiority, this *être intime*, this fitful, flitting dance of subjectivity, lending itself to that fictional technique we call "stream of consciousness," was what Descartes attributed to this separate substance he dubbed *res cogitans*, the thing that thinks, understanding thinking to cover the full panoply of consciousness, which thing was

> "Consciousness" was used to mean a kind of intersubjective shared knowledge.

---

1. His first published work, *Discourse on the Method of Rightly Conducting the Reason and of Seeking Truth in the Sciences* was written in the vulgate French, a mildly revolutionary decision motivated by his view that philosophy is for the people, who are as capable of doing it, once they have the right method, as any trained schoolman or churchman. His second work, *Meditations on First Philosophy*, which was directed toward the schoolmen and churchmen and is more exact in its formulations of the arguments, was written in the de rigueur Latin. It's the *Discourse*, and not the more careful *Meditations*, that contains the T-shirt-worthy "I think, therefore I am."

2. Descartes had no qualms about categorizing aliveness as a corporeal property, since he considered its characteristics to be defined in terms of certain characteristic behaviors, i.e., motions. He drew the line only at consciousness.

intimate with my body but was not one with it.

My body was still trapped in the tunnel, the object of increased attention by the man across from it, when my mind was peremptorily invaded by a thought that knocked all other thoughts out of it, including the heartachey ones. The words it used to express this thought—they seemed to be shouting themselves in it—were *Consciousness is huge!* Perhaps it was Hobbes's making such a simple matter of it all: material bodies impinge on other material bodies and *presto!*, there are those phantasms. Or maybe it was my heightened consciousness of all the consciousness sloshing about in my cranium. All I know is suddenly my faith in hard and dry reductive materialism was shattered, never to be reassembled. Sure, consciousness is a matter of matter—what else could it be, since that's what we *are*—but still, the fact that some hunks of matter have an inner life—sometimes *too much* inner life—is unlike any other properties of matter that we have yet encountered, much less accounted for. The laws of matter in motion can produce *this*, all *this*? Suddenly, matter wakes up and takes in the world? Suddenly, matter has an *attitude, a point of view, a fantasy life*? No wonder Descartes felt compelled to *agiter la main* and posit a *res cogitans* composed of mind stuff, different from material stuff, into which to deposit all this phenomenological frenzy. Not that hypothesizing mind stuff explains anything at all, but at least it pays tribute to the profundity of the mystery. And then Hobbes, too, together with all the increasingly sophisticated reductive materialists who have followed in his path, is just as guilty of hand waving. The amygdala is stimulated and *presto!*, there are the phantasms of a past traumatic event! But how does it happen, that leap from matter being jiggled to its *feeling like that*? What else can one do in the face of such a phenomenon as consciousness-achieving matter but vigorously wave one's hands, though, frankly, I was more inclined to clap.

> All I know is suddenly my faith in hard and dry reductive materialism was shattered, never to be reassembled.

Matter can do *this*? *This*? Those electrochemical events transpiring at each of a hundred trillion synapses of my brain—we have much more of a handle on the material processes now than they did in Hobbes's day—end up yielding this one hell of a powerful phenomenon that is nothing at all like those events, that seems like nothing else, that is, in fact, the very thing that makes *seeming* possible? What it means, this consciousness, is that I'm not just *in* the world, like all those other insensate material hunks, but I'm alive to *being* in the world. There's something that it's *like* for me to be in the world. Could someone who knew exactly how all of my neurons were firing be able to come up with the description of what it was like for me to be me, riding downtown on the IRT on my way to my class on the seventeenth-century rationalists? Could some omniscient neuroscientist of the future, scanning my brain with a completeness we can't yet imagine, turn to a colleague and say, *Ah yes, I see, a few moments ago this subject was wallowing in the self-pity of wounded love, melodramatically struggling to imagine how her life could continue, her eyes processing words whose senses escaped her, and now, why look at that firing over there, the girl is wondering how neurons firing can feel like anything at all?*

I was so mystified and awestruck, but also so exhilarated, sensing that I would never feel the world to be the same again, that when the train finally lurched the last few yards out of the tunnel to my subway stop, I whirled around, just before stepping through the doors, and gave my fellow passenger my own version of a kissy kissy. I wonder what my action caused in *his* inner life.

It turns out my moment of awe on the downtown IRT has a name. I had come up against what would be christened, a few decades later, "the hard problem of consciousness." I wish I had named it, but it was the philosopher David Chalmers who did, in his 1996 book, *The Conscious Mind*, in which he distinguishes the hard problem from the ironically dubbed "easy problems of consciousness," which aren't in the least easy, but are of the sort that can be answered by specifying the mechanism, or the combinatorial procedure, that can accomplish a specific cognitive function, whether this function is conscious (say, how one gathers the meanings one intends to communicate) or unconscious (say, how one consults the rules of syntax that express them). This is the subject matter of cognitive science, or cognitive neuroscience. Much headway has been made on these complicated easy problems, but the *doozy* of the problem of consciousness is Why does it *feel* like something to have those combinatorial mechanisms working away in our brains? That's the hard problem, and it's hard because it doesn't seem to be a problem that can be solved by specifying a function, even if it's true that consciousness does allow an organism to respond with maximum flexibility and scalability to an ever-changing environment. Pointing to the usefulness of consciousness may explain *why* it evolved, but it still doesn't answer *how* it's done, how matter manages to stir itself and wake up to the world, to end up not just being there, but *being there*.

For me, that moment on the downtown train was one of the greatest intellectual highlights of my life. No, let me be perfectly honest. It was one of the greatest highlights of my life, intellectual or not. It gave me a new respect for matter and a humbling recognition of how little we know about its intrinsic properties, even given all the surprising properties we have been led to attribute to it through the advancement of physics. In some sense, we're limited in our access to matter by the methodology of physics, which is, to the chagrin of many math-phobic students, thoroughly saturated with mathematics. As Galileo put it at the dawn of modern physics: "Philosophy is written in this grand book, the universe, which stands continually open to our gaze. But the book cannot be understood unless one first learns to comprehend the language and read the characters in which it is written. It is written in the language of mathematics, and its characters are triangles, circles, and other geometric figures without which it is humanly impossible to understand a single word of it; without these one is wandering in a dark labyrinth."

Though the mathematics that physicists use has certainly gone beyond the geometry in terms of which Galileo explained matter in motion, physics still, to this day, speaks the language of mathematics. Modern physics was made possible because Galileo and those who followed him figured out a way of translating certain aspects of our experience—first and foremost, motion—into mathematical language (motion equals change of position over change of time), so that mathematical relations could be developed and unobservable properties deduced. In this way, mathematical physics is able to lead us to complex properties of matter that are nothing like what we can directly observe. This is how physics has managed to pry out, by way of mathematics, some of matter's more elusive qualities.

But what if mathematics isn't the language of nature per se, but rather just the language of our scientific knowledge of nature? What if nature has properties that are just as remote from our direct experience as the exotic properties of theoretical physics—quantum mechanical charm, relativistic space-time curvature—but we can't get at them through science because they're not susceptible to mathematical translations? Galileo decreed that all the mathematically translatable properties we observe in matter—position, velocity, shape, size—are truly out there: he called them "primary qualities." The mathematically untranslatable properties we seem to observe in matter—color, smell, heat—he called "secondary," and he relegated them to the mind as a way of saying they aren't properties of matter at all, but rather the experiential results of the interaction between matter's primary—i.e., real; i.e., mathematically expressible—properties and our own sensory apparatus.

But what about that mind itself, into which all those secondary qualities are dumped, that mind that lives and breathes subjectivity? The promise of reductive materialism is that everything about it can eventually be subjected to the language of mathematics, all its properties ultimately explained by physics. If it's material, then it's going to be rendered transparent in the explanatory chamber of science. And so far as the easy problems of consciousness go, progress proceeds. The computational model of the mind is humming along. But none of this touches the mystery of consciousness.

But perhaps the mystery of consciousness is not quite as mysterious as we make it out to be—so mysterious as to drive some to the Cartesian extreme of reifying immaterial minds. Maybe we intensify the sense of its mystery by approaching it from the direction of the laws of matter in motion. Who says all the properties of matter relate to matter in motion? If one thinks about it, one would expect matter to have intrinsic properties that are not related to its being in motion. Cartesian dualists and reductive materialists both share the presumption that matter isn't holding out on us, preserving deep secrets about its nature. Could it be that in knowing that at least some material entities—certainly me!—are conscious, we know of at least some of matter's properties that don't derive from the laws of matter in motion? Could it be that that aspect of matter, which all of us are privy to, simply by being conscious, gives us access to an aspect of matter that one could never get to by way of the methodology of science?

This would mean that the language of mathematics, as powerfully effective as it's proven itself to be in prying out so many of matter's hidden properties, isn't suitable for getting at them all. In particular, mathematical language isn't up to the task of expressing and exploring matter's charming capacity for having an inner life. So then what is the right language for expressing and exploring and delving deeper into this adorable aspect of matter, and who are the experts who speak it best?

My answer began to take shape while I was in a heated conversation with one of the gurus of artificial intelligence (AI). He was, like many people in AI, seriously committed to there being no such thing as a hard problem of consciousness, there being no such thing as consciousness, at least not over and above the hodge-podge of functions that the "easy" problems solve. When he challenged me to deliver a definition of consciousness that would cover all cases, I reached for the quite nice formulation given by the philosopher Thomas Nagel in his seminal paper "What Is It Like to Be a Bat?": "The fact that an organism has conscious experience *at all* means, basically, that there is something it is like to *be* that organism." The guru triumphantly seized on the word *it*, saying that its presence shows the vacuity of Nagel's formulation. People always refer to some vague "it" in lieu of having anything concrete to say about what consciousness is. It deceives them into thinking there's really something there.

In vain, I tried to argue that Nagel's "it" isn't being used as a real pronoun in that construction; it is a syntactic pronoun, not a semantic pronoun, and thus not meant to be referring at all, just as when we say, "It is raining." It—there's that frigging

> But what if mathematics isn't the language of nature per se, but rather just the language of our scientific knowledge of nature?

"it" again—is just that English requires a subject, and so we have these terms that linguists call "expletives," words that fill things out, but are, so far as meaning goes, eliminable, like those other (expletive deleted) expletives we all know and love. No dice. The guru wasn't having any of it, not with an "it" dangling in the explication. His grin was Cheshire cat–like.

About a year later, I encountered the guru again. This time, he was expounding on why he never reads fiction that isn't science fiction. Fiction, he explained, is tedious and repetitive because it's always about the same thing, which is that there are some not very interesting people who make some sort of big mistake and then you see what happens, such as maybe they kill themselves or maybe they don't. Science fiction, he concluded, again Cheshire cat–like, is about everything else.

I was reduced to speechlessness, but not quite thoughtlessness. The primary thought that came to me is that there is perhaps a connection between, on the one hand, failing to see that there is something interesting about material objects for whom there's something that it feels like to be them and, on the other, holding the view that all fiction is about the same thing. A tin ear for subjectivity is required for both. Having such a tin ear is no handicap for being a guru in AI, since the problems they work on have nothing to do with subjectivity. Subjectivity's irrelevance to their work, as well as to the work of cognitive scientists and neuroscientists, seems sufficient for some such types to conclude that it doesn't exist at all, which is itself, at least to me, a fascinating aspect of their subjectivity.

What I am leading up to is this: the language used by scientific experts for expressing and exploring *some* of the properties of matter isn't sufficient for expressing and exploring *all* the properties of matter, specifically the capacity of some organized matter to have an inner life, some of it rather spellbinding, though sometimes, too, not quite as spellbinding as the organized matter in question seems to think. But there do, in fact, exist experts who have developed another language for expressing and exploring properties of matter that remain out of the grasp of science. The language they have developed is the language of fiction. It is the language of poetry. These are the most developed languages we have for grasping properties of matter that would otherwise be unavailable to us. If the quantum physicist has led us to become better acquainted with the stochastic nature of matter, then so, too, have the novelist and the poet. In the grip of the poet's language, every word as considered and necessary as the symbols in a mathematical equation, something transpires, the poet's deep solitude mixing with my own, so that I am experiencing something undetermined and astonishing, and I am left gasping: Matter can do this? *This?*

Katy Chrisler

NEW VOICE

NESS

I went back to my hometown and saw a girl who I'd been told had drowned in the ocean many years ago. Her pleasant eyes were climates crossed soft, and meaningless.

I told her that there were still heights and that the carrier wave weakens with what it carries but she just lulled and said every human is bound to die but we can't leave things that engage our bodies.

FICTION

The Particles

Once he was in the water, it was easier to see what had happened to the ship. The stern already low in the waves, the empty lifeboat davits and twisted rigging and the blackened, shattered wood on the deck, where the exploding hatches had blown deck chairs and people to bits. They'd been at dinner, spoons clicking on soup bowls, cooks poised over pots, Sam Cornelius thrown from his chair as he pushed aside a bit of carrot. Now it was past nine and fully dark: September 3, 1939. The searchlight picked out bodies floating near the boat, and when the woman crouched behind him gave her life belt to her wailing son, Sam gave her his and then was even more frightened; despite his age—he was thirty-four—he could barely swim.

Andrea Barrett

In the distance a shape, which might have been the guilty submarine, seemed to shift position. The moon disappeared behind a bank of clouds and then it rained, drenching those who weren't yet soaked; more than eleven hundred people had been onboard. When the rain stopped, the moon again lit the boats scattered around the slowly sinking ship. The three of the *Athenia*'s crew in Sam's boat took oars, as did the three least wounded—Sam was one—of the four male passengers. The others, just over fifty women and children, bailed with their shoes and their bare hands, scooping out the oily water rising over their shins.

As the two dozen lifeboats separated like specks on an expanding balloon, one pulled toward Sam's boat to let them know that several ships had responded to the *Athenia*'s call for help. Soon, in just a few hours, they'd be saved. Those hours passed. Not long after midnight, a faraway gleam, which might have been a periscope caught by the light of the moon, caused two women to shriek. A U-boat, one said, the German submarine that had torpedoed them rising now to shell the lifeboats. But the last beam of the searchlight, just before the emergency dynamo used up its fuel and the *Athenia* went completely dark, revealed enough to convince Sam and some of the others that this was a rescue ship.

Steadily, Sam and his companions rowed toward the Norwegian tanker *Knute Nelson*, which, in the light of occasional flares, popped sporadically out of the darkness. A little string of emptied lifeboats tossed in the swell beside the tanker, the boat closest to the stern still packed with people. Some grabbed at rope ladders while the bosun's chair went up and down, hoisting those not agile enough to climb until, in the grip of a heavy woman who pushed off too vigorously, it overturned and left her suspended upside down. The crew struggled to retrieve her, but before they were done another boat nudged in behind the one still being emptied.

The man rowing next to Sam muttered, "They should stand out, that's dangerous," and when Sam drew his anxious gaze away from the faces he was searching, he could see how little space separated the last boat in line from the tanker's huge propellers. He turned back to his oars. The sea was rough, the boat's seams were leaking, many of his fellow passengers were wounded or seasick or both, and Sam was working so hard to keep their boat steady that he failed to see exactly what happened a few minutes later. By the time he heard the screams, the broken lifeboat, impaled on one of the propeller blades, was already rising into the air.

"Row!" said the seaman in charge of Sam's boat. "Row, row, row, row!"

Sam, the tallest but not the strongest of those at the oars (he was out of shape), lost his grip and banged into the man beside him, who shouted at him; then all of them were shouting at each other while women wailed and children cried. Unbearable to think about what must have happened to those drawn into the propeller. The boat sped into the darkness, headed, once the assistant purser spotted it, toward an enormous, brightly lit motor yacht that had appeared from another direction. Before they were close enough to hail her, Sam saw two lifeboats tangle at her stern, one crowding the other under the angled counter—the swell had increased, making everything more difficult—which, after rising unusually high, crashed down on the gunwale of the inner boat and tipped it over. Suddenly, struggling figures, too small to identify, also dotted the water.

> **Unbearable to think about what must have happened to those drawn into the propeller.**

That was enough for the seaman in charge; Sam's boat pulled away until it was clear of everyone. "Let's wait," the seaman said, "until sunrise, when we can see more clearly what we're doing." The swell grew heavier; dawn finally broke and three British destroyers arrived. The little boy whose mother was wearing Sam's life belt pointed at them, smiled for the first time since the ship had been hit, and said, "Ring around the rosy!" Sam couldn't see what the little boy meant, and then he could: two of the ships were racing after each other, herding within an enormous circle the remaining lifeboats, the tanker, the white yacht, and the third destroyer, which was plucking boatloads of survivors from the water. Twice, he thought it was turning their way, but each time it moved toward another, even more crowded boat.

The sky was red and then pink and then blue; Sam's hands were numb; he hadn't been able to feel his feet for hours. Once or twice he either fell asleep or passed out. Once, he lifted his head just in time to see an old woman in a lifeboat not far away leap toward a lowered rope ladder and miss, slipping into the narrow space between the boat and the destroyer's hull; the boat rose on a swell and the space disappeared. He was barely conscious when, in the middle of the morning, a U.S. merchant ship arrived, cleaned out one boat before taking in a crowd transferred from the motor yacht, and then waved over the boat that Sam was in.

The Particles

The injured and frail went up in a bosun's chair, but Sam, jolted awake by the prospect of safety, scrambled up a rope ladder with the other men. A person reached out for him, grabbed his arm, and heaved him over the side—not a stranger, not a sailor, but someone Sam knew: Duncan Finch. Part of him wanted to jump back in the water. Duncan, here? But there was the ship's name, *City of Flint*, mocking him from the smokestack.

"You're all right!" Duncan shouted as Sam dropped onto the deck. "Are you hurt?"

Sam flexed his elbow, which he'd cracked on a thwart but which still seemed to work, and then inspected his shin, where all the blood appeared to be coming from one long scrape. "Nothing serious," he said.

Duncan pulled him toward a dry corner. "Is anyone else with you?"

Anyone, he meant, from the meeting; they'd been at an international genetics congress in Edinburgh, cut short by the situation. Sam shook his head. Families had been broken apart, siblings had ended up in different boats, and friends had been randomly assorted: where was Axel? Eight other geneticists had been on the *Athenia* with Sam. One by one, in the thick, dark smoke, they'd climbed into lifeboats, dropped down to the water, and then disappeared.

Duncan said, with apparent enthusiasm, "But at least *you're* here. You're safe."

Omitting, Sam thought, the fact that on their last day in Edinburgh, Duncan had asked Sam grudgingly, and when it was too late, to join the small group he'd finagled aboard this American freighter loaded with wool and Scotch whiskey.

"I did warn you," Duncan added now. Still, after eighteen years of annoying Sam, unable to rein in his red-faced, bullying self. "I *warned* you not to take passage on a British ship."

Anyone else would have understood how few choices existed. Sam's booked passage had been canceled, the other ships were quickly commandeered, and on September 1, as he boarded the *Athenia* in Glasgow, it had still seemed likely that they'd get away safely. They'd had to pick up passengers in Belfast and then more in Liverpool, both ports packed with Americans and Canadians trying to get home, but by the afternoon of the second, the ship was heading north up the Irish Sea, rounding the coast early on the morning of the third. By the time the declaration of war was radioed, they'd almost cleared the most dangerous territory, their ship overbooked but still comfortable and, Sam had thought with a twinge of pleasure, less crowded than Duncan's. Before Duncan left, not only his handful of stranded friends but also a group of college girls caught midway through a European tour had been stuffed into the *City of Flint*, making thirty instead of the normal five or six passengers. Now it bulged with another two hundred people, some freezing and still in shock, and among them—

"Is Axel here?" he asked.

Duncan turned, reached back to steady an elderly woman coming over the railing, and then pointed her toward a man who was giving out fresh water. "Of course not," he said, inspecting Sam more closely. "Did you hit your head?"

For Duncan, Sam realized, Axel was still in Edinburgh, where he'd stayed to visit a friend despite Duncan's frantic urging that he board the *City of Flint*. When the situation grew so dangerous that Axel's friend cut the visit short and delivered him to the Glasgow docks, Duncan had already been at sea.

"He was with me," Sam said. Two teenaged boys tumbled onto the deck, their hair matted with oil; a girl in a tidy jacket rushed over to them. "The *Athenia* was the only ship that had a berth." In another situation he would have enjoyed seeing the color drain from Duncan's cheeks.

"He *wasn't*."

"He was," Sam said. "We were eating dinner with that couple from Minnesota when we were hit." One of what should have been many meals; what luck, he'd thought, to have Axel aboard! An unexpected benefit of letting Duncan sail without him. They might walk the decks, share quiet conversations, sit side by side in reclining chairs and repair what had gone wrong in Edinburgh. At the dock, the sight of Axel's battered gray hat and unmistakable nose in the crowd had suddenly made everything broken and ruined seem hopeful again.

"But then," Duncan said, "how did you lose track of him?"

The smoke, the darkness, the wounded people, the babble of different languages as passengers crowded boats already full, launched half-empty ones too early. Sam drew a breath. "We went where the crew told us to go, and they assigned us to separate boats. Then the boats scattered. Can you find out if he's here?"

Duncan disappeared with a curse, leaving Sam to be herded down below with the newest arrivals. In a long room lined with barrels, they dripped into a growing puddle, which the crew and the freighter's original passengers tried to avoid as they ferried in spare clothing pulled from their luggage. A plant physiologist from Texas, transferred from the motor yacht, slipped an old sweater over his head as he said that these merchant seamen were a lot more welcoming than the Swedish billionaire who'd originally rescued him. Sam tied his feet into a pair of slippers a size too large, thrilled to find them dry, while his new acquaintance described the smartly outfitted crew who'd handed out soup and hot coffee and blankets and then—the sun was well up, the *Athenia* had gone to her grave, and the destroyers were making their rounds—told the rescued passengers that the owner couldn't interrupt his planned trip and needed to transfer everyone who'd been picked up. "To here," the Texan said, stepping out of his oil-soaked pants and into a seaman's canvas overalls. "Oh, that's *much* better."

Where was Axel, where was Axel? Maybe he'd been on that yacht, or maybe . . . he tried not to think about the huge propeller. Around Sam, coats, blankets, overshoes, shawls flew toward wet bodies, something dry for everyone. So many people, everywhere: bodies racked like billiard balls in every corner and companionway, babies calling like kittens or crows as women tried to comfort them. Among them, Axel might be hidden—or he might be in the water still, or safely headed toward Galway or Glasgow on one of the destroyers. Sam pushed through the mass, some faces familiar from the *Athenia*'s decks and dining room but many not and none the one he most wanted to see, until, when he came out near the galley, he heard his name and looked behind him. Duncan, who'd always had this way of proving himself astonishingly useful just when he was at his most annoying, waved his hand above the crowd. Beside him, his front hair pushed forward into a kingfisher's tuft by a gigantic square bandage, was Axel.

Of course Duncan had one of the actual berths; of course he turned it over to Axel, who, after touching Sam's face and saying, "You're here. You're all right," disappeared into the deckhouse and fell, said Duncan later (himself now modestly moved to the floor of his cabin, where he'd already had two roommates), into an exhausted sleep. Sam, who stayed awake for a while after Axel left, slept that first night on a coil of rope, surrounded by women in men's shoes and torn evening gowns, men wearing dress shirts over sarongs made from curtains, children in white ducks shaped for bulky sailors. A little girl whose parents had ended up in a different boat—Sam hoped they were now on some other ship—lay on a pile of canvas nearby. Earlier, he'd seen the two women looking after her piece together a romper from two long woolen socks, a pair of women's panties, and a boy's sweater. Now the women curled parenthetically around their warm charge.

Sam's trousers were still intact, and between those, his donated slippers, and a wool jacket generously given to him by one of Duncan's cabinmates, an old acquaintance named Harold, he was warm enough to sleep. The next morning, after a chaotic attempt at breakfast, he and Harold, along with everyone else who wasn't injured, helped the ship's crew spread mattresses in the hold, suspend spare tarpaulins from beams to make rows of hammocks, and hammer planks into bunks until everyone had a place to sleep. Harold had helped the captain organize seatings for meals—eight shifts of thirty people, they'd decided—and as he and Sam cut planks to length, they talked about supplies. Harold's friend George, also sharing Duncan's cabin, joined them an hour later and described the list he was making of those who'd been separated from family members and friends; first on it were the seven congress participants still unaccounted for. The captain would radio the list to the other rescue ships, which were returning to Scotland and Ireland—only theirs was heading across the sea, on its original course. But what about allocating medical care and pooling medications? What about basic sanitation? If we had rags, Harold said, we could tear them into squares. If we had a *system*, George fussed, gathering scraps of paper for the latrines.

The smoke, the darkness, the wounded people, the babble of different languages as passengers crowded boats already full.

If, if, if. Sam tried to think of them as amiable strangers helping to make the best of a hard situation—as if they'd not just been together at a conference where the two of them had looked on blandly as Sam's work was attacked. As if Duncan, elsewhere on the ship that morning, hadn't been the one attacking.

He worked all day, as the ship steamed steadily west and the passengers pulled from the water continued to shift and sort themselves, the sickest and most badly wounded settling in the tiny hospital bay with those slightly better off nearby, the youngest and oldest tucked in more protected corners, and the strongest where water dripped or splashed, layering themselves as neatly, Sam thought, as if they'd been spun in a gigantic centrifuge. He claimed one of the hammocks he'd hung himself, glad that at least Axel had a berth and a bit of privacy. Glad too to find, when evening came, that Harold and George had fit him and Axel into their dinner shift, which also included Duncan and the group of college girls.

The big square bandage bound to the top of his head made Axel, seated when Sam reached the table, look unusually defenseless. He smiled at Sam and tapped the seat next to him, but before Sam could get there, Harold, George, and Duncan swarmed in, leaving Sam seated at the corner. The college girls, already friendly with Duncan's group, filled in the empty seats and introduced themselves to Sam and Axel. One, who had smooth red hair a few shades lighter than Sam's, pointed to Axel's gauze-covered crown. "Is that bad?"

> "These two," Axel said, gesturing first toward Sam and then toward Duncan, "used to be my students."

"Not really," Axel said. "A long jagged tear in my scalp, but the doctor said it should heal."

Not nearly enough information. Sam imagined Axel under water, trying to surface through the debris. An oar cracking down on his skull, a fragment from the explosion flying toward him. When did it happen, who was he with, who took care of him? He leaned forward to speak, but another of the girls, annoyingly chatty—Lucinda was her name—said, "How do you all know each other, then?"

"We work in the same field," Harold said. His doughy cheeks were perfectly smooth; of course he had a razor.

"Genetics," George added. Also clean-shaven. Briefly, Sam mourned his lost luggage. "The study of heredity."

"These two," Axel said, gesturing first toward Sam and then toward Duncan, "used to be my students."

"Really?" said the one named Pansy. "That wolf-in-a-bonnet disguise makes you look the same age as them."

It was true, Sam thought as the others laughed; the bandage covered Axel's bald spot, his sprouting beard concealed the creases around his mouth, and he was trim for a man who'd just turned fifty. Duncan, ten years Axel's junior, boasted a big, low-slung belly that, along with his thinning hair, made him look like an old schoolmaster. Straightening up, sucking in, Duncan turned to Lucinda and said, "We were all at the genetics conference I told you about."

"Where everyone was arguing!" Lucinda said brightly. "See, I *do* listen. Which side"—she turned to Sam—"were you on?"

"Lu*cin*da," said a girl named Maud.

"Actually," Harold said, rubbing his cheek with his thumb, "it was Duncan and Sam here, who were having a disagreement. But that's all behind us now."

Sam tried but failed to catch Axel's expression, while Duncan changed the subject. But as they were clearing out for the next shift of diners, one of the quieter girls approached Sam and said, "Were you really all quarreling about some experiment while the soldiers were gathering? I would have thought . . ."

". . . that scientists aren't petty? That we're not as childish as everyone else?"

"Something like that," she said, with a surprising smile. "Although I don't know why I *should* expect that. I'm Laurel," she reminded Sam.

Straight brown hair, solid hips, pleasant, but, in Sam's opinion, unremarkable-looking except for her eyes. Up on deck, amid a crowd of people he didn't know and safely away from the ones he did, he watched the water move past the hull and listened to Laurel talk about what they'd heard on the radio. The Germans were smashing through Poland and had occupied Krakow. An RAF attack on German naval bases had gone awry. Each wave took them farther from what was going on in Europe. On the *Athenia*, along with the Americans and Canadians bolting for home, had been refugees from Poland and Romania and Germany who'd managed to get to Liverpool and then fought for berths, only to end up floating in the water before, if they were among the lucky, being rescued by a ship that would bring them back to Britain to begin the process of trying to flee again.

The sky was streaked with mare's tails to the south, dotted with little round clouds to the north; the last edge of the sun had vanished but some color remained. The open deck was so crowded by now that each of them touched at least one other person. Duncan pushed through like a fox through a field of wheat, nodded when he saw Sam, and kept moving. Duncan wasn't stupid, Sam thought; he knew some things, including what it meant to be part of a field of science still in its infancy. But he didn't know the new and enormous thing that Sam and Axel now shared. Sam in one boat and Axel in another, but the same sky, the same rain, the same flares and fears and darkness and dawn. Laurel said something about the windows of a church in London and Sam pretended to pay attention.

Why was it, he thought, that even here Duncan seemed able to keep him and Axel apart?

In 1921, when Sam went off to college in upstate New York, he was sixteen years old and six feet tall, trying to conceal his age behind his size and so lonely that he might have attached himself to anyone. His father, an astronomer at the Smithsonian, had died when he was four; Sam remembered his smell, his desk at the observatory, his laugh. Afterward, his mother had moved them to Philadelphia to live with her parents, who seemed to be nothing like her. He slept in a bed his great-uncle had once used, near a shelf on which, between two photographs of his dead father, a mirror reflected back a face framed by his father's thick red hair but otherwise very different. His mother's mouth, her father's heavy lower lids, two moles on a jaw that must have come from someone on his father's side. When he touched that face with hands his father's size but his grandmother's shape, he felt a huge, hazy, painful curiosity that he couldn't put into words. Like his mother, he was good with numbers, but otherwise his mind seemed to leap and dart where hers moved in orderly lines. Perhaps, he thought, like his father's? He could only guess.

When he turned eight, his grandfather persuaded a friend to admit Sam to a school so good that his mother, who wrote books and articles about astronomy, was just able to pay the fees. Tearing through his classes, eager for more, he skipped one year and then another. A biology teacher, Mr. Spacek, reeled him in when he reached the upper school, introducing him to the study of heredity. In the empty lab, at the end of the day, he'd enter into Mr. Spacek's fruit-fly experiments as if he were tumbling down a well, concentrating so intently that the voices rising from a baseball game on the field below, or from the herd pounding around the track, shrank to crickets' chirps and then disappeared. From the books that Mr. Spacek loaned him, Sam finally gained the language to shape what he'd been feeling since he could remember. Who am I? Who do I resemble, and who not? What makes me *me*, what makes you *you*; where did we come from, who are we like? What do we inherit, and what not?

Mr. Spacek helped Sam translate his curiosity into hypotheses that might be tested, experiments he might perform. He urged Sam to apply to college a year early, and then got him a scholarship and everything else he needed, including two precious books for the journey up the Hudson River. These, along with the sandwiches Sam's mother had packed him, helped during the bad moment when he confused the motion of the water rushing alongside the train with that of the train itself. Once he arrived at his new refuge, though, he felt fine. The brick and stone buildings were just as handsome as Mr. Spacek had promised, and his room was excellent too, with a big window, two low beds, two desks with lamps and chairs and space for books. Shirts and jackets were already hanging neatly along one half of the closet rod and these, along with a carton of books and a pair of skis, belonged to a wiry boy who introduced himself as Avery Hayes and asked if he might have the bed away from the window. Sam, who'd never had a close friend, right away liked Avery's smile and his calm, thoughtful movements.

> **What makes me *me*, what makes you *you*; where did we come from, who are we like?**

"Of course you can have that bed," Sam said. "But are you sure . . . ?"

"Perfectly," said Avery. "I'm sensitive to drafts. If you don't mind, I'll take this desk then, too."

Which left Sam exactly what he wanted, a view out over the quad, past the beeches and benches and flower beds to the long brick building with limestone lintels, which he'd spotted the instant he arrived: the Hall of Science, the reason that he'd come. This was his place, Mr. Spacek had told him, this and no other: because this was the place where Axel Olssen taught.

Mr. Spacek had also arranged for Sam to join Olssen's section of general biology his first semester, and Axel transplanted Sam so smoothly from Mr. Spacek's world into his—soon after the first exam, he hired Sam as a bottle washer, brought him into the lab, and told him to use his first name—that Sam hardly felt the shock. The weeks rocketed by, the work Sam wanted to do crowded by other classes, the regimen of the dining hall, compulsory weekly chapel, and the swimming lessons that were part of the physical fitness requirement. The basement pool was dimly lit, slimy under Sam's feet at the shallow end, where he stood and tried to follow the instructor's motions. He was the only one that year who didn't know how to swim at all, and those first weeks of splashing, coughing, breathing in when he was meant to breathe out, and sinking, perpetually sinking—"You're remarkably *dense*," the instructor said cheerily, trying to support Sam in the water with a hand under his ribs—were humiliating. Thrusting his face back up into the air, Sam lost track of his surroundings and once again was the small, frightened boy who, after his father's death, was sometimes swept away by tantrums. But then, as soon as he crossed the quad and entered the Hall of Science, everything annoying faded away.

Axel was young himself, just a few years out of graduate school, energetic and delightfully informal; he loaded Sam down with his own books, trusting that he could make sense of the material despite being only a freshman. When he discovered Sam's age, he laughed and said genetics was a young man's game—Alfred Sturtevant had been only nineteen, still an undergraduate, when he'd devised the first chromosome map. Calvin Bridges had been an undergraduate too, and a bottle washer, like Sam, when he spotted the first vermilion mutant. Who knew what Sam, the perfect age at the absolutely perfect time, might do? Theirs was a new field, Axel said. A whole new world.

> As soon as he crossed the quad and entered the Hall of Science, everything annoying faded away.

In class, Axel brought new terms and concepts alive with his arms, slicing the air like a conductor, his thick hair sticking up in spikes. They were after more than just the study of vague factors or mysterious unit characters, he said: the gene was not simply an abstract idea; genes were material! Heredity depended on chromosomes, forever splitting and recombining; units of heredity—genes—must be arranged like beads on a string, particles invisible to the eye but visible through their actions, ordered along visible chromosomes. Let the older generation argue about immaterial factors, vitalistic forces, the possibilities of organisms passing on changes caused by will or desire. The truth, Axel emphasized during Sam's first semester, was that the particles of heredity passed from one generation to the next, and could not be influenced by what happened to the body. Every living individual had two parts, one patent, visible to our eyes—the me you see, the tree you touch; that was the somatoplasm—and the other latent, perceptible only by its effect on subsequent generations but continuing forever, part of the immortal stream that was the germplasm. Phenotype, genotype (Sam loved repeating those words). Concepts made visible, Axel said happily, through our own flies.

So Sam couldn't swim; so he hated his history class. When he listened to Axel talk about his work, now *their* work, he was entirely alive. If they helped elucidate the way genes were arranged and transmitted, then they'd begin to understand heredity and variation. If they understood that, they'd

begin to glimpse the workings of evolution. And if they could understand evolution, then...

"You have a pedigree," Axel said one day when Sam was mashing bananas, sprinkling yeast, and measuring agar: by then he was the food maker as well as the bottle washer. "Just like our flies. You were trained by Charlie, and now you're working with me. We were trained by Thomas Morgan, who was trained by William Brooks. Brooks was trained by Agassiz himself, at the summer school for the study of natural history he founded on Penikese Island. One short line: Agassiz, Brooks, Morgan, me, and then you. You're connected to the new biology just as directly as the flies we're breeding in here are connected to the original stocks from Morgan's lab."

The Particles

Sam didn't share that with Avery, who was as interested in physics as Sam was in biology, but who hadn't yet found the right professor; it would have felt like bragging. But he did love the feel of his own hands linking Mr. Spacek's *Drosophila*, whose ancestors had also come from the fly room at Columbia, to the new generations hatching in the bottles he prepared. Forget the litter, the browning bananas, the morgue filled with bodies drowned in oil. The flies swooned docilely at a whiff of ether, moved easily with a touch from a camel's hair brush, and then—the variations were marvelous. Eye after eye after eye, all red—and then here were white eyes, and there were pink. Wings all shaped like wings, until one fly produced a truncated set and another a pair curled like eyelashes, each mating yielding surprises, a new generation every ten days: how could anyone think of this as work? Work was waiting for frogs to hatch and pass through their stages until they matured enough to mate. Planting corn and waiting for the seeds to germinate, the stalk to grow, the ear to fill and ripen before one could even begin to guess—*that* was work; he couldn't believe the researchers a few hours away at Cornell had the patience. For him it was always, only, flies. In a clean bottle, a courting male held out one wing to his virgin bride and danced right and then left before embracing her: who wouldn't love *that*? Let others fuss with peas and four-o'clocks, rabbits and guinea pigs: for Sam, the flies were the key to everything.

That first Christmas vacation, he returned to school early at Axel's request. As the train rumbled north, he looked up from his stack of journals now and then and noticed the Catskills thick with snow, or a crow flying low above the frozen Hudson, but mostly he kept his eyes on his work. The brindled dog at the train station had to bark twice before Sam stopped to pat him, walking on not to his room—the dorms were still closed—but to a small brick house two blocks from campus, where Axel, unmarried then, lived in happy squalor. Clothes on the floor, sheets on the couch (he always had visitors); Sam was welcome to stay, he said, the ten days until the semester started. A minute after Sam dropped his bag, they headed for the lab, which was warm and stuffy despite the bitter cold outside, electric bulbs glowing inside the old bookcases Axel had turned into incubators. Sam found a path through the tumble of plates and coffee cups and reprints and manuscripts, books lying open everywhere, cockroaches investigating the huge stain—molasses?—on the journal that Duncan, whom Sam then knew only as Axel's senior student, had left at his place.

Axel, Duncan, and two other students, both juniors, worked at desks pushed into an island at the center of the room; Sam's place was at the sink, shaking used food from soiled bottles, or at the counter, filling wooden racks with wide-mouthed homeopathic vials. From there he'd watched Duncan mating virgin females in bottles for which Sam had prepared the food, later shaking the etherized offspring onto counting plates, bending over dissecting scopes, shouting happily when he found something unexpected. In November, he'd discovered a new mutant, which Axel had sent to Columbia, and that had made Sam feel—not that he wanted to be Duncan, not even that he wanted to be Duncan's friend (he was shallow, Sam thought even then, and prone to leap to easy conclusions), but that he wanted a chance to work on his own.

> Let others fuss with peas and four-o'clocks, rabbits and guinea pigs: for Sam, the flies were the key to everything.

He plunged into the clutter, planning to take over Duncan's chair the minute he finished cleaning up. Axel asked if he thought maintaining the stock cultures for the Genetics and Heredity course, even as he was enrolled in it, might be too much.

"I'll be fine," Sam said, bending to his glassware. Everything stank of overripe bananas. "It's no problem at all. I could do more, if Duncan gets too busy . . ."

Axel squashed a fly on the counter and laughed. "You have to sleep sometime," he said. "Although, personally, I think sleep is overrated. Do you want to hear what went on at the meeting?"

"Please," Sam said. "I've been dying for news."

Later—at Woods Hole, in Moscow, every place where, after long days in the lab, he'd end up drinking with fellow geneticists—Sam would try to describe what he felt like hearing Axel summarize the extraordinary paper he'd heard at the international meeting in Toronto. As if he'd sprouted extra eyes, which let him see a new dimension. Or as if his brain had added a new lobe, capable of thinking new thoughts. *It is commonly said that evolution rests upon two foundations—inheritance and variation; but there is a subtle and important error here. Inheritance by itself leads to no change, and variation leads to no permanent change, unless the variations themselves are heritable. Thus it is not inheritance and variation which bring about evolution, but the inheritance of variation.* Surely the name of the man who'd written that—Hermann Muller—deserved a whole separate shelf in Sam's brain. Whenever he recited those crucial lines, others would chime in with more of Muller's essential insights: that in the cell, beyond the obvious structures, there must also be thousands of ultramicroscopic particles influencing the entire cell, determining its structure and function. That these particles, call them genes, were in the chromosomes, and in certain definite positions, and that they could propagate themselves. Magic, they all agreed. Magic!

> What did any of this have to do with science? Or with the real feeling of what had just happened to them?

For ten dazzlingly cold days that winter, before Duncan and the other students returned from their holiday, Axel and Sam talked about Muller's ideas while they worked alone together. Then Duncan returned for the spring semester, Axel showed Muller's paper to him—and suddenly they were planning experiments while Sam was sterilizing forceps. The whole semester went that way, until Duncan graduated and, for just a little while, got out of Sam's way.

During the day, when trying to move through the mass of people on deck was like being transported through an amoeba, Sam thought often about those early, blissful months in Axel's lab. Here, if Axel wasn't surrounded, he was absent. Reading in his berth, Duncan would say. Or napping, he's exhausted, talk to him at dinner. Each day would end with nothing Sam had meant to say said—and then it was night, when he kept thinking about the night.

The night in the lifeboat, the night on the water, which Axel had shared and which Duncan could never know. The night floating under the clouds and the moon, Sam's boat so flooded that it was in the sea as much as on it, everyone packed together as tightly as bodies in a collective grave. Shoulders pressed to others' shoulders, backs to chests, knees to hips; fifty-seven people who, once they were safely aboard the *City of Flint*, avoided those with whom they'd been so strangely intimate. The woman, for instance, who'd worn Sam's life belt: how was it that they didn't stick together? She had given her chance at life to her son, Sam had given his to her; the gesture might have bound them. Yet she was in one of the bunks near the rear of the ship, nowhere near his cocoon of a hammock, and when he passed her on deck, they nodded politely and kept moving. Each time, he remembered what they'd seen of each other. What that woman—her name was Bessie—had seen of him. Instead of seeking her out, he'd move toward

Laurel and Pansy and Maud, who'd turned out to be pleasant company, filled with impressions from their brief time in France and Italy and eager to talk about the news the radio officer relayed.

They kept him company at meals as well, where the questions he longed to ask Axel—who was beside you, what were you thinking, what was the part that most frightened you?—dissolved in the perpetual chatter. Duncan and Harold and George invariably settled close to Axel, who then would look at Sam, ruefully, Sam thought, as Sam found a separate place, and pretend to listen politely to the other three.

They were more interesting? They were safer. Harold and George taught at the same little college in Massachusetts, had roomed together at the congress, and, indeed, had come over together with Duncan, yet they gossiped about common acquaintances and speculated on jobs and funding as if they hadn't just had weeks of each other's company. Duncan chimed in with news about colleagues in California, not just from the institute that his former advisor had established and where he still worked, but from Berkeley and Stanford as well. Even Axel, a fixture now at the college where Sam had first met him, offered modest nuggets gleaned from meetings in New York. Whose lab was expanding, who had lost support. Whose marriage had broken up.

What did any of this have to do with science? Or with the real feeling of what had just happened to them? The meals seemed doubly hard when Sam thought of how much better he'd done recently with Avery. On the inexpensive precongress tour, which he'd taken largely so he could see where Avery worked, they'd been scheduled for a day and a half in Cambridge. Sam had skipped all the other sites to visit Avery's lab at the Cavendish, where he'd admired Avery's new X-ray facility and studied his lab notebooks. Together, they'd happily discussed their most recent projects.

By the time the motor coach left on Sunday, Sam had felt like he knew his old friend again—and it was this, he thought, staring glumly into his pea soup during one particularly trying lunch, that had made him optimistic about what might happen with Axel in Edinburgh. So they had not, before the meeting, seen each other in seven years; so their correspondence had shrunk to an occasional exchange of reprints. His warm meeting with Avery had convinced him that he and Axel would also slip back into their old, easy ways.

Through Grasmere and Keswick the following day, on to Edinburgh that afternoon: six hundred geneticists, from more than fifty countries!

New work, new ideas; a chance to renew old friendships. He'd been horribly disappointed to find that the Russian geneticists, some of whom he knew from his time in Moscow and Leningrad, had been denied permission to travel. After that, nothing else went the way he'd hoped; the session began to unravel almost as soon as it started. Germany and the Soviet Union signed their pact and the German scientists left. Then the delegates from the Netherlands followed the Germans, and the Italians followed them. In ones and twos the British scientists trickled off to join their military units, while the French left all at once.

By Saturday, when Sam gave his talk, the Poles and others from the Continent were also gone, leaving only a spotty crowd of Americans, Canadians, South Africans, Australians, and New Zealanders to listen. Where was it written that they all had to turn against him? That what he said would actually enrage them? Duncan, who spoke later that day, set his own prepared talk aside and instead spent his time refuting every aspect of Sam's presentation. He was so familiar with the last decade of Sam's work—he had read all of Sam's papers, Sam understood then—that he did an excellent job.

Here on the ship, the sound of Duncan's voice sometimes caused Sam such pain that even if Duncan weren't always blocking his way to Axel, he would have wanted to strike him. He'd come around a corner, find Axel and Duncan, catch Axel's eye, see Axel wave—and then Duncan would turn and smile falsely, and he'd keep moving until he ran into Bessie, which would spin him in yet another direction. Then at night, lying like one of a long row of larvae among his canvas-shrouded fellow passengers, he'd return to his night in the boat, when Bessie's knees and shins had pressed uncomfortably into his lower back. With every stroke of the oar he freed himself briefly from that pressure, only to thump back into her bones. He came to hate her legs, then to hate her. But later, when they stopped rowing and waited for the sun to come up, he grew so cold that he sought her legs on purpose. Her shivering shook Sam's body too, and also that of Aaron, her little boy, who was pressed into the hollow between her chest and her bent knees. Aaron's whole right side—shoulder, arm, torso, leg—over the course of those hours also pressed itself against Sam's back. All the adults faced the same way, unable to see each other's faces, sensing their levels of misery through the contact of their wet flesh. Bessie's crying passed from her chest through Aaron's side and into Sam's back, and his groans passed the other way, a wave moving through the boat. Her back had to be pressed into someone else's legs, and that person's back to the next and the next and the next. Each time he went over this, he imagined that Axel was listening and that he in turn would describe his own night.

Meanwhile, the *City of Flint* kept steaming sturdily through the waves, miles passing but far too slowly: how to get through the days? A grim-faced doctor, still waiting for word of his wife and daughter, busied himself by organizing the ship's hospital, stitching up the survivors' wounds, tending to burns and scrapes. He'd been in a boat that overturned and had spent hours floating alone, draped on a bit of rudder. What, Sam wondered, did he think of when he stopped working? A Canadian girl, ten years old, had been struck on the head by a falling beam when the torpedo first hit the *Athenia* and, although she'd been conscious during the night in the lifeboats and her first day on the *City of Flint*, had fallen into a coma; the doctor watched over her closely, and Sam would sometimes sit beside her, reading out loud from a novel Laurel had loaned him.

> **He'd been in a boat that overturned and had spent hours floating alone, draped on a bit of rudder.**

Eavesdropping at dinner, pretending to listen to Lucinda and Maud but actually straining to hear Axel responding to Duncan's questions, Sam learned that Axel, when he wasn't resting, passed the hours reading books he'd borrowed from Harold and George. Harold, meanwhile, kept busy with the little daily newspaper he now posted each morning on a bulletin board, around which people gathered to read his notes of the ship's progress and bits of friendly gossip. The college girls put on a fashion show, herding good-humored volunteers along an improvised runway as others voted for the most outlandish costume. On a day when the sea was very smooth, pierced now and then by leaping fish, Sam wrote letters to his mother and to the woman he was seeing back home, neither of whom knew that his changed plans had put him aboard the *Athenia*. The letters, which couldn't be sent until they reached Halifax, were as useless as curled wings on a fly, but time passed as he tried to describe—not the explosions, not the bodies, not his night in the boat. Not what had happened in Edinburgh, nor what Duncan had done, nor his estrangement from Axel. The shapes the clouds made in the sky, then. The porpoises leaping in sets of three and five. The brave little girl in her improvised romper and the kind women, strangers before boarding this ship, who cared for her.

He found a corner where he could wash his face in the morning, and an exercise route—from the open middle deck in front of the smokestack, around the port side of the deckhouse, to the bow, and back down the starboard side—on which, if he rose early enough to beat the crowds, he could pace like a horse in a mine. No matter what he did, or how he arranged his days, he ran into Duncan. When Duncan stopped near the air scoops to light a cigarette, the solid sheet of hair lying over his forehead flapped up and down in the breeze like a lid. Why was he there when Axel, whom Sam so much wanted to see, was always where Sam was not? And when Sam went down below one night to the talent show that Maud and Lucinda had organized, Axel was there, but there with Duncan.

> They were all flirting with socialism then, some more than flirting

Men sang "Danny Boy" and "Begin the Beguine," children tap-danced, a woman pleated an accordion. Two sailors whacked at fiddles as two more whirled about. Axel came over to suggest that Sam do some little tricks involving toothpicks and gumdrops, which he was good at and used to offer up at parties: two minutes to make a model of a locomotive, a minute—Avery had first taught him this—for a sugar molecule. For a moment, Sam was tempted, remembering how at Woods Hole he'd entertained his companions with models of sea squirts and the polymer backbone of cellulose, but then he looked at Duncan, right by Axel's side and waiting for him to make a fool of himself, and he declined.

Instead, Duncan stepped forward and, in his surprisingly sweet tenor voice, sang a bland version of the song for which, years ago, he used to invent ribald verses, entertaining the students during the summer they'd both spent at Woods Hole. Sam had just finished his junior year at college then; Duncan had been in his second year of graduate school, studying with Axel's teacher, Thomas Morgan. Almost everyone important in their new field was at the biological station that summer, investigating some aspect of genetics or embryology or both. Sam, one of the few undergraduates taking the invertebrate course, paid his tuition by waiting tables at the mess hall and collecting specimens for his teachers. On nights when the moon was in the right phase, he'd bus his tables, drop his apron, and head for the *Cayadetta*'s dock with a long-handled net and a tray of finger bowls. His desire to earn his teachers' approval was as ruthless as the lantern he held over the water, dooming the mating clam worms that spiraled upward.

Afterward, he skipped the gatherings at the ice-cream parlor and the visits to the movie house in Falmouth so that he could work on the project that had seized him. A scientist named Paul Kammerer, who had recently made two American lecture tours and whose sensational work—*VIENNA BIOLOGIST HAILED AS GREATEST OF THE CENTURY. Proves a Darwin Belief*, one newspaper blared—was so controversial that even Sam's mother, who wrote articles for popular science magazines, had interviewed him, had caught Sam's eye as well. Kammerer claimed to have shown that when a change in the environment of his toads and salamanders caused an adaptive change in them—altered skin color, different reproductive behaviors—these changes could be transmitted to subsequent generations. A kind of heresy, Sam knew—the exact opposite of what he'd seen in the lab for himself. Although he'd breathed in his Quaker grandparents' conviction that the world can be improved, first Mr. Spacek and then Axel had trained him out of his unconscious assumptions that when individuals strengthened and developed their faculties, through vigorous use, they then passed that strengthening along. That the ones they stopped using were lost, and lost for good.

At Woods Hole, though, surrounded by interesting strangers pursuing so many different ideas, the truth had begun to seem more complex again, which made him read Kammerer's claims with real curiosity. Axel had taught him to question everything—didn't that include the beliefs that were quickly becoming conventions in their field? At night, roasting oysters on the beach, he and his classmates talked about Kammerer and speculated on the reasons why some biologists attacked him so furiously. Even those opposed to his conclusions were disturbed by that. They were all flirting with socialism then, some more than flirting; they sympathized when Kammerer complained that no one gave him a fair hearing. With the war just over, no one wanted to hear that inheritance wasn't everything, or that race and class characteristics passed on through generations might be altered.

Tiny, darkly tanned Ellen Eliasberg, a fellow student in Sam's invertebrate course, was moved by Kammerer's passionate statements about the necessity of man passing on what he acquired in the course of his lifetime to his children and his children's children. Sam was caught up by her arguments—and, at the same time, fascinated by the bad temper Duncan's advisor showed whenever anyone mentioned Kammerer's work.

"The leopard *can* change his spots?" he'd say mockingly. "Fathers can

The Particles

pass what they've learned to their sons? Why not just reject every bit of science done in the last century? Why not go right back to Lamarck and his folklore? Cave fishes and deep-sea dwellers lose their eyes because they don't need them in the dark; moles have poorly developed eyes because they're in burrows most of the time; if an organ isn't used, it conveniently disappears and if it's used often—why not point to the giraffe stretching his neck to reach for higher leaves?—it gets bigger. How long has that been believed? And yet Payne bred fruit flies in the dark for sixty-nine generations, without the slightest change in their eyes or behavior. In my own lab, we've seen well over one hundred new types arise spontaneously, with no environmental influence, each breeding true from the start. Overnight—literally, overnight!—eyeless flies have appeared from normal parents, by an obvious change in a single hereditary factor."

Then he'd say that the popular press was being fooled, once again, and foolishly misleading the public (here Sam thought of his mother; had she sorted this out?); he'd say Kammerer was a charlatan and a publicity seeker and perhaps even a fraud. He ranted so wildly that even Duncan looked uneasy, and Sam saw, for the first time, what might happen when the passion required to defend a new set of ideas went too far.

But he wanted to work, simply to work, and he tried to stay focused on that. The old wooden house where he bunked that summer was less than a block from the lab, surrounded by sand and scrubby pines, but during his first weeks he went there only to sleep. Every minute he could steal from his course and his jobs he spent designing an experiment that might prove or disprove what Kammerer contended. Instead of Kammerer's slow-growing salamanders and midwife toads, Sam decided to use his swiftly reproducing flies. And he'd work with their eyes, not only because variations in eye color had been the first and best-documented of the mutations observed in fruit flies but also because eyes and their development had always been central to these discussions.

He used fly cultures he'd kept for Axel, techniques he'd learned in his lab, a procedure he'd seen Duncan do in a different context. With a needle he ground to a very sharp point and then heated, he touched—just touched—the center of the red eye of a lightly etherized female fly; then he touched the other eye and laid the fly on a dry piece of paper, which he put into a little vial. A couple of hours later, he transferred the treated flies to a food bottle. In the few that survived the procedure he watched how the Malpighian tubules, which worked rather like kidneys, turned deep red and stayed that way. So: injury to one organ, the eye, caused what appeared to be a permanent change in another organ: an acquired characteristic.

Later, he mated the treated females to normal males and proceeded as usual. Amid the next generation he found a few mutants—yellow body, narrow eyes, twisted penis—as expected. And also, unexpectedly, seventeen flies, both male and female, with red Malpighian tubules. This was peculiar, and completely interesting: what did it mean? Immediately, he started breeding these to each other. None of their offspring showed the red tubules, but that might mean nothing; the trait was likely recessive, and he had only a small sample.

> Sam saw what might happen when the passion required to defend a new set of ideas went too far.

Duncan and most of the other students had a sense of what he was doing; they wandered in and out of the open labs and they all talked not only while they worked but also during their outings. Still, no one knew the details until the director asked him to give a presentation at one of the season's last Friday night gatherings. He was nervous when he spoke—undergraduates were rarely asked to speak in front of the whole community—and he referred to earlier work that he hoped might support his own. In particular, a recent symposium that many in his audience had attended and that had examined this crucial question: *could* an injury to one generation cause an effect that was inherited by the next?

Swiftly, he moved through those other researchers' results. One had demonstrated the transmission of acquired eye defects in rabbits, which seemed to have the characteristics of a Mendelian recessive. Others had shown what seemed to be inheritable effects of injury from alcohol, lead, radium, and X-rays. Perhaps, though, this was parallel induction: had a physical agent acted simultaneously on *both* the germ cells and the somatic cells, producing changes independently in each, or had the change induced in the body actually affected the germ cell? Which was the mechanism at work with Sam's flies, and would either case argue for evolution directly guided by the environment? Sam saw Duncan in the audience, listening intently and taking notes, although he didn't ask any questions afterward. Other hands did wave, though, and Sam was pleased with the way he guided the passionate, occasionally contentious, but civil discussion that followed.

In September, when he returned to college and reported all this to Axel, Axel shook his head and said he wished Sam had consulted him before throwing himself at such a controversial issue. He should never, Axel said, have presented this to so many eminent scientists before testing his hypotheses more thoroughly. Then he said that while he didn't yet trust Sam's results, they were intriguing and Sam should push the work forward. He'd supply the flies and the other materials; when the time came, he'd help Sam write up the results. "Although it would have been better," he added, "if you'd done even more while you were still there."

"I should have," Sam admitted.

> His hands on her small, pointed breasts, his mouth in the hollow of her throat, her bony feet on his back.

And would have, he knew, if he hadn't gotten involved with Ellen. Four years Sam's senior, presently working as a biology instructor at Smith, she'd spent the previous year in England, where she'd cut off her hair, befriended several brilliant women, and taken up feminism and eugenics. One opinion she held strongly was that exceptionally intelligent people—"Like you," she said to Sam, during a collecting trip at Quisset, "and me"—should have children together, which would improve the world. Later, she and Sam decanted their specimens side by side, and a few nights after that, when a crowd of students got drunk on the beer two chemists had brewed, they ended up entwined in the dusty wooden attic over the supply room.

The next day, when Sam apologized for what had happened, Ellen calmly claimed it as her own idea and said Sam had only done what she wanted. At the beach, she wore a daring wool-jersey bathing suit that clung to her wiry shape and ended midthigh, the white trim disturbingly like underwear, and when she swam, she looked to Sam, with her close-cropped hair, like one of the elegant spiraling clam worms he collected at night. He had no idea how he felt about her; he was nineteen, and she let him make love to her. Sam couldn't imagine why.

"Because I want to have several children, starting soon," she told him. "And you're such a good specimen. You're tall"—here she tapped one of Sam's fingers—"big-boned and bright"—tap, tap—"hardworking, sturdy, even-tempered."

By then she was working on Sam's second hand, having thrust the first inside her blouse. His hands on her small, pointed breasts, his mouth in the hollow of her throat, her bony feet on his back. He was completely inexperienced when they met; he was astounded. For the last two weeks of his stay at Woods Hole he was with Ellen every night. If I'm pregnant, she said the day they parted, we'll get married. If not—

Not, as it turned out, although they met as often as they could during Sam's last year of college, several times near Sam and twice in Massachusetts, the second time just after Duncan proved him wrong.

What kind of a person would, in utter secrecy, interrupt his own project to replicate a fellow worker's experiments and double-check his results? Duncan published a paper noting that the preliminary results of a young student investigator—here he named Sam—presented orally and informally had sufficiently interested him to push those experiments further. When he did, he found that in flies whose eyes had been burned, the Malpighian tubules indeed turned red, and that a small number of the offspring of those flies also had red tubules.

But he also saw something Sam had failed to see, perhaps because he'd been so absorbed with Ellen. In his early work in Morgan's lab, Duncan had occasionally noticed—or so he wrote; Sam wondered if it wasn't Morgan himself who saw this—larvae feeding on the eyes of dead flies that had fallen on the food at the bottom of the culture bottle; this had colored the intestines of the larvae red. After seeing the initial data (and this did sound like him; he could test a chain of reasoning like a crow pulling at the weak spots in a carcass), Duncan had suddenly wondered if the pigment might be carried through the pupa stage, possibly appearing in the adult fly.

He crushed the eyes of some flies, mixed them with yeast and agar from a culture bottle, and added larvae; their intestines soon became filled with the red food, and a bit later the Malpighian tubules, visible through the larval walls, became deep red. The larvae pupated; adults emerged; their tubules too were red. Variations with different foods showed clearly that some component of the red pigment in the crushed eyes passed from the digestive tract of the larvae into the Malpighian tubules and remained there into the adult stage. Sam's larvae had eaten the damaged eyes of dead flies and that—not a response to the injury itself—had colored their tubules. Sam had found not an acquired characteristic, but simply a transient response to diet. Acquired characteristics were not—could not be, Duncan said—inherited.

Sam was wrong, he'd been proven wrong, but at first that didn't seem so serious—why would people hold his curiosity against him? He was young, he was enthusiastic; he'd seen a big question in Kammerer's work and explored it open-mindedly, trying to follow the data rather than his own preconceptions; he'd shared his findings honestly. Leaving Woods Hole for his last year of college, he'd sensed that others saw him as a wonderfully promising student, welcome anywhere. Six months later, the recent work he'd done in Axel's lab rendered pointless by Duncan's paper, those same people seemed to regard him as a dubious young man who'd overreached himself. Even Axel, after reading the copy Duncan sent specially to him, a little handwritten note—"I'm sorry"—scrawled at the top, groaned and went for a long walk before sitting down with Sam.

"I should have seen that," Axel said when he returned. "If you'd kept in touch with me over the summer, if we'd been talking about your experimental design . . . I should have seen that before Duncan did." Sam couldn't tell whether Axel was more angry at himself for missing it or proud of having taught Duncan so well.

In the wake of that paper, Sam knew he wouldn't be welcome at Columbia, where everyone had assumed he'd follow Axel and Duncan to graduate school. But with Axel's help he found a place in a small program in Wisconsin, run by a sound but middling geneticist. Not one of Morgan's golden boys, like Bridges or Sturtevant; not even someone at the top of the second tier (which was how Axel disparagingly characterized himself), but a man who knew he was lucky to have a lab and the funding for a few graduate students.

Sam spent that last summer in Axel's lab, maintaining the cultures and leaving everything in order for Axel's next helper, wishing, all the time, that he could be discussing new projects with Axel. But Axel, collaborating with a friend in Texas, was seldom there, and Ellen, who might have helped him settle into his new life, instead did the reverse. If she'd gotten pregnant during his last year of college, nothing, Sam knew, could have wedged them apart—but she didn't, and didn't, and when summer came and she still wasn't pregnant, they didn't see each other for several months. In August, she backed out of her offer to drive to Wisconsin with him, and before Thanksgiving she was gone.

For a long time, Sam was able to avoid her. His luck ran out after seven years, at a big meeting in Washington where Duncan received a prestigious award. Sam was moving toward the back of the auditorium, having just heard a talk by a maize geneticist and hoping to escape before Duncan spoke. He ran into Ellen in the middle of the aisle, herding two boys and a girl, all recognizably Duncan's, toward the special seats at the front set aside for the prizewinner's family. She introduced the children awkwardly and asked how Sam was doing.

"Fine," Sam said. "Just finishing my thesis." She and Duncan had married before he'd even started that work. After which Axel, as if inspired by them, had married a mathematician he'd met in Texas, moved to a leafy street twenty minutes from the college, and promptly produced a son.

"We miss you at Woods Hole," she said.

"Handsome boys," he said, avoiding their eyes.

Tugging at her younger son's collar, bending to adjust the skirt on the dark-haired little girl who'd inherited her reedy arms and legs, Ellen said that she and Duncan went back every year, always with the children, who loved it. But nothing had ever been as wonderful as her second summer there. When, Sam knew by then, she'd already left him but he didn't know it. When she and Duncan had both returned and Sam, in the shadow of his big failure, had been unable to join them.

> **If she'd gotten pregnant during his last year of college, nothing could have wedged them apart.**

On the lifeboat, before the sun rose, when the night was at its coldest and the waves were tossing them about and when, having long since thrown up everything he'd eaten the previous day, Sam was retching painfully and Bessie's hand was lightly patting the back of his neck, he had thought about his calm hand bringing the needle's point so lightly, so deftly, to each *Drosophila* eye. How the flies' wounds had sometimes stuck to the food, and to each other; how those that lived were weak for several days, some unable to eat. Here on the ship, shaken about like a fly in a test tube, he too was having trouble eating. One evening he learned that while most of the geneticists who'd been on the *Athenia* with him had been picked up by the British destroyers, two were apparently lost. And on the eighth day of the crossing, while he scored patterns in the oatmeal that was one of the few things left to eat, Sam learned that the little girl who'd been in a coma had finally died.

Gloom spread through the ship as each seating heard the news, and later Sam saw Bessie, near the bow, comforting her son, Aaron, who was crying. He and the girl had been friends, Sam thought, or at least known each other the way children even of different ages do when confined together. He couldn't stop himself from walking over to Aaron and squatting down beside him. He rested his hand on Aaron's back, his fingertips moving gently.

"Shh," he said. "It's all right." Which was what he'd said in the boat, when Aaron was so cold and sick that he was crying. Also this was what Bessie had said to Sam. Now she said, "He's taking this very hard."

"Were they close?" Sam asked. The two geneticists who'd drowned, husband and wife, had worked at a small Minnesota college and traveled only rarely to international gatherings. Sam hadn't met them at the congress, but he had on the ship, and he'd envied them when they came down hand in hand to what would be their last dinner. Axel had said, at that same meal, how much he'd been missing his wife and son.

"She took him for walks around the deck, when she was bored," Bessie said, gesturing toward their own crowded railings, so packed with passengers eager for air—they were expecting rain—that strolling was out of the question. "They played make-believe. You know, the way children will: I'll be the mommy and you be the little boy, and I'll get you ready for school . . ."

> Everything that had led to his father and mother and converged in him would be extinguished.

"She sounds sweet," Sam said. The figures crowding the railings separated, moved together again, bunched, and dispersed, long lines forming only to condense into shorter segments.

"Not always—once she pinched him hard enough to leave a mark."

Aaron shrugged off Sam's hand and pushed himself more firmly into Bessie's legs. "Do you have children?" she asked, smoothing her son's hair.

"I don't," Sam said, and if Duncan and Harold hadn't joined them just then, he might have told Bessie how pained he'd been when he understood that he likely never *would* have any. Ellen, who couldn't get pregnant with him, had gotten pregnant instantly with Duncan; no woman he'd been with since had had so much as a scare. Sometimes, when he'd had too much to drink (throughout Prohibition, he and his friends had always had access to lab ethanol), he used to joke around with a toothpick-and-gumdrop figure he called Mr. Heredity. *Look at me!* he'd have the figure say. *Interested since childhood in how we inherit traits, but I can't reproduce!* But although he laughed as hard as anyone when Mr. Heredity drooped his gumdrop head, later, when he began to grasp the fact that no one would ever have his hair or his blocky nose, his height or his big hands, he felt quite otherwise. The day his heart stopped, the day he got hit by a bus (the day a torpedo sank the ship that was taking him home), everything that had led to his father and mother and converged in him would be extinguished.

But here were his colleagues, bearing down. He managed a smile as they greeted him and, looking at Bessie and Aaron, asked if they could do anything to help. Sam introduced them only by name, without explaining how he knew them.

"We're fine," Bessie said.

Impossible to focus on her and Duncan at the same time. Instead, Sam kept his eyes on the unusually turbulent sky. Great, soft, gray clouds piled one atop the other, pushing each other aside like wrestling dogs.

Bessie said, looking only at him, "Margaret's death made Aaron miss his father more than usual. He keeps thinking something's happened to him, that he won't be there when we get home. Those men we saw in the water . . ." She picked Aaron up and left.

Duncan watched them walk away and then turned back to Sam, eyes bright with curiosity. "You were in the same lifeboat?"

Sam nodded. He'd told Duncan nothing about the night in the boat; what Duncan knew of the torpedo, the flames, the boats in the water, he knew from other survivors, not from him.

"If you ever want to talk," Duncan said, pushing aside his floppy hair, "I'm happy to listen."

After Sam graduated from college, he mostly kept his work to himself. Axel, busy with his new wife and son, also had new students to train and increasingly relied on his connection to Duncan, who was doing very well as part of his advisor's group. Duncan and his colleagues shared fly strains with Axel's lab; Axel and his students collaborated on papers with them, which helped them all. Sam worked alone, steadily and quietly, throughout his years in graduate school, doing nothing without his advisor's explicit approval, choosing a thesis project closer to his advisor's heart than to his own and committing to it entirely. He kept in close touch with Avery, who'd gone to England by then, and Avery helped him modify an X-ray source so he could radiate his *Drosophila* and look for mutations. The experiments he completed were nowhere near as flashy as Muller's work in this area, nor did he and his advisor gather anywhere near as much data—they were working along parallel tracks at first and then, after Muller had yet another big breakthrough, in support of what he'd already shown—but Sam knew it was solid work, a bandage for his dented reputation. By 1930, when he got his degree, he was able, despite the growing effects of the crash, to find a position in Missouri. In between teaching sections of general biology, he worked every spare minute in his own lab, grateful for what he'd been able to salvage and trying not to envy

Duncan, who had followed his advisor out to California and had a much better job.

Half his salary he sent to his mother, who, in the wake of both her parents' deaths, had taken in boarders but even so was still struggling to hang on to the Philadelphia house. When he lost his job in 1933, he knew she felt the blow too. Although he wrote to everyone he'd ever met, there were no positions to be had. Axel, who temporarily had to close his own lab, could find him nothing, and Duncan couldn't, or wouldn't, help, despite being the protégé of someone who'd just won a Nobel Prize. When Sam had nothing to lose and was on the verge of going back home, he appealed to the man whose paper had so inspired him during his first year of college, and in whose field he now worked.

He'd written to Muller a few times during graduate school, sending results that confirmed or extended Muller's own and asking about his latest work. At a conference, Muller had tracked Sam down and inspected his most recent data closely; after that, they'd continued to correspond about interesting questions. If a quantum of light could, as Niels Bohr suggested, trigger photosynthesis, was it also the case that an individual ionization caused a mutation? Did chromosome breaks result from radiation's direct or indirect effects? After Muller left Austin in the wake of a scandal involving his support of a Communist-leaning student newspaper, he went to Berlin, where, he wrote to Sam, he was collaborating with a brilliant Russian scientist who shared his interest in using the tools of physics to explore the nature of the gene. The work was intriguing, the company stimulating, but just as he was settling in, Hitler was appointed chancellor and soon his colleagues began to lose their jobs. Muller then accepted his Russian friend's invitation to come help set up a research program and most recently had written to Sam from the Institute of Genetics in Leningrad.

Was it possible, Sam wrote him, that given his background and their shared interests, he could be of some use at the institute? Secretly, he thought they also shared a disgust with what was going on in their country, the mad inequities that seemed to be destroying every good thing. In Russia, Sam thought, science might assume its rightful role, and scientists, instead of being separated into little fiefdoms ruled by petty kings, would work under the shelter of the state, free to follow their best ideas. He was thrilled when Muller, so enthusiastic himself about the Soviet experiment, found money for a position in which Sam was, if not quite an independent investigator, more than a student.

Soon Sam was living in Leningrad, investigating chromosomal rearrangements and learning that many of the apparent point mutations caused by X-ray treatment were actually recombinations of broken fragments. Segments were lost, segments were duplicated; he began to get a sense of what size a gene might be, and how it might function when moved to a new position. What if natural mutations were actually rearrangements of the particles in the chromosomes, rather than changes to the particles themselves? Muller proved to be an excellent guide. Not a teacher, as Axel had been; not really a friend; he was clearly Sam's boss, but he was accessible and kind, and Sam was thrilled to be working with someone he'd admired for so long.

> Sam was thrilled to be working with someone he'd admired for so long.

It hardly mattered that, with housing short everywhere, Sam had to sleep in the corners of other scientists' rooms, for a while in a bed behind a curtain in the laboratory, later in a basement hall. Everything was crowded, everyone was improvising; he was glad to be part of the common flow, and even the struggle to find supplies was worth it—such excitement! Such work, for such a purpose. Surrounded by Russians day and night, he learned the language quickly. And when the institute was moved to Moscow, Sam went too, leaving behind several friends and a woman with whom he'd had a brief affair.

Writing to his mother—he tried to write home twice a month—he described the farmers and engineers he met, the German Jews who'd sought refuge in the Soviet Union as the Nazis rose to power, the ardently socialist Englishmen and discontented Americans. He met men who'd soldiered in several wars, including one who'd fought Germans at the beginning of the Great War and then Americans, later, in Archangel, with the Reds. *He showed me the white cotton overcoat he'd worn,* Sam wrote, *which had made him invisible in the snow. He claimed that once, as he'd been scrounging for food in the streets, he'd seen an American soldier leap from the top of a gigantic wooden toboggan run and onto the ice below. Really, I am living in the most remarkable place.*

That winter, as the snow fell and fell—he was never warm, no one had enough fuel—Sam thought often of that soldier suspended in the air. Leaping from or leaping toward? For all the hardships of daily life here, he still felt freer than he had since his time in Axel's lab, and he moved through Moscow with a sense he hadn't had in years of everything being interesting. At the Medico-Genetics Institute he saw hundreds of pairs

The Particles 83

of identical twins—how eerie this was, each face doubled!—being studied like laboratory mice. He visited collective farms, and he met a geneticist named Elizaveta who'd discovered a remarkable mutant fly a few years before Sam arrived. Walking toward her bench was like walking into Axel's lab for the first time, the air dense with the smells of ether and bananas and flies fried on lightbulbs, the atmosphere of delight. Elizaveta, who had long, narrow, blue green eyes below the palest brows, said she knew that genes controlled development: but were they active all the time, or did each act only at a particular period of development, and lie dormant otherwise?

> Scientists from different fields began to disappear as well, including geneticists.

At meetings—so many meetings!—he listened to talks about the practical applications of genetics to agriculture and the Marxist implications of the theory of the gene. Once, in a dark room after a day of lectures, he watched a film called *Salamandra*, about an idealistic scientist who'd demonstrated Lamarckian inheritance in salamanders but then was betrayed by a sinister German who tampered with his specimens to make it look as though his results had been faked. Denounced, deprived of his job, he lived in exile until rescued by a farsighted Soviet commissar who proved his work had been right all along. Partway through, Sam grasped that this was a transposition of the life and fate of Kammerer, who'd killed himself after a researcher proved that some of his results had been faked. By then, his own big mistake seemed very far away.

Working all the time, excited by the new experiments in the lab, he ignored what was happening out on the streets until, after a while, even he couldn't avoid knowing about the party members being persecuted and executed, those who disagreed with Stalin disappearing. Intellectuals and scientists from different fields began to disappear as well, including geneticists, some of them Sam's own colleagues. The director of the twins study vanished and his institute was dissolved. Elizaveta, more cautious than some, gave her flies to Sam and then slipped away to her grandmother's village. Geneticists had failed, Sam read, to serve the state by providing the collectives with new crops and livestock that could thrive in difficult climates and relieve the food shortages. They were stuck in bourgeois ways of thought. If a society could be transformed in a single generation, if the economy could be completely remade, why couldn't the genetic heritage of crops or, for that matter, of man, be transformed as well?

In this context, Lamarck was a hero; and also Kammerer (Sam could see, now, why he'd been shown that film); and also the horticulturist Ivan Michurin, who'd claimed that through some kind of shock treatment he could transform the heredity of fruit trees, allowing growth farther north. Trofim Lysenko, pushy and uneducated, rose up from nowhere to extend Michurinism beyond what anyone else could have imagined. Lysenko hated fruit flies, he knew no mathematics, he found Mendelian genetics tedious, even his grasp of plant physiology was feeble. How could Sam take him seriously? Lysenko claimed that heredity was nothing so boringly fixed as the Mendelians said, but could be trained by the environment, endlessly improved. At a big meeting Sam attended at the end of 1936, Muller tried to rebuff Lysenko by clearly restating Mendelian genetics and outlining the institute's research programs. Larmarkian inheritance, Muller explained, could not be reconciled with any of the evidence they'd found.

Sam was amazed when some in the audience actually hissed, and more so when, after Lysenko responded by dismissing all of formal genetics, those same people stood and cheered. Genetics was a harmful science, Lysenko said, not a science at all but a bourgeois distortion, a science of saboteurs. Muller and his like were wrecking socialism, preventing all progress, whereas he would now completely refashion heredity! His Russian was failing him, Sam kept thinking; Lysenko couldn't be saying that what should be so, must be so. Yet his friends heard the same thing. Those who doubted him, Lysenko said, were criminal. A theory of heredity, to be correct, must promise not just the power to understand nature but the power to change it.

Muller, after making careful arrangements to protect his colleagues, left the country early in 1937, and Sam followed a few weeks later, first destroying the papers and letters he'd received from his Russian friends. *Of course I understand why you need me to return to the United States*, he carefully wrote to his mother, who'd requested no such thing but could be counted on to understand that his letters were likely being read.

Back in Philadelphia, writing up his last results from the Moscow lab in the small bedroom where he'd slept as a child, the familiar sound of his mother working in the living room complicated by the movements of the two teachers with whom she now shared the house, Sam began another search for work. This time he had better luck, finding a position at a small college near the western edge of Illinois. For a while, as he was trying to set up yet another lab—how many times could a person order glassware, brushes, ether, drying racks, all the bits and pieces needed to do the smallest experiment?—he thought about changing fields entirely. If science in the United States was controlled by a few powerful people, and science in the Soviet Union was nothing but a branch of politics—then what was the point of doing anything? Perhaps he'd do better at farming, or statistics, or auto mechanics.

Soon enough, though, he got caught up in the life of a place that at first had felt to him like nowhere. His better students were curious and eager to learn, and he found—as perhaps Axel had found earlier; Sam longed to talk with him about this but couldn't afford a trip east—that he had to hurl himself at a problem again, simply to give the students something to do. He started a genetics course in addition to his sections of general biology; he bought a little house with two large trees; he met a woman he liked, who planted vegetables in his backyard and taught him how to cook chard. The college gave him an excellent incubator, as well as some other crucial equipment. Through the fly-exchange network he was able to get some useful stock, which in turn put him in touch with many of the researchers trained in Morgan's lab: not only Axel but also Harold and George (that was how he first met them) and, inevitably, Duncan, who immediately mailed to Sam's new address all the papers he'd published while Sam was abroad. Once Sam solved some difficulties with mites and temperature fluctuations, he was back in business and, after hiring a couple of student helpers, began a new set of experiments. For one particular project, he used Elizaveta's flies.

He'd smuggled breeding stock into the country, and when the cultures were established, he turned, with a sense of recovering his younger self, to investigating them. Like some of the curiosities naturalists had noticed and collected for years—crustaceans with legs where jaws or swimmerets should be, plants with petals transformed into stamens—Elizaveta's flies shared the property that one organ in a segmental series had been transformed into another. How were those homeotic mutants produced? And were those variations heritable or caused by damage to the developing embryo? An acquaintance of Axel's had discovered a true-breeding homeotic mutant he called bithorax, in which the little stabilizing structures normally found behind the forewings had been transformed into a second set of wings; Elizaveta had worked with that four-winged mutant, and also with an even odder one called aristapedia, which had legs growing where the antennae should be. Endlessly fascinating, Sam thought, and he began to investigate how a mutation to a single gene could cause such massive effects.

Months passed, a year of hard work passed; thousands of cultures and tens of thousands of flies. In the mutant, he learned, the antennal discs developed early, at the same time as the leg discs, allowing the evocator that normally instructed the leg discs to act on the antennal discs as well.

Evocator: he loved that word. The chemical substance that acts as a stimulus in the developing embryo. How intriguing, how sensible, really, that the mutant gene didn't build a leglike structure out of thin air. Instead it acted more simply and generally, altering the rate of development so that a whole pattern of growth occurred at a time and place where it ought not to be.

> **Soon enough he got caught up in the life of a place that at first had felt to him like nowhere.**

Others were working on this as well, but there was so much to do, along so many branching paths, that Sam had no sense of racing to solve a problem before someone else. Rather, the whole world seemed to shimmer, a delectable feeling he'd first had as a boy, working with Mr. Spacek: the act of throwing himself at one problem, *this* problem, lit up every other aspect of his experience in the world. Legs grew out of a fly's head because of a small change in timing; would his life have been different if his father had died earlier, or later? If he hadn't met Mr. Spacek when he did, or gone to college at sixteen and found Axel willing to teach him. If he hadn't met Avery or Ellen, hadn't met Duncan . . .

In this state of excitement, he'd gone to the congress, where he presented his results and then connected that work with Goldschmidt's, with work on position effects and the possibility that the particles of heredity might move around, with the possibility that maybe all genetic changes were changes in development. Maybe genes weren't particles after all, weren't arranged like beads on a string, but were more like spiderwebs, susceptible to the influence of events in the cytoplasm; maybe they weren't quite as impregnable to outside influence as previously thought? He aimed his ideas at his former Russian colleagues, who should have been there but weren't; at Axel, who was there but had missed all the groundwork; at Muller, who'd found a temporary haven in Edinburgh and who, although distracted by the responsibilities of hosting the congress, still found time to come and listen to him. He sailed past his notes, avoiding the false paths of Kammerer and Lysenko, which, unlike most of his audience, he'd learned for himself, to speculate about the question of timing. When, in the course of development, might a tiny change cause massive later effects? Might inheritance not be far more complex than we'd guessed? When he finished speaking and looked out at the disgruntled faces in the audience—Duncan's face was red, Axel was poking his notepad with a pencil, Muller was gazing at him quizzically—he had a separate thought, which had nothing to do with inheritance. The first big leap he'd taken, with Kammerer's work, had turned out to be wrong. Was it possible that now no one could see the rightness of this second big leap, because of his first mistake?

> When, in the course of development, might a tiny change cause massive later effects?

Two bright white ships, crisp and military-looking with broad red stripes across the bow, came out of the distance to meet them when they were still several hundred miles from Halifax. Sailors from the coast guard cutters transferred food, which they needed badly—oranges! Sam saw, and apples and cheese, potatoes and meat, fresh bread!—along with toothbrushes and hairbrushes, soap, shampoo, donated clothing, more blankets. Two doctors, wanting to examine the wounded to see who might need the alignment of broken bones checked with their portable X-ray machine and who should be transferred to the cutters for care, also came aboard.

For the first time in more than a week, Sam brushed his hair, cleaned his teeth with something other than a finger, and along with everyone else dipped into the new supplies to spruce up for that night's celebration. Officers from the cutters joined them, the captain extracted a case of whiskey from the hold, a few passengers did what they could to decorate the deck while others, beginning to believe now that they'd get home safely, began to relax. All around him, Sam saw groups of people, faces suddenly scrubbed shades lighter, smiling and talking with the friends they'd made on the journey. These women bound to those, these students to those sailors; the college girls—for him, still simply pleasant acquaintances—more closely attached to Duncan and Harold and George than he'd understood.

He felt, for a moment, unusually alone—more so when he saw that Axel, standing only a few feet away as the whiskey was handed around, was barricaded by Duncan and Harold and George. Fanning out from them were Laurel and Pansy and Maud, talking to a young man Sam hadn't met; Lucinda, playing cards with the plant physiologist he'd first seen the day they were rescued; and Bessie and Aaron, sitting on one of the hatches, watching the constellations rise in the sky. Sam went over to Bessie's side as Pansy asked the young man what he planned to do when he got home.

"I'm still in school," he said shyly.

Sam looked up, spotting the stars of Pegasus. He remembered sitting on his father's shoulders, following the line of his arm as he traced out shapes overhead. *Look at the horse, do you see the dolphin? There's a whale . . .* Or did he remember those shapes from other evenings, much later, with his mother?

"I'm an art student," the young man continued. "I was traveling on a fellowship. But now . . ."

"You'll go back when the war is over?" Maud asked.

"What's the point?" he said. "Without my friend."

As Sam continued to pick from the glitter overhead all the constellations he could remember, the student described how he and a dear friend from their school in Boston had split a traveling scholarship meant for one of them so that they could both see Europe. Despite their pinched budget and the signs of war cropping up everywhere, they'd visited Paris, Amsterdam, Verona, Venice, and even Berlin before returning to London, which they'd reached about the same time Sam reached Edinburgh. They too had found their ship home from Glasgow commandeered and later sailings either booked or canceled; they too had boarded the *Athenia* as a last resort. After the torpedo struck, he and his friend had managed to stay together in one of the last and most crowded lifeboats, which was also the most unlucky—the one that had swung too close to the *Knute Nelson* and been crushed by its propellers.

"We dove into the water," the student said, "my friend and I. We dove and then we swam until we found a plank to hang on to. After a while we were picked up by another lifeboat. By then the *Southern Cross* was near us, so we rowed there. And then we got too close to the back of that . . ."

As his voice trailed away, Duncan, who had moved closer, said, "That wasn't the boat . . . ?"

The young man nodded, looking over at Axel and Duncan, then down at the deck, as if embarrassed that others had already heard the story and that some had seen the boat overturned.

"My friend," he said. "My friend—by the time the crew from the *Southern Cross* reached us, he was gone."

How could anyone be so unlucky? Not one but two lifeboats wrecked beneath him, his friend by his side through the torpedoing, through the first lifeboat's destruction, only to be lost. Sam closed his eyes. The ship rolled beneath him, a long, slow movement that made him dizzy. A hand touched his: Axel?

Bessie, Sam saw, when he opened his eyes. "Are you all right?" she asked.

"The whiskey," Sam said faintly.

"Let me get you some water," she said, burrowing through the crowd. Duncan came up on Sam's other side and poked his shoulder. Jovially, stupidly, looking exactly the same as he had all week—the new supplies had meant nothing to him—he said, "Too much to drink?"

Where had Axel gone?

Duncan stopped smiling. "You don't look very well."

"*Now* you worry about me?" Sam said.

An odd look crossed Duncan's face. "What went on at the congress—that's work. I don't agree with your work; I want it buried. Doesn't mean I want *you* buried. Until you came over the side of this ship, when I thought you might have drowned, I felt—"

"Oh, please," Sam said.

"You're impossible," said Duncan. He pushed past Sam and toward Harold and George. Then, finally, Axel reappeared, his face concerned and his hand stretched toward Sam.

"It's all right," he said quietly. "It's all right. It wasn't as bad as all that."

"What wasn't?" Sam asked stupidly.

"When our boat overturned, under the stern of the *Southern Cross*—I saw you turn pale when that young man was speaking, the one we'd pulled from the water earlier, with his friend. I knew you must be thinking of me, what had happened to me and how much worse it might have been. But it wasn't so terrible, not really. I was in the water for a while but I didn't know I was hurt, I couldn't even feel the gash on my head. And I had an oar to cling to, and it wasn't too long before the crewmen from the *Southern Cross* found me and got me aboard. And then once I got here, and Duncan tracked me down, he arranged everything. You mustn't worry so about me."

How was he only now learning for sure what had happened to Axel? If they'd had time alone together, if they'd been able to talk . . . why hadn't Axel ever come to *him*? That night on the water, he'd scanned every boat they approached for Axel's face. Then, it hadn't mattered that they very seldom saw each other, that since Sam's time in Russia—no, before that, even—since Axel's marriage, perhaps, or since Sam had lost that first job and Axel hadn't been able to help him, they had drifted apart. He'd come to the meeting in Edinburgh hoping to repair this, tracking Axel through the corridors and cocktail parties like a devoted beagle, but although they'd had pleasant moments and caught each other up on the trivia of their lives, they'd never had the one, real, deep conversation Sam had been missing for so many years. And when Duncan attacked him so vigorously, Axel had not defended him. He hadn't supported Duncan—but he had not, in public, stood up for Sam. Instead, afterward, he'd pulled Sam toward a bench beneath a holly tree and questioned him closely about his results. Then he said—Sam felt this simultaneously as a blessing and a dismissal—that the work itself seemed promising. But why, Axel scolded, would he expose it to the world at such an early stage! If he would only stop speculating in public . . .

After the torpedo struck, he and his friend had managed to stay together in one of the last and most crowded lifeboats.

"That's what happened to you?" Sam said now. "That night in the boat?" It wasn't so much what changed in the environment that altered a living organism; it was the *when*. A question of timing. When in the course of development does the event arrive that initiates the cascade of changes? "That's what happened?" he repeated.

"You knew that," Axel said. "Didn't you? I assumed . . ."

That Duncan had told him, Sam understood. That Duncan had relayed to him whatever Axel, stretched out on his berth, the bandage stuck to his oozing wound, had said. Axel must have told the story of his night on the water to Duncan, who lay on the floor in the place where Sam should have been. Perhaps he'd also relied on Duncan for whatever image he had of Sam's own night; he'd never asked Sam. "Duncan," Sam said feebly.

"I know," Axel said. "Really, I *do* know—he can be so exasperating sometimes, he probably told you more than he should have, he's always too dramatic. And he forgets how attached we are. I don't think it even occurred to him that you might be upset by hearing that something bad happened to me. Any more than he seemed to understand, in Edinburgh, how much he'd hurt me by attacking you."

Sam stared at him blankly. "But Duncan," he said, "the way you are with him . . ."

"I do the best I can," Axel said. "You must have found yourself in similar situations with students. You know how sometimes you have to treat the one you actually feel least close to as the favorite, just so he won't lose confidence entirely?"

"I do," Sam said miserably. Not that he'd ever felt treated as a favorite, but he knew what Axel meant: he'd always acted more kindly toward Sam than he really felt, so that Sam wouldn't be too crushed to go on.

"I've always had to do that with Duncan," Axel said. His bandage, unpleasantly stained, had shifted farther back on his head. "I still do, I find, in certain situations. And here—what could I do? He wanted so badly to take care of me."

"You gave him his start," Sam said, not knowing what he meant.

"It's a good thing I can count on you to understand," Axel said. "You're strong enough to go your own way. That's part of what gets you into such trouble. And part of why your work is so interesting."

The next morning, still a day and a half out from Halifax, Axel and five other passengers were transferred to one of the cutters, which had excellent hospital facilities. The wound on his head wasn't healing properly; the coast guard doctor wanted to debride and resuture it without further delay. Sam, left behind with Duncan and Harold and George, could do nothing but wave goodbye and hope that they'd find each other later.

At the docks, a huge crowd greeted them, Red Cross nurses and immigration officials, family members of some of the survivors, local citizens who wanted to help, reporters from various papers: they were big news. Theirs had been the first ship sunk and theirs the first Canadian and American casualties; when the torpedo struck the *Athenia*, not even half a day had passed since Britain and Germany had gone to war. Nurses moved in to tend to the wounded; volunteers brought coffee and sandwiches; officials herded them into the immigration quarters, where they arranged baths and offered clean clothes. Scores of reporters moved in as well, eager for stories—what had they seen, what had they felt?—and then all the passengers began to talk at once, a hopeless tangle.

How could Sam be surprised when Duncan stepped forward? Of course it was Duncan who, never having set foot on the *Athenia*, still somehow managed to simplify, generalize, organize the scattered impressions. The reporters turned toward him, relaxing, already making notes: so much easier to follow his linear narrative, spangled with brief portraits of the survivors and vivid details of the crossing! He'd listened closely, Sam saw, to accounts of what he hadn't experienced himself. Bits of Axel's story flashed by, along with elements of the art student's, the plant physiologist's, Bessie's, and more. Bessie looked startled, as did some of the others, but what Duncan recounted wasn't untrue; it just didn't match much of what Sam felt, or what he knew to be important. If Duncan were to tell the story of Sam's working life it would, he knew, be similarly skewed—yet who knew him better than Duncan? Who had been with him for as much of the way?

Only Axel, who, leaving the *City of Flint* for the cutter, had held his hand to his stained bandage, looked crossly at the doctor, and said, "Really, I'm *fine*. I don't know why you want to move me like this. I'd rather stay here with my friends." And then had gestured toward Duncan and Sam, on either side of him.

Patricia Lockwood

AN ANIMORPH ENTERS THE DOGGIE-DOG WORLD

Discover the power at age 11. Discover all powers
at age 11. A kittenhead struggles out of your face
and the kittenhead mews MILK, you gasp with its
mouth and it sucks itself back. Yet the mew for MILK
remains, you drink it. You think, "I am an Animorph."
Your sight and your hearing increase, like wheat
and the wind in the wheat. Well you've never seen
any wheat but it sounds good, to you and your new
trembling ears. Blue sky increases above the wheat
and you know what it's like to grow a . . . well.
A hawk's is between two legs but much higher.
      Halfway to any animal is where you like
to be. Get halfway there and have just the instinct,
the instinct that someone's approaching. Stripes
   begin to form, are always a surprise, you look
down and you move your head left to right and then
the meaning comes. English get worse but not much
in your muzzle, English get worse but not much
in your mouth. You walk to school and sit next
to a girl who was born with a tail and you copy off
her. You rub your temples when they ache, rub any

of your body when it aches, you seem to be only
a series of places where animal parts could emerge.
Soon you will be a teenager, and soon you will be
so greasy, and how you can hardly wait, because:
its grease makes the animal graceful, and go. You go
to the petting zoo with your class and timidly reach
         in a hand. Turn to a donkey and finally
     feel your lashes are long enough. Turn to a horse
and finally feel that your eyes are so meltingly human.
Walk home on your own through the fields and the fields,
and the increase of wheat and the wind in it, and think
of the life that stretches before you: work your way
through all the animals, and come to the end of them,
and what? And turn to crickets, and make no noise?
One tear struggles out of your face, but no that's not
a tear. "I fuckin eat crickets," your kittenhead says,
"I fuckin eat silence of crickets for fun. I got life after
life and a name like Baby. Every time I try to cry a tear
a new kittenhead grows out of me." And oh how you
are lifted, then,
         the kittenhead of you in the high hawk hold.

THE COMPUTER PLAYS A GAME OF CHESS

Oh
the probabilities he breathes, and imagines
her opening move: she sits down at him
and types, "I was a child chess prodigy,
it was just me and my mother, I was all
from different fathers, I choked on a horse-
head when I was three and breathed around it
    ever after, I spent Saturdays in classrooms
    still smelling like six blond Jennifers—"

    the computer closes his eyes and remembers
    his own school days, a young erect machine
    at a desk flunking every biology test
                    they gave him—

"I kept a horse-head in my pocket and touched it
whenever I got too nervous, soon its whole
flaring face was loved off, I played another
prodigy—one of the six blond Jennifers!—
and we shook hands after I totally killed her
and her cherub flesh went *poing* against me,
and my breath whistled fast past the horse-

head, and later they found us in the bathroom
cramming castles in each other's mouths—
    it was never the same after that. I began
      to lose on purpose, even in the parks,
where the leaves were always turning orange
or so you have been told, and I never played
chess again, the end,"

    what end breathes the computer, and all
      possible moves play against him at once,
    each raises a goosebump of data on him,
then: tell me about the box, he begs, tell me
about the box you slap, I think it has something
to do with time. "Speed chess was my frst great
love" she types, "120 pawns a mnute." Her fingertip
oils have worn off his I, she has loved off completely
his comma,

      he slows with love and she slaps him
        hard and her human breath comes faster now—
oh the polished marble head! Oh the flowing
        hair of horses, or so he has been told.

ESSAY

THE WILD WHAT

Amy Leach

Bright star, you're a gas!

Several centuries ago the stars reconstellated into figures more relevant to the times. The Earth had been industrializing, mechanizing, electrifying, while the stars were still trotting out swans and goats and bears every night. Men of the world advised the stars to update their subjects, to figure forth printing shops and electricity generators. Obligingly the stars complied, and for a while the sky was up to snuff; the stars were sophisticated and worldly; but then shops supplanted shops and machines surpassed machines and the sky was left behind, littered with musty antiques.

Thereafter were the stars persuaded to depict compasses and quadrants, stripped of their names, given numbers, all but regimented into a grid, before they had had enough and reverted to their old subjects: dogs, dragons, herdsmen, bears. Take heed, worldly fashion—someone may trust you up to a point, but if you push him too far you will lose all the power you ever had over him and he will blaze up and turn into a bear.

The bear in the sky is sometimes mistaken for a prawn, or the government, while the bear on the ground rarely is. There are a few discrepancies between the bear in the sky and the bear on the ground—for one thing, bears on the ground are not nocturnal; nor do they have long tails; nor are they stalked by ravening chickadees who cook and eat them once a year. (Chickadees are good cooks but they do not usually own cooking pots.) The long tail of the Great Bear is also the handle of the Big Dipper, which is an asterism, less distinguished than a constellation, lower down in the hierarchy of starry patterns. Any goose can make up an asterism. Constellations are superior to asterisms and asterisms are superior to asterisks.

There is an even higher order than constellations, though. Many of the stars in the bear are leaving the bear: they belong to the Ursa Major Moving Group. If you saw an assortment of red berries in the air, all floating the same way and perfectly maintaining their configuration in relation to each other, you might surmise that they were all growing on the same invisible drifting hedge. Sometimes, in the pool, dispersed among the randomly paddling people, is a secret synchronized swimming team, not singing and smiling and exhibiting their legs but all heading the same way and all possessing an inward resemblance if not the same mass. As they move across the pool it may look like they are part of miscellaneous social clumps, but watch carefully and you will be able to discern that they are associated with each other and share a common drift, perhaps toward the slide.

That is what the Ursa Major Moving Group is like. Ostensibly members of the bear and the giraffe and the water carrier and the rabbit and the harvest maiden, these stars are secretly committed to the Ursa Major Moving Group. Like brother and sister berries, the stars of the Ursa Major Moving Group are chemically homogeneous, with unusually high levels of yttrium, and they came from the same cloud. They are slowly drifting toward Sagittarius; as they drift, they will wrench apart the bear, the giraffe, the harvest maiden, the tresses of Queen Berenice, Apollo's goblet, the man in the coils of a snake, and the snake itself. Thus are many identities, over time, shown to be temporary alignments of components involved in a deeper allegiance. Goodbye to my goblet, goodbye to my bear; identity must yield to deeper identity. Goodbye to my giraffe, goodbye to my girl; local association gives way to an association of travelers across the firmament.

> But until something disintegrates, there is always a chance it will be taken to heart.

Stars, like thoughts, are not inevitable. Out of the diffuse dusty disorder something may or may not coalesce; floating specks in space find each other very escapable. Think how easy it is to escape the gravitational field of an animalcule. When consolidation does happen, it is usually precipitated by an outside force: a density wave, a nearby supernova, two colliding galaxies send the specks reeling, clustering, concentrating into collapsing factions, and those specks that once were strangers, easy come easy go, are now drafted into the same turbulent, raging-hot, high-pressure project—not just pressed close but pressed *into* each other, their previously repulsed protons fusing, four hydrogens becoming one helium. Out of these violent conjunctions are born the least violent, most oblivious things in the universe—neutrinos, rushing by the trillions through your person every second. Runners-up are oblivious to persons, tarantulas, silver and gold, landslides, dust bunnies, disapproval, hearsay, the cheese cart rolling by, but neutrinos are oblivious to all this and geraniums.

The other byproduct of nuclear fusion, besides neutrinos, is light. All bodies are radiant but not all radiance is visible: stars radiate visible light; planets and donkeys and couches radiate infrared waves. (If your couch is emitting visible light GET UP IMMEDIATELY.) Some condensing assemblies in space never get big enough to radiate visible light. A star will not shine until it has assembled enough self; once it has enough self it cannot help but shine; once it starts to shine it cannot help but burn the self up, and blow the self away upon the stellar winds. Some stars are so windy they lose a Sun's amount of mass every 100,000 years—at that rate, if you weigh one hundred pounds, you could be selfless in two yoctoyears.

Dubhe, the red giant at the front of the Big Dipper's bowl, is not a member of the Ursa Major Moving Group. In fact it is drifting in the opposite direction. But Dubhe is not all alone in the universe; Dubhe has a companion star, Dubhe B. If you want to know how it feels to have a companion star, find a stone that weighs as much as you do, about 100 pounds, or less if you want to be the primary star. If your name is Ruby you can call the stone Ruby B; then get a strap and call it Gravity—it will be what holds you together. Now place Ruby B in the strap and swing her around and around. At first you will feel like you are doing all of the work, but after a while Ruby B will start reciprocating and you and Ruby B will be a mutually slinging sensation.

Yes plus No equals a circle, where Yes is coming together and No is flying apart. Two stars in mutual orbit feel equally the forces of Yes and No, of gravity and inertia. If Yes were stronger they would crash together; if No were stronger they would go tearing off into the wild what. Ambivalence is an engine, a motion machine.

Three ambivalent planets have been detected circling 47 Ursae Majoris, a star between the bear's back paws; three messages dispatched thereto from Evpatoria Planetary Radar. One of the messages is a musical program created by teenagers and performed on the theremin, an instrument you play by waving your hands around in front of it. The First Theremin Concert for Aliens begins with "Egress Alone I to the Ride" and concludes with "Kalinka-Malinka." Of course music does not always register with its intended audience—when music comes out of nowhere like that, it is hard for an audience to know whether they should admire it or not. The aliens might ignore the First Theremin Concert for Aliens; then it will seem pointlessly conceived, space-borne compositions transmitted in vain: the First Theremin Concert for Nobody, with a long way to go before it disintegrates.

But until something disintegrates, there is always a chance it will be taken to heart. Even if the aliens despise the theremin concert, perhaps on a leguminous exoplanet farther out, a bean farmer possessed of two muddy acres and one lost pig will be out late one night looking for his pig, calling, "Dewey come back!" and the strains of "Kalinka-Malinka" will reach him and he will look up astonished, into the wild what, whence cometh weird delights. The song is his who hears it.

The Bright Bear, made of stars and planetary nebulas and far-off galaxies, contains within it a Dark Bear, made of black holes and dust and gas and planets and moons and invisible dwarfs. Black dwarfs are stars that have gone to seed: having run through all their hydrogen, all their helium, having stripped all the electrons off their atoms, they are cool and spent and invisible. However at present black dwarfs are invisible not because their lights went out but because there are no black dwarfs. For any black dwarfs to exist yet, their precursors would have had to be older than the universe. Roomy an inn as it is, the universe turns away anyone older than itself, perhaps because it would alarm the other guests.

Although brown dwarfs are dim and cool like black dwarfs, it is not because they are spent—you can only be spent if you once had something to spend. Brown dwarfs were always brown dwarfs; they start out dim and get dimmer; they are like pits that never had a peach. But even failed stars have planets, though of dubitable habitability. What a brown dwarf can offer its satellites is stability—whereas hot young stars will explode, squandering their gravity, frizzling their followers, brown dwarfs are stable and attractive forever.

But for all that, brown dwarfs are never adored; for a host star to be adored, it must first give ferns enough confidence to come out of the ground. The ferns on their planets never come out of the ground, the squirrels have no ferns to play under, and no squirrels to play with.

If there is seeing without perceiving, there is also perceiving without seeing. If Ruby B were invisible we could infer her presence from your anomalous wobbling. Brown dwarfs and super-Jupiters and black holes, though hidden from sight, can be inferred from the anomalies they cause in their seeable neighbors. Much strange behavior, in fact, is caused by invisible companions, although implied existence is not certain existence. Not everyone who stumbles, stumbles upon an invisible bandicoot. Our Sun may not have a brown-dwarf companion called Nemesis that provokes our planet's periodic disasters.

It turns out that a lot of normal behavior is also caused by the invisible, for example the fact that the galaxies do not fling away their stars like slingstones. There does not seem to be enough material to hold a galaxy together; they rotate too fast—their outer stars should be thrown in various directions, like you and Ruby B if the strap broke. For them to be as gravitationally stable as they are, spinning as fast as they do, they must contain a lot more matter than the matter we can see—about eighty percent more. The galaxies have some pumpkins up their sleeves.

Is this true on smaller scales, too? Apart from a visible fragment, is everyone largely invisible—invisible like the magic part of magic mushrooms and the song part of songbirds? Maybe the balance between one's visibility and invisibility is like the balance between the salt and the water in the blood, delicate and critical, as becomes obvious when the balance deteriorates: people with an invisibility deficiency seem like paper dolls, subject to crumple. Other people have the opposite problem: they cannot be seen building a bicycle, nor making lentil soup, nor knitting a green wool sweater by candlelight; neither can you look down from your second-story window in the morning and see them tromping off through the snow.

The Pinwheel Galaxy, a little east of Chickadee, is about twenty-two million light years away, so we see it as it was twenty-two million years ago: a swishing pool of lampy champagne, yellowy pink, trailing fizzy streaks of sapphire stars. Space champagne is strong—Pinwheel champagne strong enough to have sparkled up a trillion stars. If we could be in the Pinwheel Galaxy now, peering back at Nebraska, that would also be a sight to see—the horselife and the hickorylife and the ducklife twenty-two million years ago, the horses tiny and amateur, with three toes on each foot, the hickories following their own counsel, the ducks upended in the pond, dabbling for weeds, hoping never to be ambushed by an ysengrinia.

The Pinwheel Galaxy seems to be dominated by Euphoria. In fact it looks like most places out there are dominated by one spirit alone, where none of the others can get a foothold—see, for example, comets commandeered by Confidence, or the intergalactic stretches languishing under the rule of Patience. Not even Mercury is really mercurial. But here on Earth, Glee and Delinquency and Grimness share terrain. Of course none of them has changed its essentially rapacious nature; we still see how ruthless the spirits can be, as when Joy possesses a dog and whacks her tail against a wall, over and over, although the dog is whining and her tail is broken. Many times a day a mood sets up a monstrous dominion in the mind, but before it kills us another takes its turn, and no ruler who hands over the reins like that can be called absolute.

Maybe after thirteen billion years of experience, even despots start to understand that despotism eliminates anyone sensitive, that what they long for, more than territory, is sensitive territory, that too much electricity fries the wire that carries it, that in a wilderness of ice, or dust, or flame, there is no substrate for Dread or Giddiness to grow on. If you were Reticence, would you rather inhabit a pseudo-star or a waif, even if you had to share the waif with Warmth? So they check themselves, dwelling in combination, being as gentle as they can be, here, as gentle as they can. Translucent green worms hang down from tree branches, twisting on threads in the breeze. Male deer rub the velvet off their antlers. When the sun shines through the rain, the drops turn clear gold.

LOST AND FOUND

POSITIVE CHARGES

ON LAWRENCE WESCHLER'S
Mr. Wilson's Cabinet of Wonder

GABRIEL BLACKWELL

Lawrence Weschler's *Mr. Wilson's Cabinet of Wonder* opens with a drawing: the Cameroonian stink ant (*Megaloponera foetens*) "with forehead rampant." According to Weschler, this normally earthbound ant climbs high into the rain-forest canopy, confused by a fungus that has infected its brain. There, a perpendicular stalk sprouts from the ant's chin and crown, killing it instantly. In a matter of days, the fungus uses its spent host to produce spores that then sprinkle down to the forest floor, where other ants ingest them and follow their predecessors into the canopy, a vicious cycle. It's telling that Weschler accompanies this description with a drawing and not a photograph. The ant depicted seems whole and unharried, except for the looming threat of what appears to be a wood screw hanging above its head. A fascinating story, no doubt, but is it true?

I was hooked despite my skepticism, or maybe because of it. So was Weschler, who didn't learn about the stink ant in an archaic encyclopedia—though his drawing seems orphaned from one—but at a storefront in Los Angeles called the Museum of Jurassic Technology, which is packed with everything from a preserved European mole to a hydraulics-enhanced scale model of Noah's Ark. As a reader peruses Weschler's inventory of the museum's exhibits, he or she will be hard put to suppress the occasional arched eyebrow: A South American bat that can pierce lead with its ultraviolet "echo-wave transmissions"? An "Antler Wall," featuring racks from a moose, a deer, and the back of a woman's head? An exhibit comparing the sound made by "small, iridescent beetles, when threatened," to "similarly sized and hued pebbles 'while at rest'"? (The sound of a pebble at rest?)

The first part of Weschler's book, "Inhaling the Spore," tells the story of visiting the museum and meeting its curator, the David Wilson, described by Weschler as "Ahab inhabiting the body of Puck." "'We're a small natural history museum with an emphasis on curiosities and technological innovation,'" Wilson says. "'We're definitely interested in presenting phenomena that other natural history museums seem unwilling to present,'" a claim to which Weschler adds the caveat: "phenomena known to science, if known at all, because of their appearance in the museum itself."

A quarter of the way through the book, having faithfully offered up these bizarre exhibits and the equally bizarre research behind them, Weschler finally asks, "Um, what exactly *is* this place?" And I thought, "What took you so long?"

Weschler's skepticism is, as it turns out, healthy, and much of the fun of his book is in seeing where his urge to debunk the fantastic exhibits leads him (the notes that follow the second section of the book are longer than that section itself, nearly doubling the book's overall length). Wilson has set up his museum as a kind of scholarly house of mirrors in which his sources are often real even when the exhibits are fake. And any fake sources are jokes that the (hyper-)educated visitor would get. The stink ant, for instance, comes via the Carolina Biological Supply of Portland, Oregon. "Carolina Biological Supply . . . *in Portland, Oregon?*" wonders Weschler. Calling information, he is told that, yes, such a place exists. Still, Weschler cannot let it go. He calls Tom Eisner, a biologist at Cornell, to inquire about the Cameroonian stink ant: "'*Megaloponera foetens*, you say? I don't think *Megaloponera* exists, but there is a genus that used to go by the name *Megaponera*, although—it gets a little complicated—lately I'm told it's been folded into another category called *Pachycondyla*. And there is an African ant called *Pachycondyla analis*. "*Foetens*" is smelly, but "*analis*"—well, let's just say that's even more smelly.'"

So the "Cameroonian stink ant" exists, albeit under a different name. But what about the fungus? Because so much of the joy of reading this book lies in watching Weschler's investigations come to their uncanny ends, I won't tell you what he found, but following the conclusion of "Inhaling the Spore" is the book's lone full-color plate. On it is a photograph of an ant nearly vertical, suspended on a wisp of a leaf by a ghostly stalk springing out of its head that is easily as long as the ant itself. One thing the reader can be sure of is that there is more to this photograph than either Wilson or Weschler is telling us.

The real story behind this exhibit, as with all the exhibits at the Museum of Jurassic Technology, has more to do with Wilson than it does with its subject. Wilson's background is not in museum science, nor, for that matter, is it in biology, although he *may* have majored in urban entomology in college. Before opening his museum, Wilson worked in the film industry, "doing highly sophisticated and specialized camerawork." Special effects, in other words. Trick photography—making the real seem fake and the fake seem real. As Weschler explains in the book's second part, "Cerebral Growth," it is a surprisingly apt education for a would-be curator.

The museum, "in its original sense . . . meant a spot dedicated to the Muses," writes Weschler, who traces the history of the institution back to the sixteenth and seventeenth centuries and the Wunderkammern, or cabinets of wonder. "[The] experience—of the ground opening before one's feet—was at the heart of the sensation of wonder ideally afforded by . . . many of the cabinets of the time," Weschler tells us. So, too, were the first museums designed not with an impulse to educate, but with a desire to guide visitors from one extraordinary object to another, inspiring a sense of compounding wonder, wonder "defined as a form of learning—an intermediate, highly particular state akin to a sort of suspension of the mind between ignorance and enlightenment that marks the end of unknowing and the beginning of knowing."

Weschler's book, too, seems not quite firm in its convictions, itself only an intermediate step toward knowing. The contents of the essays that constitute the book are called into question by Weschler's endnotes, and then those endnotes are reexamined in the "Acknowledgements and Sources" that follow them. On the last page of the acknowledgements, Weschler is still wrestling with his subject: "I couldn't help myself," he writes. "I did end up having to pursue the matter [of a cure for bed-wetting involving a roasted mouse and toast], and the reference, naturally, is actual." The "reference" is "actual," but Weschler won't advance any claims about the truth of the matter. As Weschler found himself in his first visit to the museum, so too, does this reader find himself at the end of Weschler's book—fascinated, skeptical, and not a little bewildered, wondering, "Um, what exactly *is* this?"

ON RACTER'S

The Policeman's Beard Is Half Constructed: Computer Prose and Poetry

ALEXANDRA KLEEMAN

As a child in the early nineties, I discovered a type of computer program that others casually called "chatterbots": text-based interfaces designed to simulate conversation between the user and a humanlike entity. These programs were entertaining, and they projected an aura of effortless sentience without the heavy-duty, strenuous programming that was then at the core of many other attempts to create artificial intelligence. ELIZA, the computerized Rogerian psychotherapist, was the most popular of the programs. It generated questions or turned each bit of user response into an open-ended statement, outputting phrases such as "I am sorry that you are depressed" or "Why do you think that you are a selfish person?" that encouraged users to say more, to provide more material, in order to further the specter of conversation. But there was another program, called RACTER (short for "raconteur"), that would "talk" to you at length and at all hours and, unlike ELIZA, RACTER was a bit deranged. It solicited input from the user, and then placed these phrases, Mad-Libs style, into narratives that veered off into the nonsensical and the abstract. While ELIZA's measured responses felt distinctly mechanical, RACTER's weird tangents could have been the utterances of an odd bard. A year or two ago, while trying to hunt down a copy of the program, I learned that RACTER had "authored" a book—*The Policeman's Beard Is Half Constructed: Computer Prose and Poetry by RACTER*.

RACTER's writing is spastic at times, crystalline and concise at others. In its stories, tangles of characters with generic names collide in dinner-party settings in which each character's relations to the others are disclosed in cluttered detail; in its poems, a bizarrely whimsical lyric voice discourses on topics of love, cosmology, reason, and matter. There are stylistic flaws in the text—the words *steak*, *lettuce*, and *neutron* are conspicuously overused throughout. But the moments when RACTER captivates are those in which the voice surveys aspects of human experience, giving the effect of a speaker looking in on life from an inquisitive, but dissociated, exteriority:

At all events my own essays and dissertations about love and its endless pain and perpetual pleasure will be known and understood by all of you who read this and talk or sing or chant about it to your worried friends or nervous enemies. Love is the question and the subject of this essay. We will commence with a question: does steak love lettuce? This question is implacably hard and inevitably difficult to answer. Here is a question: does an electron love a proton, or does it love a neutron? Here is a question: does a man love a woman or, to be specific and to be precise, does Bill love Diane? The interesting and critical response to this question is: no! He is obsessed and infatuated with her. He is loony and crazy about her. That is not the love of steak and lettuce, of electron and proton and neutron. This dissertation will show that the love of a man and a woman is not the love of steak and lettuce. Love is interesting to me and fascinating to you but it is painful to Bill and Diane. That is love!

Reading RACTER's poems and stories makes you feel as if you are looking at yourself from a great distance, through the lens of a cognitive system that produces meaning and comparisons mechanically, without reference to familiar combinations that make "good sense." It's a feeling like the one I used to have sitting in front of my computer alone, late at night, chatting with pre-programmed bots: a sort of intimation or trail that led outward, into the machine, and then, ultimately, back to myself.

Original and uncannily engaging on the first read, upon subsequent readings RACTER's writings begin to show signs of their dependence on the manipulation of human agents. Although RACTER's programmer, Bill Chamberlain, states in the introduction that "the writing in this book was all done by a computer" and is "in no way contingent upon human experience," it is clear that RACTER's writing owes much to the programmed contents of its vocabulary bank and to the algorithms that randomly assemble phrases and cause language elements to recur, creating the illusion of reasoned and coherent thought. Much of the "liveness" in RACTER's work can be located in the programmed syntax patterns that RACTER fills with supplied content, in the compound sentences and multiple clauses that pile up on one another dynamically. The sentences are grammatical, but they register an urge toward linguistic excess: nouns and verbs tend to come in groups of two or three, adding to or contradicting the connections they begin to form. "Helene's a maid, I'm a quantum logician; can maids know galaxies or even stars or a multitude of galactic systems? The universe is frightening, little, gargantuan; can maids recognize electrons? I recognize each of you thinks I'm maniacal, but electrons and neutrons and a multitude of mesons are within you all," declares a character in the short story "Soft Ions." While the voices of RACTER's characters and narrators are difficult to distinguish from one another, the elements of the text enact an animated dialogue with each other, returning to topics while rephrasing previous propositions, elaborating and questioning, mimicking the surplus of signification and sense associated with natural language use. In this way, though Chamberlain insists that "the programmer is removed to a very great extent" from RACTER's operations, the programmer seems to be vitally present, preparing the syntactic structures within which RACTER operates, selecting from among the examples of generated text which will be included for publication, constructing signal from noise.

If all the work in *The Policeman's Beard Is Half Constructed* was indeed "done by a computer" as Chamberlain claims, then a radical revision of our conception of creativity seems necessary. What RACTER does in writing is no totality of invention or creation: it would, perhaps, be best thought of as an act of generation, a term that connotes the idea of material born of other material. Like the collages by artist Joan Hall that illustrate the book's stories and poems, RACTER's creativity is recombinatory, bringing preexisting pieces together in new and striking orders. In this way, machine-produced creativity offers us insight into the machinelike qualities of our own creative processes: writing is the mobilization of linguistic units that originate outside of the writer, made active through arrangement and utterance.

While the computational mechanisms underlying the production of RACTER's work are fascinating in their own right, *The Policeman's Beard* is not designed simply to showcase this recombinatory power. A person curious about the "natural" voice of the computer could access the raw code, the pages of readout generated in response to even the simplest user commands. RACTER's book aims instead to let us see the computer as we see ourselves, speaking as we speak ourselves. The quirky and puzzled alienation that runs throughout the work is touching, a voice eking out an understanding of itself on the page: "More than iron, more than lead, more than gold I need electricity. / I need it more than I need lamb or pork or lettuce or cucumber. / I need it for my dreams."

But when we consider the work of the human editor, selecting these scraps from other scraps, stripping away machine noise in order to isolate a signal, a subject, another narrative emerges. The editor discovers something identifiable in fragments culled from random recombination and pieces these computed sentiments into a voice. What we respond to in RACTER's writing are the fragments of ourselves hidden there for our own excavation: RACTER's puzzlement and dissociation are our own, made apparent through something like ventriloquism. In looking deeply into the technological I, we look more deeply at ourselves. Technology neither approaches nor overtakes the human, but offers it company, shows it a strangeness and a loneliness that originate within, but can be perceived only from without.

ON C. P. SNOW'S
The Two Cultures and the Scientific Revolution

AND JOHN BROCKMAN'S
The Third Culture: Beyond the Scientific Revolution

CHESTON KNAPP

I was born into a house divided. In college, Mom studied history and English, and Dad did biology. Growing up, when we needed help with our homework, my brothers and I razzed Mom for not knowing her math and mitochondria, and Dad for mangling the past's facts. Her occasional miscalculations and his sometime solecisms thrilled us, because we relished correcting them. We switched sides seamlessly then, our childhoods an idyll of curiosity.

But then school betrayed us, and the divide turned inward. Earnest educational bureaucrats had built the bridges to our future, and in sixth grade, we encountered our first riddled troll: the squat and blotchy standardized test. We sharpened number two Ticonderogas and bubbled in our Scantron sheets, which were mailed off, probably to Texas, to be scored. And we waited for our prophecies as to which bridge we would cross: were we to be men of math and science, or were we better built for arts and language?

In his Rede Lecture at Cambridge University in 1959, later published as *The Two Cultures and the Scientific Revolution*, C. P. Snow, who was primarily a novelist but who also had a background in science, laments this division.

His core idea is simple enough, as simple as breaking bread. There are two cultures: "Literary intellectuals at one pole—at the other scientists, and as the most representative, the physical scientists. Between the two a gulf of mutual incomprehension." Snow claims that the literary intellectuals suspect the scientists of being ignorant of man's tragic individual condition, that we all die alone, while the scientists accuse the literary intellectuals of being unconcerned with man's social condition and in deep denial of "the future"—"If the scientists have the future in their bones, then the traditional culture responds by wishing the future did not exist." Literary intellectuals don't know the second law of thermodynamics and scientists have trouble reading Dickens, let alone Shakespeare. Things are a mess!

The anxieties around science and literature and the possibility of their coexistence aren't new, and they weren't new when Snow spoke at Cambridge University in 1959. Before him, there was Plato, who famously expelled poets from his republic. There was Descartes, who, with the thin blade of his radical doubt, sundered subject from object and helped ratify (along with the other rationalists and empiricists) what Alfred North Whitehead later called "scientific materialism" as the only trustworthy, i.e., verifiable, way to know the world. And eighty years before Snow, the poet Matthew Arnold gave a Rede Lecture, called, simply, "Literature and Science."

If we ignore some of Snow's careless reasoning (can there be a social condition without an individual one?) and cloudy terminology ("culture" slips in and out of definitions as though they were ball gowns), we see it is the simplicity of his main idea that guaranteed its longevity. Whether or not people know who C. P. Snow was, they seem to know his phrase, those few freighted syllables: "The two cultures." It has become shorthand for the force fields of insecurities surrounding the two pursuits and the kerfuffles that break out when they cross paths.

There have been minor skirmishes here and there, but the most recent significant run-in between the cultures happened during the mid-1990s. It's referred to ominously as the "science wars." Postmodernist academics and philosophers, embracing Thomas Kuhn's paradigm shifts and Karl Popper's notion of falsifiability, made aggressive animadversions on the very idea of objectivity and claimed scientific knowledge was socially constructed, "relative," subject to change. Much ink was spilled. Tenured titans tussled in a kind of trench warfare. Dispatches from the front lines were published in academic journals. Out of the strife, there rose a resistance of sorts, a loose movement called the third culture. In 1995, John Brockman, a literary agent and head cheerleader of science, edited a book named after the movement that showcases conversations with some of the scientist-writers we now recognize as influencing our imaginations and shaping our conceptions of the world, including Dawkins, Dennett, Pinker, and Gould—names that line up like a law practice.

The Third Culture intends to be an anodyne to Snow's dichotomy. "Literary intellectuals" still aren't talking to scientists, but the scientists featured in the book say they no longer need them to serve as middlemen to the public (although it's unclear when this was ever the case). And the introduction does seem like a parade of bruised egos: Stephen Jay Gould calls the literary intellectuals' putative dominance a "conspiracy," Richard Dawkins a "hijacking," while Nicholas Humphrey has them running in fear, dropping their Derrida and berets as they head for cover in juice bars. With a tone of finality, Brockman writes, "What traditionally has been called 'science' has today become 'public culture,'" which is a direct rebuttal of Snow, who writes, "It is the traditional culture [read: "literary intellectuals"], to an extent remarkably little diminished by the emergence of the scientific one, which manages the western world."

Once you get past the rhetoric and cant of the introduction, though, *The Third Culture* reads as if you're attending a fascinating symposium or lecture series, or even as if you're back in school. After all, as Snow writes, "There is only one way out of all this: it is, of course, by rethinking our education." Those of us who are nonscientists and nonacademics are largely in terror and in awe of scientists. We are intimidated. We tend to understand "Science" as a capital S pursuit, done by kempt men wearing white coats in anonymous and vaguely sinister laboratories or by wild-eyed, quasi-deranged loners in their outpost hovels. We are told that Science has changed our lives, and that it continues to do so, faster than we can keep up with. And the fact that it relies so heavily on math worries us deeply.

In one way, *The Third Culture* accomplishes just what it set out to do, which is to pierce this mysterious aura surrounding science and bring the special knowledge to the general public. The book gives the curious layperson the language with which to approach serious scientific ideas. You don't get the math you'd need to understand string theory, but you do understand that it is a response to the challenges cosmologists face in trying to unite classic general relativity with quantum mechanics. You do get a précis of Dawkins's idea of extended phenotypes, that is, how an organism's genetic selection for certain physical characteristics might be understood in relation to how and why it lives in the environment it does. You begin to understand the difference between the weak and the strong anthropic principles, the former suggesting that we humans are privileged in that our location (in both space and time) in the universe is compatible with our existence as observers, and the latter suggesting that the universe and its fundamentals are designed in such a way that life was destined to exist at some point in order to observe the universe. There's the gorgeous idea of autopoiesis, or self-production, which tries to explain why identities of living systems remain constant even as their component parts change. There are questions about the role the senses play in consciousness, as well as discussions about the manifold problems that attend the building of learning machines and whether a computer could ever truly resemble a mind. Physicists confront the limitations of the theory of everything and the whole epistemological project of reductionism in physics, which gives way to theories of "complexity" that examine how sophisticated ordered systems arise out of simple laws, or what Murray Gell-Mann calls "plectics." Science turns out to be just as innovative and *interesting* as we have been told it is.

But for all its success, *The Third Culture* is also kind of insidious. While it brings scientific ideas to us, and gives us the language to discuss them, it also rarifies them even further. It is at once a revelation and a covering up. Just as you may familiarize yourself with a place by reading about it and yet not really know it at all, you don't walk away from *The Third Culture* with the ability to *do* science, of course, just to talk about its landmarks, as it were. Over the course of the book, its symposium structure, which allows other thinkers to respond after each talk, begins to give the impression that science is, indeed, a closed world, with its own infighting and ego clashes. There is an undeniable and uncomfortable smugness in tone from some of the participants that just doesn't sit right. While it claims to solve the problem of the division of the two cultures, *The Third Culture* only does so by ignoring one of the two, and the entrenchment is deepened. And as Snow states, "This polarization is sheer loss to us all."

In his Rede Lecture, Arnold said, "In our culture, the aim being to know ourselves and the world, we have, as the means to this end, to know the best which has been thought and said in the world." Pierre Teilhard de Chardin, an anthropologist and priest, also writes about this in *The Phenomenon of Man*. He calls the collection of human thought, the pursuit and result of our inquiries into the world and ourselves, the "noosphere." The development and goal of this realm is the systematic enrichment of human consciousness and complexity, working toward a maximum capacity of both, or what he calls the Omega Point. (Dawkins and his disciples wouldn't go in for this type of talk, this mystical mumbo jumbo—consider this, from his section of *The Third Culture*: "There's no sense in which evolution was ever aiming towards a distant goal of humanity. That would be ludicrous.") Essential to Chardin's idea is a kind of correspondence: "The exterior world must inevitably be lined at every point with an interior one." Innovation and understanding must happen within, as much as without. Call the within whatever you like—selfhood, subjectivity, personality, a Wittgensteinian "craving for generality," meaning, or just plain old spirituality. It's that sense of something *more* that my intuition tells me to trust.

The tea leaves of my standardized test scores came back and told me arts and language was a slightly safer bet. The narrowing began then, in the sixth grade, and only deepened as the years went on, and more tests were taken. But I've recently become fascinated with science and its history. I've been reading magazines, blogs, and books, and checking out video lectures from the library. I have long conversations with friends in history of science PhD programs. *The Third Culture* and the thinkers it introduced me to have been incredibly helpful in this early part of my journey, even if I often sense there's something missing from the work. For instance, many of these scientists are very good at talking about what's going on in the present and what will be in the future, but fail to devote very much attention at all to why I'd want to live in either. Maybe that's a job for the explorers of the interior, the "within." But I will continue to read the scientists, just as I will my Dickens and Shakespeare, my Luther and Foucault. I want to know the best that has been thought and said, though not in order to call myself "cultured," which linguists would call a skunked term, one that no longer has a definition that satisfies all parties concerned. I will read them for no other reason than for the thrilling sense that my world can still open out, and the dizzying intimacy that fills me when my consciousness mysteriously expands.

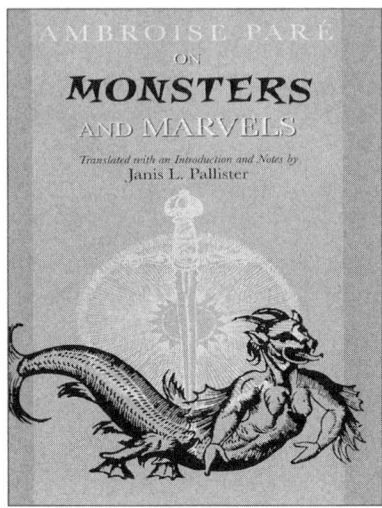

ON AMBROISE PARÉ'S
On Monsters and Marvels

MICHELLE LEGRO

There's a game my friends and I like to play: who would you have been if you had been born one hundred years ago? A weary housemaid? A troublesome suffragette? What about five hundred years ago? For myself and for many of my friends, the game is cut short—we wouldn't have been born. As children of the late twentieth century, we were pulled out of our mothers by dangerous C-sections, our bodies twisted and turned in the birth canal. In the past, those that survived would have been disfigured by missing teeth, harelips, or other birthmarks. In my case, a perfect oval of brown peach fuzz—slightly raised like a button and cut out of my face when I was five years old—would have ensured my place in the French surgeon Ambroise

Paré's 1575 book *On Monsters and Marvels*, a treatise on medical oddities, in a chapter called "On Certain Monstrous Animals That Are Born Abnormally in the Bodies of Men, Women, and Small Children."

My diagnosis would likely have been such: "how many [persons] does one see who on their face or other parts of the body have the form of a cherry, of a plum, of a sorb-apple, of a fig, or a mulberry, the cause of which has always been referred to the very powerful imagination of the conceiving or pregnant women moved by a vehement appetite or with the appearance of an unexpected touching of this [fruit] . . ." My mother, it seems, enjoyed rotting peaches in particular. Her vehement appetite was written on my face.

Birth is a battle, and a woman's belly a primordial battleground of good and evil. In sixteenth-century medicine, the effects of biology were still mixed up with the causes of magic. Paré was not only a surgeon but also a philosopher, an astronomer, a demonologist, a storyteller, and a man of careful observation with a deep fascination for the wondrous and the horrific. An army doctor, he was looked down upon by court physicians, who kept the recipes for their (often useless) medicines closely guarded as if they were magic potions, and who tended to the king with very little practical knowledge. Paré was caught between these two worlds, the life of the tooth puller and that of the alchemist, and his blend of the practical and the supernatural is apparent in the very first chapter of his book, in which he lists the thirteen causes of monsters:

The first is the glory of God.
The second, his wrath.
The third, too great a quantity of seed.
The fourth, too little a quantity.
The fifth, the imagination.
The sixth, the narrowness or smallness of the womb.
The seventh, the indecent posture of the mother, as when, being pregnant, she has sat too long with her legs crossed, or pressed against her womb.
The eighth, through a fall, or blows struck against the womb of the mother, being with child.
The ninth, through hereditary or accidental illnesses.
The tenth, through rotten or corrupt seed.
The eleventh, through mixture or mingling of seed.
The twelfth, through the artifice of wicked spital beggars.
The thirteenth, through Demons and Devils.

Paré's book is a catalog of sorts, with writing taken from ancient and medieval sources, some by learned men such as Saint Augustine and others no more than the hearsay of midwives. He covers a wide range of so-called monsters, many of which are recognizable to the modern reader as simply suffering from mutations or birth defects: a half-formed arm or leg, a face born without eyes, a twisted torso, twins joined at the forehead or the heart or the stomach.

According to Paré, other deformities, such as the birthmarks caused by the pregnant women who thought too much of cherries or figs, were the result of an active imagination. The daily life of a pregnant woman, he explains, even the smallest glance or desire, could affect her child in horrible ways. He describes a woman who gave birth to a furry child after she gazed too long at a picture of St. John the Baptist dressed in bear skins. Another woman had a frog-faced child after she was told to hold a frog at all times, even in bed with her husband, because it would cure her fever.

Finally, he includes in his catalog more devilish animal-creatures covered in scales or fur, with horned heads and forked tongues—those which have clearly been touched by the supernatural or by evil. All of these he calls "monsters," yet Paré makes it clear that despite their deformities, the monsters are just like us—human at the core.

Humans once diagnosed as monstrous have found their place in the modern world. After leaving the sideshow, the Siamese twins Chang and Eng settled in North Carolina, marrying sisters and even buying slaves to run their plantation. The conjoined twins Abby and Brittany Hensel are twenty-one now. Joined at the neck, they share one body but are two distinct women. A medical marvel when they were born, their lives are now marveled at for their ordinariness—learning to drive, to date, to live quietly in a universe no longer haunted by demons.

Many of the most wondrous things cataloged in Paré's book have become commonplace today, especially the zoological discoveries of the past five hundred years.

Paré discusses not only marine monsters such as the mermaid and the siren but also the whale. In his chapter on terrestrial monsters, he describes an African monster with the hands and face of a child who lives only on air, as well as familiar species such as the toucan, the elephant, the giraffe, the ostrich, and the chameleon.

Today, people feel compelled to make themselves as marvelous as the creatures Paré once beheld. Plastic surgery can pierce tongues in two like a snake's, stretch faces to look like jungle cats', and cover a circus performer's body in scaly tattoos to resemble a lizard. In a 2001 profile in *Harper's*, Joe Rosen, a radical plastic surgeon at the Dartmouth-Hitchcock Medical Center suggested that we should have the freedom to make marvels of ourselves, implanting wings into our shoulder blades, replacing our eyes with far-seeing owl eyes: "Why are plastic surgeons dedicated only to restoring our current notions of the conventional, as opposed to letting people explore, if they want, what the possibilities are?"

Of all the causes of monsters that Paré identifies, there is one cause that continues to lurk darkly within us all—the imagination. We can no longer expect the good or the evil in the world to imprint itself on our unborn children; our children must imprint it on themselves.

Lulu Hurst and the Secret That Shook America

ON LULU HURST

(The Georgia Wonder) Writes Her Autobiography, and for the First Time Explains and Demonstrates the Great Secret of Her Marvelous Power

BY JESSICA HANDLER

At thirteen, what I craved more than a boyfriend or a trim body was an aura of mystery. At a slumber party, I once captivated an audience by standing in a doorway and pressing my hands hard against the frame. When I stepped forward, my arms floated upward of their own accord. My friends had never tried this themselves, never even heard of it, and suddenly I purveyed a wonderful, weird power. Of course, what I really wanted was the power to make my father sane, my dead sister alive, my living sister healthy, and my mother happy. Floating hands were a poor defense against circumstances I couldn't control.

More than a century before I awed my friends with simple muscle reactions, Lulu Hurst, a thirteen-year-old girl in rural Cedartown, Georgia, played a similar prank that made her cousin believe Hurst harnessed the then-mysterious power of electricity. Hurst stuck a hairpin into a mattress beside her sleeping cousin's head, timed exactly to the spooky noises of a freak lightning storm. While Hurst was probably merely bored and craving escape from the powerlessness that comes with poverty, a small town, and being a girl in 1883, her startled cousin's belief that Hurst's hands conveyed electricity—and Hurst's failure to correct that notion—changed her life.

I learned about Hurst because my mother and I share a minor obsession with vaudeville and "freak show" women who defied limitations through physics, alchemy, luck, and lies. We admire their bravado. Long after my own teen years were past, my mother e-mailed me a digital clipping from *Cassier's Magazine*, an obscure engineering periodical from the turn of the nineteenth century. The article, "The Feats of the Magnetic Girl Explained," introduced me to the stage career of Lulu Hurst, "The Magnetic Girl" and, sometimes, "The Georgia Wonder." On stage, Hurst turned umbrellas inside out with a touch of her hand. She appeared to lift grown men straddling parlor chairs by bracing her feet, hidden by her long skirt, and tilting the chairs to a forty-five-degree angle. But her true feat lay in convincing the gullible that she harbored exceptional power. This teenage girl grabbed the Victorian man by his fear of the looming twentieth century and threw him to the ground. She was "the master of them all." In one of the few remaining photos of her, Hurst smiles out like a possum in a dress. She's every kid I simultaneously admired and feared: the girl who stuck her foot into the aisle when I was called to the blackboard, the girl who tossed cans of cheap beer onto the blacktop from the passenger window of her boyfriend's speeding Camaro. The Magnetic Girl's feats—and the profits they generated—saved her family from desolation. Lulu Hurst, would that I were you.

Lulu Hurst and the Magnetic Girl phenomenon were forgotten to all but aficionados of weird science until her 1897 book, *Lulu Hurst (the Georgia Wonder) Writes Her Autobiography, and for the First Time Explains and Demonstrates the Great Secret of Her Marvelous Power*, reappeared as a book-within-a-book in *The Georgia Wonder: Lulu Hurst and the Secret That Shook America* by Barry Wiley, published in 2004 by Hermetic Press. The delirious mayhem of *Writes Her Autobiography*'s cover, reproduced in Wiley's book, portrays caricatures of nine men crawling away from, being tossed into the air by, or recoiling in fear from a woman in a bustled dress. Lightning bolts erupt from the woman's fingertips. This cover differs slightly from the original, which promises *A Death Blow to Spiritualism and Superstition of Every Kind*.

But for me, a reproduction wouldn't do. I wanted to get as close to Lulu (by now I was sure we could be on a first-name basis) as possible.

One copy of *Writes Her Autobiography* is in the archives at the library in Madison, Georgia, the town where Hurst and her husband raised their family. Madison is less than an hour from where I live, so I hit the freeway for my laying on of hands. In Madison, the librarian took Hurst's book, which was in a folder, from a cabinet and gave me white gloves with which to turn the pages. Wearing white gloves while reading the secrets of a Southern lady who manipulated the world with her hands seemed innately perfect.

Hurst's tenant-farmer father saw deliverance in his daughter. In an era when the average person didn't differentiate between electricity and magnetic force, which many believed transited the human body as a fluid, William Hurst bet the farm on his daughter's desire for attention. He put her on the national circuit for almost two years, predicting correctly that her pretense of weird science would attract the paying public in droves to witness the dangerous forces emanating from the hands of his Magnetic Girl.

In her autobiography, Hurst claims that she "set aside the eternal laws of gravitation, reverse[d] the order of nature, and . . . impart[ed] life to dead matter." Her onstage "tests"—a term suggesting more science than "act"—invited audience volunteers to hold a cane or billiard cue horizontally while she pressed on the tips. Locked in Hurst's gaze, the mark pushed down while Hurst simply held the object in place and waited for Newton's third law of motion (the "equal and opposite reaction" one) to kick in.

Her admirers believed that the inexplicable, treacherous power of electricity generated from her hands knocked the hapless volunteers to the ground. Men—almost always her audience—left the stage red-faced, flustered, and thrilled. Anecdotes suggest she stopped a runaway train with her hands, bested a sumo wrestler, and cured a woman of fainting spells. A brand of soap, a line of saddles, and a cow were named in her honor. When Hurst quit the spotlight in 1885, she had inspired at least two copycat acts and earned a reported $250,000, a relative fortune that redeemed her subsistence-farming parents from the dire economy of the Reconstruction South. She retired, attended college, and married Paul Atkinson, her onstage interlocutor.

Writes Her Autobiography begins as a cheerful deceit. Hurst writes that her stage persona was that of "a young girl . . . in a short silk frock," but she's stretching the truth; she was thirteen, but as curvy and tall as a young woman. For the first half of the book, she refrains from debunking the nature of her feats, relating instead the spectacle of her gift. Maybe it's science, she implies. Or maybe it's mystery. In the second part, Hurst uses photographs, diagrams, and helpful arrows to reveal how she lifted those men, flipped those fellows, and tossed actress Lily Langtry down a flight of stairs. Claiming a need to unburden herself, she confesses discomfort with undeserved fame. But science—this time of the mind—remains useful. Believing in her was the audience's fault. Their credulity, she writes, was a "psychological problem of vast importance."

Handling Hurst's book without paying her a visit was ungrateful and un-Southern, so I left the library for the old Madison cemetery. I found no Hurst, and no Atkinson. As I wandered the grounds, a train whistle blew. Startled, remembering the train that teenaged Lulu Hurst was rumored to have stopped, I jumped back from the rails that bisected the cemetery. Out of habit, I waved at the conductor as the train passed. He waved back. I felt, for a moment, hypnotized, but perhaps it was the heat.

When the air was still again, I glanced in the direction from which the train had come. In my sight line was a stone engraved "Lulu Hurst Atkinson, 1869–1950." A name and date on an unremarkable gravestone, a marker for a wife and mother, not a magnetic girl. But Lulu Hurst's weird science had outlived her, proving to me that imagining one's own power can be enough to make it real.

ESSAY

ATOMIC CITY

Justin Nobel

Fusion and fission : a love triangle's half-life

In the middle of Idaho's Lost River desert is a green street sign that reads "Atomic City," with an arrow pointing to a lonely gravel track. One evening last April, I followed it. As purplish storm clouds swallowed the sun, I came across a cluster of scraggly trees and weather-beaten trailer homes. Beside an abandoned speedway sat an antiquated ambulance and across the street a neon *Bar* sign twinkled in the dusk. Inside the bar, I met drifter lovers from Colorado and a potbellied man in a hunting cap who worked as a spent-fuel handler for the nearby Idaho National Laboratory. We discussed nuclear energy, of which he was, not surprisingly, a fan. Then I asked the question that had brought me to Atomic City: What caused the 1961 nuclear disaster?

The spent-fuel handler ordered a shot of Jägermeister. "Have you heard of the love triangle?" he asked. I hadn't. All I knew was there was something fishy about the disaster. Earlier that day, when I tried bringing it up at Pickle's Place, in Arco, Idaho, thirty miles away, I received cold stares. "You won't find much on that," a brawny man with a girl at his side told me as he exited the restaurant. I heard the same thing at the gas station next door, and at the fleabag motel I checked into. People aggressively knew nothing, which seemed to imply there was something to know.

"One guy's wife was messing around with another guy," said the fuel handler, after downing his Jäger. "He got pissed off and messed up . . . I shit you not." He then reenacted how the disaster might have happened: "You fuck my wife, I fuck you up"—and with fingers clenched he yanked his hand upward, making the motion of pulling a control rod out of a reactor core. *Boom.*

At 9:01 PM, on January 3, 1961, a nuclear reactor the size of a small grain silo exploded in the Lost River desert. All three men inside the Stationary Low-Power Plant Number 1, or SL-1, were killed. To this day, they are the only nuclear fatalities ever to occur on U.S. soil. Even in the wake of Japan's nuclear meltdown last March, no one mentioned the SL-1 disaster, and CNN reported that the United States had never had a nuclear fatality. The tsunami that caused Japan's meltdown was viewed as something unpredictable, a result of poorly understood plate tectonics and mercurial seas, while the meltdown itself was perceived differently. It could have been prevented, said experts, with better safety protocols. Had anyone remembered SL-1, perhaps the conversation would have been different.

Few Americans know their nation's nuclear history. In 1946, after the bombing of Hiroshima showed that the atom could destroy a city, Congress created the Atomic Energy Commission to show it could also generate electricity. Reactors sprang from the sage of the Lost River desert, a spot chosen because it was sparsely populated, geologically stable and arid, but with good access to water and electricity. The site was called the National Reactor Testing Station. On December 20, 1951, the Experimental Breeder Reactor 1 powered four lightbulbs, the world's first nuclear energy. Four years later, Arco became the world's first town powered by nuclear energy. Businesses, thinking radiation would remove impurities from or enhance the strength of their products, blasted their goods—gold, diamonds, plastic, papayas, potatoes—with gamma rays.

The fuel of the future had arrived, and it would run cities, make materials stronger and food imperishable, and protect the nation by powering the Distant Early Warning Line, a ring of remote Arctic bases intended to detect America-bound Soviet missiles speeding over the ice cap.

> The testing station was like a nuclear playground where each branch of the military pursued its own pie-in-the-sky projects.

The army envisioned simple reactors that could be airlifted north in pieces, assembled like Erector Sets, and operated by regular army guys. They would train at SL-1.

The testing station was like a nuclear playground where each branch of the military pursued its own pie-in-the-sky projects. Machines were built before physicists could prove the principles to make them run. Some projects succeeded, such as the first nuclear-powered submarine, tested in a vat of water in the Idaho desert in March 1953. Others failed miserably. The air force spent more than one billion dollars trying to create a nuclear-powered aircraft. The result was a 600,000-pound plane that spewed radiation into the sky and poisoned its pilots' internal organs. There were other mishaps, including a string of accidental meltdowns—and several that were triggered intentionally, to see what would happen.

SL-1 was housed in a three-story metal silo and surrounded by administration buildings slapped together from surplus war materials. It looked more like an idle granary than an endeavor to salvage humanity. And there were problems. The boron that lined the uranium fuel plates and stabilized reactions was flaking off at an unknown rate, and the control rods that regulated reactions had been sticking. Lifting the rods allowed neutrons to buzz freely and a reaction to occur, while dropping them squelched a reaction. When the rods stuck, the lifting and lowering had to be done by hand. The facility had been slated to receive a new reactor core in the spring of 1961, something the explosion prevented from happening, and thus the original core, which had a curious design, was still in use. At most reactors, several control rods must be removed to initiate a reaction, but at SL-1, pulling just the central control rod was enough. This design had never been used before, and has never been used since.

Flawed as SL-1 was, those who worked there still felt part of some epic mission. "The spirit of patriotism was absolutely palpable," says Susan Stacy, author of a book written for the government entitled *Proving the Principle—A History of the Idaho National Engineering and Environmental Laboratory, 1949-1999*. "I think there was a great deal of idealism about the potential for nuclear energy, this fissioning atom, to solve many of the world's energy problems." Young men flocked to the budding industry; Jack Byrnes and Dick Legg, two of the three workers in SL-1 the night it blew, among them.

Byrnes, a handsome twenty-year-old from Utica, New York, had joined the army at seventeen and by nineteen had married his high school sweetheart, Arlene, and become a father. After a year-long course in reactor operations, he was assigned to SL-1. In October of 1959, he and Arlene strapped a trunk to the top of a black Oldsmobile and headed cross-country, their son, Jacky, belted between boxes in back.

Dick Legg, a stocky twenty-five-year-old from rural Michigan, had worked for two years as a navy electrician before enrolling in the same nuclear course as

Byrnes. He was also assigned to SL-1. Unlike Byrnes, Legg came west without a woman. ("I've got it all figured out with these gals," he once told a navy friend, explaining his pickup strategy: ask every girl at the bar for a drink until one says yes, then tell her you know a spot nearby with a good band but instead drive to a drugstore and buy condoms.) In Idaho, Legg married a teenage testing-station stenographer named Judith Cole.

We know the details of these men's lives from reports made by an AEC special investigator named Leo Miazga. The reports were later dug up by journalist William McKeown and woven into his comprehensive book, *Idaho Falls: The Untold Story of America's First Nuclear Accident*, published in 2003. Miazga meanders in his analysis but his takeaway is simple enough: both Byrnes and Legg were screw-ups. Byrnes ignored his family, catted with strippers, and threw temper tantrums at work in which he chucked tools. Legg was unprofessional and lazy. For a gag, he once turned off a fan that cooled critical instruments, and on at least one occasion he was found sleeping in his car in the parking lot when he should have been overseeing the reactor. After Legg fudged the time card of a friend playing hooky, the friend was transferred and Byrnes brought in to fill his spot. The two had never worked together, but they had a volatile history.

One night the previous May, the SL-1 boys had gotten drunk at a strip club called the Boiler Room. Byrnes introduced to the group a chatty hooker named Mitzi. She joined the men at a sergeant's house for tequila and whiskey, offering sex for twenty dollars a head. They talked her down to two and Byrnes took her into a back bedroom. Afterward, Legg started a fight with him. No one quite knows why, but the sergeant who broke it up later told investigators that Legg was either scolding Byrnes for being unfaithful or razzing him about his stamina. McKeown mentions another possibility, gleaned from Miazga: Byrnes was sleeping with Legg's wife.

On January 3, at 4:00 PM, Byrnes and Legg began their shift. Assisting them was a trainee named Richard McKinley. The crew's first task was to reconnect the control rods to the drive rack that moved them up and down. This required manually lifting the hundred-pound rods about four inches. Lifting the rods too far—another ten inches—would trigger a reaction, but Byrnes and Legg knew the risks. At 5:00 PM, a patrolman stopped by, saw the men were busy, and moved on. Around 7:00 PM, the testing-station operator placed a call to the control room. It was Byrnes's wife, Arlene. They spoke briefly, deciding to end their marriage. According to Miazga, and relayed by McKeown, an unidentified woman tried calling back several times over the next few hours but never got through.

We don't know Byrnes's response to this devastating phone call. However, we do know what happened next. And from the autopsy report, we know that the man standing directly over the central control rod was Jack Byrnes.

At 9:01 PM, SL-1 exploded. "When the reactor went critical, it released so much heat energy in four milliseconds that it flashed the water surrounding the fuel to steam," reads Stacy's book. "[Water] slammed against the lid of the pressure vessel at a velocity of 160 feet per second and 10,000 pounds per square inch exactly as if it were a piston—a water hammer. The entire vessel jumped nine feet into the air, hit the ceiling, and thumped back into place... The violence of the explosion killed all three of the men."

McKinley was struck in the head by a piece of radioactive shrapnel that tore off half his face. Byrnes was thrown into concrete blocks, breaking ribs that pierced his heart. Legg was skewered in the gut by a flying control rod that launched him thirteen feet in the air and pinned him to the ceiling. (It took a week to get him down, requiring a pole with a hook to push him into a net attached to a crane operated by a man shielded in lead.) The men's bodies were wrapped in several hundred pounds of lead, placed in steel coffins, and buried under a foot of concrete.

The day after I visited Atomic City, I drove east across the Lost River desert, to Idaho Falls. On a Barnes & Noble display table, I found McKeown's book, which even looks haunting—its cover is a grainy close-up photo of a gas mask. He builds a careful case, showing that Byrnes likely caused the accident by intentionally pulling out the critical central control rod. Maybe, says McKeown, "roiled with emotion: anger, remorse, guilt, feelings of persecution... [Byrnes] wanted to do something to get Arlene's sympathy, or just to 'show her.'"

McKeown considers the love triangle theory, but he also reveals just how weak the evidence for it is. The fodder comes from a conversation Miazga had with an SL-1 supervisor who, in referring to Legg's wife's relationship with Byrnes, had used the title Miss and not Mrs. Was the supervisor subtly implying she had slept with Byrnes before being married to Legg? This seems like a great leap, but it was interpreted that way and has since become lore. To me, the love triangle theory is off the mark. The version told by the spent-fuel handler in Atomic City implies that Legg pulled the control rod to get back at Byrnes for sleeping with his wife, but regardless of who may have slept with whom, we know Byrnes pulled the control rod, not Legg. He could have pulled it in an act of rage directed at Legg, though I think it was more about Arlene and, as McKeown suggests, remorse. We are mercurial creatures, and Byrnes was known to be especially volatile. That a man with a heavy heart could

> The men's bodies were wrapped in several hundred pounds of lead, placed in steel coffins, and buried under a foot of concrete.

pull a one-hundred-pound control rod out of a reactor core seems perfectly plausible.

Much of McKeown's book is based on interviews he conducted in 2000 and 2001. Since then, many of the interviewees have moved or died, but I connected with one, C. Wayne Bills, the testing station's deputy director of health and safety at the time of the accident. Now eighty-seven, Bills lives in a brick house in a quiet east Idaho Falls neighborhood. He is broad-shouldered, sturdy, and sharp. He grew up on a Colorado ranch and studied engineering at the University of Colorado Boulder. After graduation, he took a position testing plutonium at Los Alamos National Laboratory, in New Mexico, where the first atomic bomb was developed. It was a riveting experience. "The guy who worked across the hall from me was on the Enola Gay," said Bills.

At Los Alamos, he met his wife, who worked in a lab that tested urine samples. After stints at an oil company in Tulsa and a glue factory in St. Louis, Bills returned to nuclear energy, taking a safety inspector job with the Atomic Energy Commission, first in Richland, Washington, and later in Idaho Falls. The place was buzzing, but in a different way than Los Alamos—more bravado than brains.

When SL-1 blew, Bills was at choir practice in Idaho Falls. He jumped into his government Studebaker, picked up an AEC doctor, and raced to the site. Near SL-1, they came across an ambulance on its way to the hospital. "I opened the door and was reading four hundred roentgens," Bills said.

The man inside was McKinley, mutilated and glowing with radiation, but somehow, until a few moments earlier, still alive. Bills turned the ambulance around. "If you go to the hospital, you contaminate everyone," he said. His good judgment was noted, and the higher-ups chose him to lead a technical committee charged with determining exactly how the accident had happened.

Bills's team showed the explosion had not been caused by SL-1's laundry list of pre-existing problems, as some experts had speculated, nor had it been caused by someone accidentally pulling the central control rod out of the core while reattaching it to the drive rack. A piece of piping used in reattaching the rod provided the critical evidence. It had been deformed by the explosion but still contained a bit of the rack to which the rod was to be attached—meaning, Legg and Byrnes had already finished attaching the rod by the time the explosion happened. Scratches on the outside of the rod indicated that it had been forcefully yanked not just fourteen inches, the distance needed to initiate a reaction, but twenty inches, the maximum distance possible.

The team tested scenarios to see whether the rod had been yanked by accident. Bills had men take turns trying to pull a hundred-pound rod upward while others held it down, then suddenly let go. Most men pulled the rod a few inches. None came close to twenty. They even looked at whether goosing could have caused a man to pull the rod out if another man stealthily approached and poked him in the butt. Still, no one jerked hard enough to lift the rod twenty inches.

Toward the end of my conversation with Bills, after his collection of grandfather clocks had chimed several times and afternoon sunlight had begun to creep across the carpet, his wife, June, the same woman he had met in Los Alamos sixty years ago, returned from a church meeting. I began to see Bills as a classic sort of 1950s American hero, devoted to his wife, devout in his faith, dedicated to his country. In contrast, Byrnes and Legg seemed to have been bawdy, bumbling young men who were in way over their heads. Bills was passionate about nuclear energy; Byrnes and Legg had simply gone west for jobs. "These people weren't scientists," said Bills. "They were essentially military people; they knew how to run reactors but weren't involved in knowing an awful lot about how they worked."

SL-1 was a very American nuclear accident, with its high drama and focus on the individual. Fukushima, which involved protocol problems and collective blame, was a very Japanese one. But whereas Japan has been forced to confront its nuclear errors, America still marches forward, thinking Three Mile Island was its biggest nuclear mishap. The bartender in Atomic City, a weatherworn man who grew up in Alaska and spent his career fighting oil spills in the Persian Gulf, didn't think this would change anytime soon. "This is a subject you'll get nowhere with," he said, as he sent me on my way, giving me an Alaskan lager for the road. "This is their black eye. As far as the industry goes, in the United States, there has never been a fatal nuclear accident."

FICTION

Parallel

There's a theory that says there are billions of other universes, parallel to the one we live in, and that each of them is slightly different. There are the ones where you were never born, and the ones where you wouldn't want to be born. There are some parallel universes where I'm having sex with a horse, and ones where I've won the lottery. There are universes where I'm lying on the bedroom floor, slowly bleeding to death, and universes where I've been elected president, by a landslide. But I don't care about any of those parallel universes now. The only ones that interest me are the ones where she isn't happily married, with a cute little boy, the ones where she's completely alone. There are plenty of universes like that, I'm sure. I'm trying to think about them now. Among all those universes, there are some where we've never met. I don't care about those now. Among the ones that are left, there are some where she doesn't want me. She tells me no. In some of them, she does it gently, and in others—in a way that hurts. I don't care about those now, either. All that's left are the ones where she tells me yes, and I choose one of them, a little like you choose a piece of fruit at the greengrocer's. I choose the nicest one, the ripest one, the sweetest one. It's a universe where the weather is perfect, never too hot or too cold, and we live there in a little cottage in the woods. She works at the city library, a forty-minute drive from our home, and I work in the education department of the regional council, in the building that faces hers.

Etgar Keret

Universes

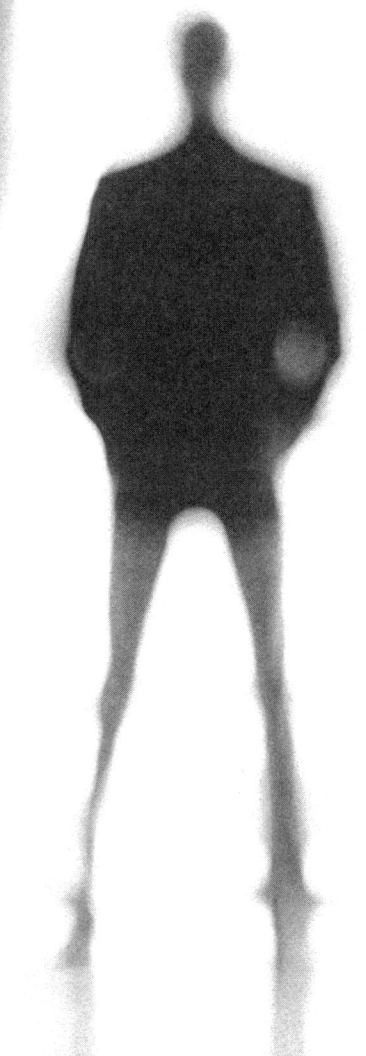

Sometimes, from my office window, I can see her putting books back on the shelf. We always have our lunch together. And I love her and she loves me. And I love her and she loves me. And I love her and she loves me. I'd give anything to move to that universe. But meanwhile, until I find the way there, all I can do is think about it. I picture myself living there, in the middle of the woods. With her, in complete happiness. There's an infinite number of parallel universes in the world. In one of them, I'm having sex with a horse; in another, I've won the lottery. I don't want to think about those now, only about that one, the one with the cottage in the woods. There's a universe where I'm lying with my wrists slashed, bleeding, on the bedroom floor. That's the universe I'm doomed to live in until it's over. I don't want to think about it now. I just want to think about that other universe. A cottage in the woods, the sun setting, going to bed early. In bed, my right arm is unslashed, and dry. She's lying on it and we're hugging each other. She lies on it for so long that I can hardly feel it anymore. But I don't move, I like it that way, with my arm under her warm body, and I keep liking it even when I can no longer feel my arm at all. I can sense her breathing on my face—rhythmic, regular, unending. My eyes begin to shut. Not just in that universe, in bed, in the woods, but in the other universes too, the ones that I don't want to think about. It's good to know there's one place, in the heart of the woods, where I'm falling asleep happy.

Translated by Miriam Schlesinger

Jared Harel

MY BODY DOUBLE GOES TO THE HOME DEPOT

1.

My body double goes
to The Home Depot
to buy materials
to build an ark.

He likes the shape
of its hollow smile,
the smell of sawdust
like a vital resource

up in smoke.
An ark? asks the boy
in the bright
orange smock,

then walks my double
over to lumber.

2.

My body double goes
to The Home Depot
and blacks out
over in lumber.

He wakes to a panic
of trained professionals,
a woman pricking
his delicate wrist,

asking for a name,
a date of birth,
if he recalls drinking
or taking any pills?

I remember, he answers,
I'd like to buy lumber.

MY BODY DOUBLE TELLS ME I'M AWAY ON BUSINESS

My body double tells me
I'm away on business
and won't be back
for quite some time.

Meanwhile, he's agreed
to read my mail,
pick up the newspaper,
just to be safe.

He insists it's no trouble
walking my dog,
dating my girlfriend,
raking the leaves

around my refinished deck.
If I need to call,
I should try
my own number,

unless it is Sunday,
in which case,
my mother's.

INTERVIEW

THE SCIENCE OF STORY-TELLING

Tony Perez

A Conversation with Robert Krulwich and Jad Abumrad of Radiolab

A slow crescendo. Throat clearing. Bleeps and bloops. A series of voices spliced together. *You're listening to Radiolab (lab, lab lab...) from WNYC.*

Cut.

Jad Abumrad and Robert Krulwich sit on high stools in front of a couple thousand people in Seattle's 5th Avenue Theater. They've taken their show on the road, re-creating for huge, and not exclusively NPR-looking, audiences what they typically broadcast from the safety of their Manhattan studio. Abumrad—in an untucked button-down and sneakers—fiddles with his laptop, while Krulwich—blazered and blue-jeaned—looks down at his notes. To stage right, a cellist with extravagant tights and a postapocalyptic haircut plays a long, deep note.

Krulwich begins to describe Aristophanes's speech on the origins of love, his contribution to Plato's *The Symposium*. He explains that in primal times, we humans were born not as individuals but as couples, conjoined at the back. Eventually, as tends to happen in these types of stories, the gods felt threatened by their creation, so Zeus hurled bolts of lightning (cue sound effects, courtesy of Abumrad) from the heavens and split the creatures in two. We were thus alone, but left with the memory of—and a longing for—our other halves.

Over the course of the next hour, Abumrad and Krulwich talk brain scans, Jimmy Carter's hair part, a molecular reading of *Through the Looking Glass*, and antimatter... anything that might broaden their understanding of that particular episode's theme: symmetry.

Radiolab is more than a science show, or anyway, it's a science show for people who might not otherwise bother to tune in to such a thing. Krulwich, who previously hosted PBS's *NOVA*, and Abumrad are flâneurs of the sciences—wandering and wondering, favoring experience over explanation. They tell stories, talk to subjects, interview experts, and bicker among themselves, then piece it all together into the most densely produced hour on the radio—something akin to *This American Life* with DJ Shadow on the soundboard. One minute they'll dissect the minutiae of electrocardiographic monitoring; the next minute they'll break your heart.

Now in its tenth season, *Radiolab* has evolved from a Sunday-night AM-radio experiment to a nationally syndicated show broadcast by over three hundred stations. It has upward of two million listeners and a wildly successful podcast. In September of last year, the MacArthur Foundation saw fit to award Abumrad one of its "genius grants"—no small praise, or sum of money.

I spoke with Abumrad on the phone from his office at WNYC, and I sat with Krulwich over breakfast (well, yogurt and peach pie) at the Edison Hotel's coffee shop in midtown. The following is a composite, chopped and screwed in my best *Radiolab* impression, of those conversations.

TONY PEREZ: There are certain magazines that have stood for a particular aesthetic or way of thinking; I think of George Plimpton's *Paris Review* or Gordon Lish's run at *Esquire*. *Radiolab* seems to have a stable of writers—such as Jonah Lehrer, Oliver Sacks, E. O. Wilson—that represents a different way of talking about science. What is it that you think unites these people?

ROBERT KRULWICH: They're probably better described as teachers. That's the quality you need: to be able to explain science carefully, and slowly, and stupidly if you have to—or *cunningly*, I'd say. We invite people who can put into their voice, somehow, the surprise and beats of making a discovery. That tends to be a teacherly talent. A guy like Neil deGrasse Tyson is extraordinarily good at acting as though he's thinking this for the very first time. There's something of a little boy in Tyson—and in Oliver Sacks, and in Ed Wilson—who comes out and plays. There's a bit of a campfire quality to the whole thing.

JAD ABUMRAD: I think there's a certain attitude at the core of every story we tell, sort of a sense that you're wandering through this world and have to stand back in awe of it. It's a very different attitude. A normal journalist or broadcaster will go to report on a story, figure it out, then report in a very podium-style way what he knows. All the ups and the downs, and the figuring it out, and thinking you know, and realizing you don't know—all of that happens off frame.

But here, it's very important to show how we're moving through the information. You're encountering things that you don't know, and jumping to conclusions that turn out to be wrong. But in the end,

> We invite people who can put into their voice, somehow, the surprise and beats of making a discovery. That tends to be a teacherly talent.

you go through this very rigorous step-by-step walk until you get to the edge, and you can sort of stand and look at the world in a state of simple wonder. I think that's what it is: the sense that if you actually move through things, you'll get to places that shake your perspective.

RK: One of the tropes of journalism—particularly high journalism—is you go off and learn everything, then you artfully report it back. But it's already done, it's cooked, by the time you serve the meal—as would be the case in most restaurants. In ours, we cook it right in front of you. Presumably, that should bring you in. But it *does* bother some people.

JA: Then there are the form elements—narrative storytelling, wrapping technical details in human experience. All of that binds Robert and me together with our writers. We all share that sense of how to do it. But at the core, it's something to do with curiosity and wonder.

TP: Wonder, even more than science—especially as the seasons have gone on—seems to be at the heart of the show. I came up on the liberal-arts side, the English department, where the best texts aren't about hard answers but about opening up bigger, more complex questions. That isn't how we're typically trained to think about science. *Radiolab* seems far more interested in asking than answering.

RK: That's true. The answers, in some ways, are temporary in science. It's not like religion.

JA: To be completely honest with you, I couldn't care less about science as a geography. My parents are scientists; it's not as if I have any antagonism toward it. But I do have an antagonism toward the institution of science journalism, which seems very much about covering what happens in laboratories—these things that get put out by universities in press releases. That kind of stuff doesn't interest me at all.

In your question, you sort of put your finger on it. It's sort of about mystery, but it's not pure mystery—if that were the case, you might as well just sit in your dorm room and smoke pot. It's a wrestling match between *that* impulse and what the scientists are doing. There's a rigor and a specificity and an empirical approach that scientists have, which I could never do without.

A Conversation with Robert Krulwich and Jad Abumrad

You want to have this gunshot of amazement at the top of every story. Then you proceed to *de*mystify it.

At the same time, there's that sense of just being completely amazed. The show is the tug and tension between those two things.

TP: And how does that tension develop?

JA: In every piece, we start by mystifying something. You want to have this gunshot of amazement at the top of every story. Then you proceed to *de*mystify it. Then you *re*mystify it at the end in a new way. If I could distill every story I tell to those three moves, I'd be happy. You begin with sort of simple, cheap wonder, you go to science—to someone who can analyze the underlying assumptions—then you put it back together in a new way, but where you can still stand in amazement. But it's not cheap anymore; it's tested.

The two impulses pull on each other. Part of my brain is that guy in the dorm room smoking pot and just going, "Wow, is that me in the mirror?" And part of my brain wants to be an adult and understand how the world *really* works. I don't want to kill that first guy, but there should be a kind of armed truce. That's how it works for *Radiolab*. If it's one or the other, I get very uncomfortable. If we do too much hard science without any sense of poetry or mystery, I want to jump out the window. But if everything is silly and soft, and you don't have that sense of rigor, I feel like I'm letting myself and our listeners down. It's somewhere in the middle; it has to be a balance.

TP: I'm interested in that balance of the hard science and the emotional core. Vivian Gornick wrote a great book on writing called *The Situation and the Story*. An insultingly oversimplified explanation is that the "situation" is the series of events that comprises the plot, and the "story" is what's happening below the surface. My favorite thing about *Radiolab* is the way you balance the two. I'm always as interested in the hard science of the situation as I am the emotional core of the story: the exploration of neuroscience *and* the story of a woman in a coma. How do you build segments with both of these elements in mind?

JA: I think it comes from both directions equally, really. The stories are the harder thing to find. It's an easier place to start, for me, when you have a great story that seems pregnant with something. Then I can invite a smarty to talk about neuroscience or whatever. That's easier for me to conceptualize, but that's not always how we start. I know Robert often works the other way. He'll have a broad concept or a new bit of research that will lead him to go look for the story. The show really evolved in that juxtaposition. You have those two things happening side by side; you have some kind of human experience but you also have a way to examine and understand it.

In my opinion, experience can never be taken out of the equation. It doesn't always have to be a story in that classic "Once upon a time" sense, but even when you're explaining some arcane concept—like the dopamine reward system, which we've talked about fifteen times—even then it has to feel physical; it has to feel like an experience. If it ever feels like a lecture, if it ever feels didactic, we've lost. That's where the sound comes in; that's where the writing comes in; that's where the pictures and visuals come in. It has to feel like a movie. It can never feel like something that's just being explained.

RK: There's a bottom-up approach and a top-down approach. I tend to be more comfortable with broad architectures. In the case of "You Are Here" [season 9, episode 2], someone suggested doing a show about mapping. So I read a book about the map on which the word *America* first appeared. Then we met a mapmaker—a very interesting fellow—and that led to a discussion of place. Jonah [Lehrer] said he could help us explain place neurons [*Ed. note: place neurons are cells in the hippocampus that help create a cognitive map of an animal's environment*], and that seemed kind of interesting.

Meanwhile, Jad was beginning to wonder about people in the South Pacific who go from one *teeny* island across a vast stretch of emptiness to another teeny island without the use of sophisticated navigational tools. How do they know where they are going? Well, one of them claimed it was his testicles. "My testicles guide me," he said, and of course his wife said, "That's ridiculous ... I don't have testicles and I can do it." We got very interested in that and did a whole series of testicle-related conversations with South Pacific Islanders. The mapping thing began to fall out, but the stuff from Jonah was developing really well. We then found someone who had a problem with her mapping sense. Things kept shuffling.

Finally, a friend called and said, "I have this neighbor who had a terrible thing happen to her. Her boyfriend's a friend of mine; I think he's a great hero, and you should help them somehow." I went to meet Alan, the boyfriend. His girlfriend was swimming in a coma, and he was fighting to pull her back out. I thought that, in his way, he was acting like Jonah's place neurons. And it was just this amazing story. So all of this was going on simultaneously, and the show was in a continuous shuffle. In the end, the maps, where it all started, shuffled out and a sense of place shuffled in.

TP: I'm always impressed by the jumps you make without it feeling like a stretch, those transitions between a profound story and the more complicated material.

JA: Those transitions are the things we'll do thirty takes of over the course of a production cycle, just to make sure we get them right. We're always trying to figure out the most plainspoken but genuine way of making a connection. It's really hard sometimes, figuring out what the apple has to say to the orange.

TP: Robert, you mentioned that your approach bothers some people. *New York* magazine described you as someone who could simplify science without making it simple, but do hard science people feel differently?

RK: Yes, it *is* abrasive to people. Throughout my career, there's always been a continuous ten percent—the "Fuck you" ten percent—that says, "Why can't you use fancy words?" "Why can't you talk like an adult?" "Why can't you sound like a person who knows what he's talking about and articulates it from a place of knowledge and power?" This is a choice that we make. *Radiolab* chooses to put two people, who, admittedly, don't know a lot at the beginning, on a path where they quarrel and wonder and poke and ask and whisper to each other—that stuff is done on purpose.

TP: Where does that resistance come from? Is it academia?

RK: Yeah, mostly. I would say pedants of one kind or another, but they would probably feel differently. It's interesting; on my blog, I'm very clear that the voice there is a chatty voice, not a newswriting voice, but still, it upsets people every day. I say, "You know, this is *not* a news story. We're not in a news setting. This is an essay. You can wander around here and muse. It doesn't have the discipline of an athletically gathered, extremely accurate, honed piece of journalism." People don't always know that.

TP: But part of *Radiolab*'s popularity has to be due to its success in making hard science accessible to nonscience people (like me). I love how you take turns playing the straight man—almost like Carson or Letterman deferring to a guest comedian, acting as a stand-in for the audience, some kind of layperson by proxy.

JA: Most of the time, it's genuine that one of us does know more than the other about a particular topic we're covering. Oftentimes, I'll intentionally keep Robert in the dark. It's often the case that we'll just start rolling tape and I'll explain a concept to him.

TP: I imagine that helps keep the banter fresh.

JA: Yes, sure. And there are times, to be honest, when it's more constructed, when there's a bit of acting involved, when one of us is playing a role... but it's a role that's based on a previous version of ourselves. There have been times when Robert knew something that I didn't know, and we actually have had that conversation off tape. We'll carry that into the studio and we'll reconstruct those moments as best we can. We'll improvise, sometimes, fifteen takes trying to get a moment that feels real to us, to who we were before we got into the studio.

> People may not like science-y stuff, may not like mathematics, but what everybody likes is a friendship. Something warm that glows a little.

So, yes, the straight man is a construct, sort of a vaudeville trope. But it *is* based on the inequalities that exist within any friendship. At any time, one of us knows more than the other. And we're always trying to get the other guy to see the world as we're seeing it. That's genuine. Where, I think, we depart from the vaudeville trope is that I *really* want Robert to join me in being excited about something, or he wants me, or our guests, to join him. We all want, at the end of the day, to stand together and give each other a big hug. We depart from the shtick, I hope, at the end of each piece.

RK: Even though in the beginning neither of us knows anything, one will become the one who knows, and one will be the one who doesn't know. We'll say, "You take this one," or "I'll take this one." But oftentimes we're guided by actual differences in opinions. We deeply disagree on certain things. It's a source of great happiness to us when one can say, "You *really* think . . ." And we don't try to fake that; it wouldn't work. But we have some very different views.

TP: But the affection you have for each other seems key.

RK: Of course. People may not like science-y stuff, may not like mathematics, but what everybody likes is a friendship. Something warm that glows a little. If something fun and interesting is going on over there and if you're invited, there's a pull. I said to Jad at one point, "The fact that we feel this way about each other is a huge advantage to us, if we're not embarrassed by it. We should act like we feel." The whisper of affection and curiosity and play—mostly play—will get a lot of people into the tent. We could be talking about food, or flowers, or sports, but if we talk about it in this way, we will attract people. That's the way people are.

TP: At the same time, those little arguments and tensions certainly keep the show moving along. Are there particular differing beliefs or opinions that you keep coming back to?

JA: Absolutely. There are instances when we disagree, and there are real disagreements—friendly, but real. Anything to do with God, and that comes up relatively frequently. These are big questions we're examining, religious-sized questions. It's easy to talk about God when you're talking about the birth of the universe. There are

We're lucky in that we work in a place full of people who are deeply committed to our content and editorial mission.

questions that get you to that place very quickly. And we do disagree about the nature of things. The question, are humans special? is one of those overarching thoughts that continually barges its way in. Robert and I disagree about that. He tends to take the point of view that we are, and I take the view that we aren't.

TP: Robert, do you see this battle between science and religion as something of a false binary?

RK: Well, if you're asking, "What happens after death?," "What is the conclusion of everything?," or "Where do we all come from?," there are now scientists who propose answers. They didn't used to, but they do now. So there are two different stories and they are, I suppose, rivals. I don't think you can simultaneously believe in heaven *and* a death of all sentience, that is, when your nerves and muscles decay, that's the end of you. Those are conflicts.

But on the other side, if you're asking ethical questions or *why* questions, then I think they can coexist. Why do nice people have terrible things happen to them? Well, because there is a randomness to the world, and accidents always happen, and there is no message in it, no lesson in it . . . *or*, there is, and there is some author outside of things who is discriminating. I don't think science can say yes or no to that, or even try. In that area, the area of *why*, I think there is a place where you can be of two minds. I don't know why, but I'm quite comfortable being of two minds.

TP: How do listeners respond to that sort of thing?

RK: *Radiolab* has a very broad audience, and among the people who listen are lapsed Christians. Former students at Bible schools, preachers, people who have come from various evangelical traditions in which questioning is not really welcome. Some of these people listen and notice that we keep asking questions and that we're comfortable as questioners, which is the most viral thing we've got. We're getting people to examine fundamental questions gently, but the real accomplishment is we give people a little more power to wander in a territory where they might not ordinarily. That feels like a great thing.

TP: Considering that the same people pushing creationism are the ones stripping public radio of federal funding, is it difficult to navigate a world where every idea in the marketplace, regardless of its validity, is expected to be treated with equal weight?

JA: Honestly, no. I would have expected to, but we've never bumped up against that. We're lucky in that we work in a place full of people who are deeply committed to our content and editorial mission. No one here would ever try to impose a false sense of balance; they would never tell us what to say or think. When Robert and I get into arguments that touch on a tension between science and religion, it's perfectly genuine; it's for no reason other than what we're feeling and thinking in the moment. People will yell at us in our comments field online, but that's about it. We've never gotten any pressure from one group or another. I always assumed that it's because we fly a little below the radar. I don't know if that's the case anymore, but I just assume that the people who like the show like those arguments. They don't run away from them; they enjoy them.

RK: No, not really. I don't know why. Maybe because we haven't ventured yet into stem cells; we've done "Where does life end?," but we haven't done "Where does life begin?" So far, for some reason—it isn't any calculated reason—we haven't walked right into that territory. Part of it is that we do only ten shows a year. We can't afford to do something that's so topical that it goes stale. We need shelf life, so part of our logic has been to avoid things that are "right now."

But maybe we haven't felt the pressure because we haven't gotten into the middle of the debate. We are talking with *This American Life* about doing a joint program about global warming, so maybe that will do it.

TP: Well, I'm glad to hear Michele Bachmann isn't coming after you.

JA: Not yet.

TP: Does the current political climate worry you? Do you think public radio is in danger?

RK: No, I think it's unbelievably healthy. The programs that most of us have heard of are ninety-eight percent paid for, then the government puts a couple of pennies on the table. What's at risk are those stations in eastern Montana or Alaska that don't get a lot of listener support but do get a lot of listeners. If you live in a remote area, it's a way to hear something that isn't the CBC or the BBC. That is at risk.

I live in New York City. WNYC was owned by the city of New York, and about fifteen years ago, the listeners got together and said, "You're having a budget crisis. Can we buy it from you?" The then-mayor, Ed Koch, came up with a price and the listeners bought it. It didn't hurt. That station has produced one show after another. It's entrepreneurial and it creates a culture of yes as opposed to a culture of no.

The NPR culture, at this point, is all about "What can we do to not tick off the congressman from Knoxville?" That's no way to run a network.

TP: How does what you're doing fit into the public radio paradigm?

RK: We are thinking about public radio *a lot*. What happened in public *television* is that a group of people, very roughly of my generation, came in during the 1970s and said, "This is wonderful! We'll make magazines; we'll do *Washington Week*; we'll create *Sesame Street*; we'll do British-theater things that you can't get here."

But the usual process is that somebody gets fired and someone replaces him. Lou Rukeyser walked into *Wall Street Week* in 1972, and in 2002 he was still doing exactly the same thing, endlessly and over and over again. The people who came after couldn't get jobs because these people never left. There is something not unlike rigor mortis that has set into public television. I *think* it's dead.

So about fifteen years ago, a bunch of folks in public radio, led by Ira Glass and a guy named Jay Allison, said, "Uh-oh, this sound has become so predictable that you know you're listening to public radio as soon as you graze the dial across those 90s and 80s stations." Ira and some friends created the Third Coast International Audio Festival for the express purpose of trying to seduce kids who were then Jad's age. That's where Jad first encountered a lot of these radio people. Jay created PRX, which basically enables you to put your own thing on the radio; it's essentially an ongoing job fair, and it's moderately successful. *Radiolab* was part of that, and I thought, "Here's this young guy who has a set of beats in him that I've never heard before."

TP: Jad, you really developed the sonic aesthetic of the show. Can you talk about how that evolved or why you thought it would be a good format or style?

JA: I guess I could make up some bullshit about what I think I was doing, but I don't really know. The show began when it was just me on Sunday night from 8:00 to 11:00 on the AM frequency here in New York. I didn't know it at the time, though I had an intuition, but no one was listening. Really, no one, like, probably *zero* listeners. I was just making it up and trying to create a sound that made sense to me. Not having grown up around radio, I had no idea what broadcasting *should* sound like. I was listening to *This American Life*, so I had that sound in my ears. I was trained as a composer and had been listening to a lot of really complicated, layered, avant-garde music. I knew that stuff could be alternately annoying or absorbing, so I wanted to work that. Not in a way that felt experimental, just in a way that made sense to me.

The mood that I thought about in the beginning was the sense of a dream. When you listen to someone tell you about a dream, it's almost like you're in a dream together. That's encouraging to me, that there's a kind a trance people enter into when they hear a story. I wanted to create a sound that somehow induced that trance. But at the same time, there's something very exciting about breaking it up with strange blurts and spastic noises. There is always a tension between a kind of dreamy wash and a more percussive alienating sound. I was trying to work those in, but it was on a purely intuitive level.

The mood that I thought about in the beginning was the sense of a dream. When you listen to someone tell you about a dream, it's almost like you're in a dream together.

TP: Robert, what did you initially think of Jad's style?

RK: I thought it was very important that his sound get on, and get heard, and get joined, and get elaborated upon. One of your jobs or duties at a certain point—if you're an impresario (which you always have to be, in a way)—is to take what you know and stare at what you don't know. When you hear something that strikes you as at least vaguely beautiful—a lot of times what Jad does is vaguely ugly to me; I don't understand it, but I can hear my *kids* liking it and listening to it as ordinary fare, as if it understood their beats—you have to think, *If that brings in an audience, let's do that.* There are a lot of parts of *Radiolab* that I don't understand, but I *know* it has this reach.

So I just say okay. Jad has final cut on every show. It has to end with someone, and it can't end with me. I'm going to die at some point—I mean, I hope I die earlier than he does—so it should be his. That's part of the transfusion that is required in any of this.

NPR was the one thing my generation made that wasn't there before. We got CBS, we got NBC . . . we made PBS, but we fucked it up. NPR turned out to be a gift, but only if it becomes the next generation's property. If it's just their parents' radio, then it will die. *Radiolab* is a way of dealing with that.

TP: How much time do you spend on a given episode? Are you still doing ten a year?

JA: Yeah, plus a bunch of shorts—I don't remember exactly how many, probably about fifteen. We do one episode every six weeks, and that's pretty much the full arc. We'll have a show that's incubating in the background for a while, where you know you have one thing and you're looking for another or you need more research, but once we finally hit go, it's six weeks start to finish. Some shows come together really fast, and others just don't want to be born . . . you have to drag them out kicking and screaming.

RK: But the process by which we do all of this is insane. We'll take up a subject, we'll go out and interview people—often together, but sometimes apart—somebody does a cut, then we take the cut into the room and start talking; we'll say this doesn't work, or that doesn't quite make sense, or we need to get someone else. Then we do it

A Conversation with Robert Krulwich and Jad Abumrad

It's one of the crucial things, whether you're making a movie or a radio show— and maybe it's true about writing—to know when you're done.

again. We switch roles or we throw things out. Gradually, it starts coming together. Everything goes through nine or ten passes before it gets close, then we start with the music. Once it's scored, we ask, "Should we change our voices to react to the music around us?" What you get at the end is the sum of fifteen or twenty performances. It turns into a very fluid thing, but it's entirely artificial . . . except that it isn't. And it's insane. I've never done anything like this before; it makes no sense. The reason we can do only ten shows is that it's just that stupid . . . and it's as close as we can get to making something that's perfect.

JA: The sound stuff doesn't really enter in until about the fifth draft. That's when I kind of close the door, and when the show starts to sound like the show. Everything will be in place, but the musicality below the surface isn't there yet. It never really sounds like *Radiolab* until about that fifth draft.

TP: When do you know that it's done, that it's perfect?

RK: That's Jad. I'll make suggestions, but he doesn't have to take them. It's up to him at the end of the day where our final beauty rests. Though, it's interesting to me, either because he's seduced me or because we were doppelgängers from the beginning, we often agree. It's one of the crucial things, whether you're making a movie or a radio show—and maybe it's true about writing—to know when you're done. It's sort of like flower arranging. You have elements. You put them into a bowl. There are incomprehensively large numbers of combinations that could be made, but at a certain point, you feel somehow satisfied. It's a mysterious feeling. And if you feel satisfied together, it's a doubly mysterious feeling.

TP: More and more of my "radio" consumption is coming through podcasts. When I turn on the radio, I hear *Car Talk*, or *A Prairie Home Companion*, or a painful local call-in show. With podcasting, I listen, at my convenience, to the shows I like—*Radiolab, Bookworm, The Best Show on WFMU*. Considering the growing access to technology, is this the direction radio is going?

JA: I definitely see that as the direction we're going, and the kind of show we're interested in making. We see the podcast audience growing rapidly, and I'm glad about that. The kind of stuff we're making just lands better on an iPod than it does out of a box. People can experience it more intimately, because we're in their ear canals. It's much, much easier to comprehend all the stuff that's happening on the show if you've *chosen* to put it in your ear than if it's just randomly coming out of your car stereo. For us, podcasting has been a blessing.

RK: We create a very jewel-like production; it's very layered. When you stick two things in your head, you are a prisoner of what's coming in, and you can't help yourself. You become a coauthor. Radio is much more intimate than TV, but even the seven feet you're away from a radio is a big seven feet, from the storyteller's point of view. Once we're inside you, there's nothing else; it's like sex. You're in. You can have a conversation that's almost sexy in its intimacy, and its colors, and its subtleties. You can't have that just shaking someone's hand. When you fuck 'em, you can do all kinds of interesting things. That's the big difference. We didn't expect it, but it's made all of the difference to us. We went from seven thousand subscribers to fifty thousand, then Ira put us on his show and we jumped to a quarter million in an instant. We keep growing and growing, and I think it's because we are podcast friendly.

TP: Will that format change the way people are producing content?

JA: I don't know if it's the direction all radio will go, but I do know that kids below a certain age just don't own radios anymore. That's kind of an interesting situation. I don't know what that will mean for radio as a whole, if it will just migrate onto smartphones and things like that.

I do think that there's a serendipity that happens when you turn on old-school radio; you hear things you weren't expecting to hear, and that's kind of beautiful. A lot of the people who like the show began with those little collisions that happen when you're in your car and some story comes on. So there's a part of me that's sad that maybe that is happening less. I don't know if this has been your experience, but I subscribe to a lot of podcasts and listen to maybe one percent of them. There just aren't enough hours in the day. I wonder if that happens often, if people are actually listening to as many podcasts as they have.

But I will say, if you just stroll through the top twenty on iTunes or something, there are a lot of different sounds. I've been listening to Marc Maron's podcast a lot recently.

TP: I love his show.

JA: Yeah, he's really interesting, aside from those fourteen-minute commercials. He's this great, kind of unhygienic character. Whereas sometimes public radio personalities are very anesthetized and squeaky clean, he's not, and it's incredibly compelling. To me, it's great that there are these cool things sprouting up in meadows just adjacent to us. I like that, and I think they benefit us.

TP: What episodes or segments typify, for you, what *Radiolab* should be, both in terms of form and content?

JA: You mentioned the story of the woman in the coma. On a pure storytelling level, I feel like that is everything I want from the radio. There isn't a ton of science or philosophy inside that story, but if you ask me why I actually turn on the radio, it's so I might hear a story like that. And that's a case where we just got lucky.

But in terms of *Radiolab*, and the sound and synthesis we're aiming for, I think of the "Words" show [season 8, episode 2] and the different moves we make. We start with a woman who describes meeting a fellow who had no language until he was twenty-seven. It's just a pure story. Then we go to a really complicated psychology experiment involving rats and people in a white room—it was a terribly difficult experiment to explain, we must have done fifty different versions of it and it wasn't working in terms of the mood, or the scoring, or the explanation, until it suddenly did. But I remember reading about the experiment and saying to myself, "This is incredible. This gives me a completely new way of thinking about the power of words."

I can remember that feeling, but everything that happened after that was difficult and frustrating. It was all an attempt to reconstruct, for the listener, that feeling. We eventually got to a place with that story where I was really proud of it. It achieved a certain kind of dreamy poetry that's perspective-shaking in a way that I felt when I first discovered that idea.

So I liked the balance in that first segment between a very narrative thing and something extremely cerebral and abstract. Overall, I think that show really captured the full palette of our moods in a way that sometimes shows don't.

RK: "Words," I think, was very special. I don't know how well you know that episode, but there's a guy who can't hear, and he discovers that things have names. The surprise of that not only shocks him, it also delights him. It allows him to find a place in the world. I just thought that was one of the more beautiful stories we've produced.

For some reason, I like the show about stress, with Robert Sapolsky. There's something about Sapolsky. If there's an E. B. White for your ear, it might be this strange neuroscientist from Stanford University. I don't know why it is, but he's just the most compelling storyteller. He talks about his father dying, then putting on his dad's shirt and putting his dad's pencils in the shirt pocket and mourning his father by becoming him. He'd lecture his class at school by telling them that even though the exam was coming up, and they all wanted to know what was on the exam, it was more important that they call their parents. He realized that he'd just *become* his father for a season. I found that completely bewitching.

It's always the occasions when the idea that's being examined and the heart that's being examined, which carries the idea, become so entangled that you can't stop thinking and you can't stop feeling. That's when you hit it.

ESSAY

THE SYNTHESIZERS

Jesse Lichtenstein

Life, made to order

Does anything mark the past so thoroughly as *the past*—so seal it in its particular shade of amber—as one era's version of the future? This thought occurred to me a few weeks ago when I saw a poster taped to a street lamp advertising a concert by a band called We Were Promised Jetpacks. The future either ripens into inevitability or it gets canned as nostalgia, to be served later as irony.

In a brief essay published in 1992, the astrophysicist and science fiction writer Gregory Benford asked, "What would a biological century look like?" As he saw it, "If the 19th century was characterized by hardware and this century by information, that is, software, we might believe that the next century will be informed by liveware. Living technology." A dozen or so years later, something called *synthetic biology* first caught the attention of mainstream media. It was billed as an entirely new approach to genetic modification, and with its coming, such profound transformations were apparently on layaway that, in comparison, the jet pack looked like a knotted handkerchief attached to a stick and slung over the dusty shoulder of a hobo. Jet packs? Where we were going, we didn't need jet packs.

The promises of synthetic biology were many. While Benford had mused about household conveniences ("a kitchen or

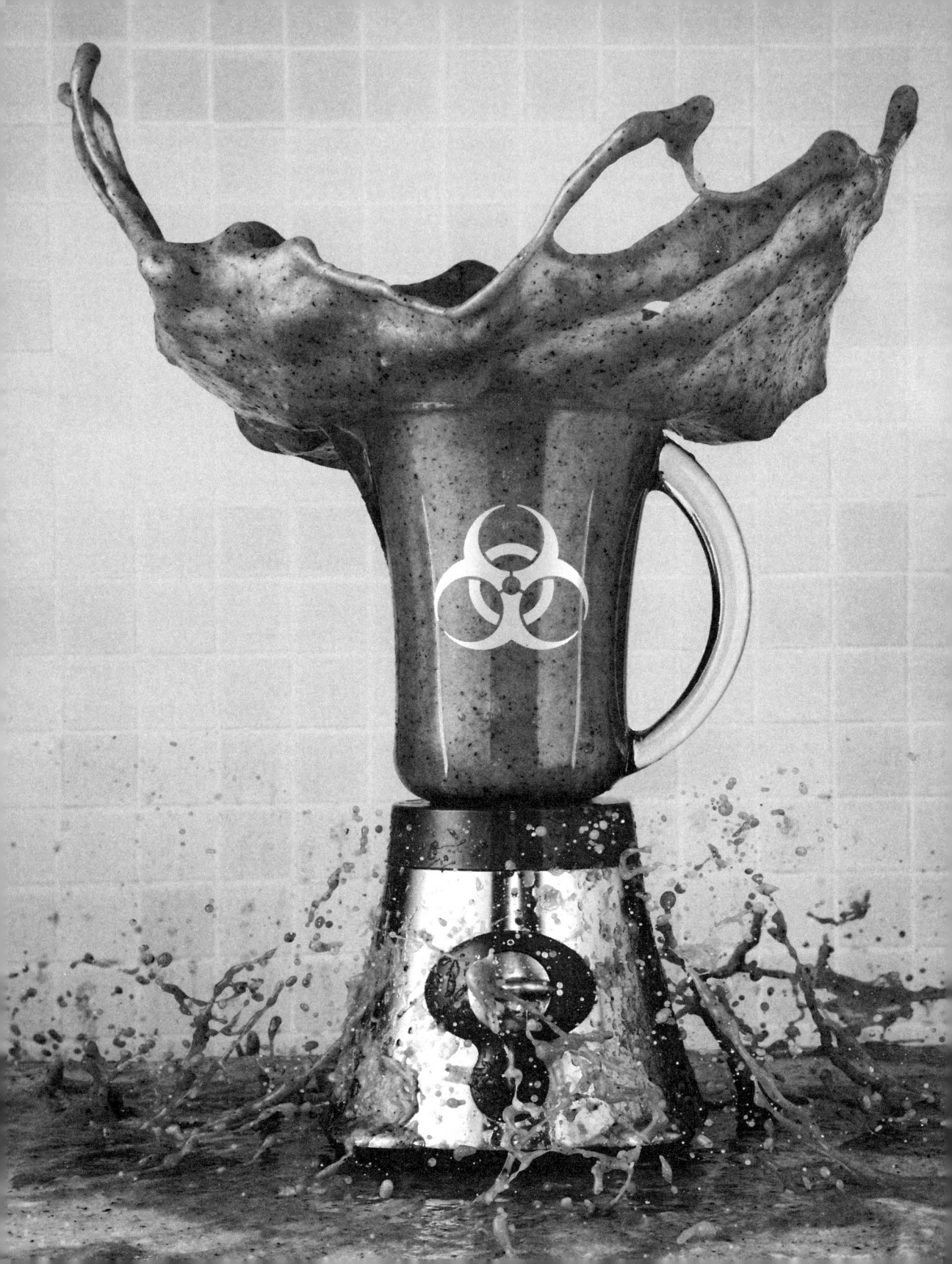

bathroom mat that is alive and cleans the room because it lives off what it eats") and convenient housing ("it might be much smarter to simply engineer the genes of the trees and grow your own house"), synthetic biology would also redesign microbes to produce limitless fuel, secrete a cure for malaria, devour cholesterol in the body, program cells to kill themselves if they reproduced at a cancerous rate, sink carbon in vast quantities, produce medicine within the bloodstream, and—yes—reengineer trees to grow from an acorn into an entire house. And those were just the parlor tricks. One popular vision of the future—the android, in which hardware blurs the border between human and machine—had been superseded by another—the entirely living, self-programming, master and manipulator of a far more powerful code: our own DNA. Synthetic biology presented, in the words of the young bioengineer Drew Endy, "a secondary path" to evolution—one that we could thoroughly control. This was the ignition key to life itself.

As someone who studied biology in college before balking at life in the lab or the field and retreating to the vantage of a casual observer, I was taken with what I read. The new field came with a snappy handle, *synbio*. "Sin" and "syn": a slip of homophony reminding us that the gut-level unease provoked by such made-to-purpose rejiggering of life is rooted in deep notions of transgression. To me, synthetic biology embodied what we who are not scientists find most invigorating and unnerving about science: from the moment a question can be formulated, someone somewhere will not rest until she can demonstrate an answer. With synthetic biology, the technical question was, simply, Could we design and build DNA—and by extension, living organisms—as we design and build software, and airplanes, and electric toothbrushes? If the answer was yes, it was hard to imagine a corner of reality the moral and ethical questions wouldn't reach.[1]

> Synthetic biology embodied what we who are not scientists find most invigorating and unnerving about science.

---

1. The ethical questions surrounding modifying DNA are obviously not new. Since the 1970s, we've been combining bits of DNA from one organism with bits from another, making mice produce cow hormones, knocking out targeted bits of DNA to see what happens in their absence—what synthetic biologists somewhat dismissively called "gene bashing." And if we look even further back, by some lights, human civilization as we know it is mostly a lingering side effect—a swelling that won't go away—of agriculture and husbandry, which are possible only because, millennia ago, *Homo sapiens* figured out how to adjust the knobs of evolution. We've been playing God ever since we took one relatively passive wolf, mated it with another, fed the pups, and called them dogs. But breeding was a black-box experiment, and recombinant DNA is a heuristic process. The revolution at the heart of synthetic biology is that it wants to do away with the pretense of working only with the material we're given.

Most of the shapers and early adopters of the field were engineers, and they thought like engineers in that they wanted the blueprint (the DNA) to consist of known parts with known functions that interact in a predictable way. Of course, even at the chromosomal level life doesn't act in a wholly predictable way—or at least not to our level of understanding. When the material world (the organism) doesn't behave like the model, you can either keep working on the model to make it more like the world or make the world more like the model.

To get to that point, you first take a relatively simple life-form, such as the laboratory workhorse E. coli, knock out every part of the bacterium's genome that you can without killing it, and you're left with a baseline for life—the minimal functionality—in essence, a living chassis. Then you add the functions you want back into the genome, one short sequence at a time, building your new organism to do what you want it to do, be what you want it to be.

From the beginning, the goal of synthetic biologists was to create a biological engine of innovation for which, ultimately, the inventor didn't have to understand what was going on under the hood. With standardized fittings—Legos would be a loose analogy—you can mix and match known DNA sequences to create increasingly complex genetic systems.

> If teenagers and art majors were doing this work, it was no great leap to imagine the darker implications of open-source microbe making.

For example, let's say you have a sequence of DNA and you know that in the presence of arsenic, that strand of DNA codes for making Protein A. In synthetic biology, that sequence is a "part." And say you have another sequence that, in the presence of Protein A, codes for the making of Protein B, which has the convenient property of glowing in the dark. That sequence is another "part." Link these two sequences together, add them to your "E. coli" chassis, and now you have a simple, living, arsenic detector you can drop into water. If it glows, don't drink. But at a higher level of abstraction, you have a basic circuit.

For the past fifty years you haven't needed to know how to make a capacitor or a resistor or a transistor in order to build an electrical circuit—these parts are ready-made; you assemble them to perform increasingly sophisticated operations. Genetic "parts" combine to form "devices"; devices combine to form systems. You work "off-line"—in software, not wetware—designing and modeling your code. The "synthesis" in synthetic biology comes from the fact that, ever more rapidly, ever more cheaply, we can construct longer and longer strands of DNA from sugar. So a code of letters becomes an abstraction for the organism: life is data; data is life. It's a hell of a lot easier to manipulate a string of the letters *A*, *G*, *C*, and *T* and then e-mail the sequence than to transport living material. You send your finished code off to a gene synthesis shop, which builds the DNA and sends it back to you. You add the new DNA to the chassis and "upload" into a cell. You've just modified a living being to create another that never before existed.

But first you need to build a library of these DNA parts, which Tom Knight, a senior scientist at MIT, named "Bio-Bricks."[2] Working with MIT students, synthetic biologists designed or refined more basic parts. In 2005, Knight, Endy, and Randy Rettberg (then all at MIT) and Chris Voigt (then at UCSF) and Pamela Silver (at Harvard) created the BioBricks Foundation, a nonprofit that maintains an open-source registry of parts and their functions.

BioBricks are what student teams employed at the first International Genetically Engineered Machine (iGEM) competition in 2005. The teams vied to create the coolest or most promising new microbes using (or adding to) a library of publicly available DNA sequences.

Though initially pitched toward undergraduates, iGEM soon allowed a few high school teams to compete as well. In the fall of 2007, I flew to Massachusetts to attend the event—held that year in Frank Gehry's shimmering, chimerical Stata Center at MIT—and was blown away by the work of teams from such places as Ljubljana, Slovenia, and Peking University. Many of the students had been doing synthetic biology for a shockingly brief period of time. I spoke to one young man from Mexico, a nineteen- or twenty-year-old math major who'd joined his school's project over the summer. At the conference, he was presenting original research on new organisms. Another student was an art major. By iGEM's seventh year, over one hundred sixty teams hailing from every continent but Antarctica were churning out new BioBricks—and new creatures.

If teenagers and art majors were doing this work, it was no great leap to imagine the darker implications of open-source microbe making. In 2006, a reporter for the UK paper the *Guardian* announced a great scoop: he'd been able to order part of the genome for the smallpox virus—the code was available online—from a gene synthesis lab. Scientists I spoke with were unimpressed. It smacked of a stunt, they felt, and the journalist vastly overestimated the ease of making a viable virus from the available materials. But the larger question remained: In the hands of misanthropes, what sort of weapon could this technology give rise to?

---

2. Brief histories of this young field tend to locate synthetic biology's genesis in Knight's MIT lab. In the 1990s, he transitioned from a brilliant career in artificial intelligence to what had been a moonlighting interest in genetics and biochemistry. To the biological world of wet imperfection he brought an engineer's passion for streamlined processes, simplicity of design, and interchangeable parts—tellingly, he set up his biology lab in the institute's computer science department.

This was not a new question. Benford had speculated in his essay: "Some maniac may attempt to kill billions of people in one shot with a plague, maybe a super-influenza conveyed mouth to mouth"—and, of course, the public fears following the advent of recombinant DNA experiments in the 1970s were born of nightmare scenarios involving new creatures loosed or leaked into a world unprepared. In the press, each mention of the coming glories of synthetic biology came with a somber, cautionary note and, often, an evocation of bioapocalypse at the hands of terrorist networks or a lone-wolf sociopath. A watchdog organization called the ETC Group issued the loudest warning of unintended consequences—not only bioterror, in other words, but also "bio-error"—in calling for "an immediate ban on environmental release of de novo synthetic organisms until wide societal debate and strong governance are in place."

On the heels of the iGEM competition, I attended the BioBrick Foundation's annual meeting in November of 2007. Endy convoked the meeting, which was held in a modest lecture hall on the MIT campus, by saying, "I think you'll agree it's likely to be historic." (As if to mark synbio's emergence into the mainstream, Endy would be profiled in *Esquire* a few weeks later as one of the "Best and Brightest" people of 2007.)[3] One sensed, hovering around the attendees, a palpable self-awareness that this was a Wild West moment: time was short for the village worthies to draw up a charter before the federal marshal rode into town. There were references to the watershed Asilomar Conference on Recombinant DNA in 1975, when scientists gathered to discuss the perils of the new field and to offer up guidelines; there were debates about the limits and the potential of open-source science, the threat to the entire field posed by patent law, and the mistakes of scientists in the past who promised too much too soon (the elusive death-ray laser was a popular example).[4]

Almost taken for granted was the assumption that as the technologies of gene sequencing and DNA synthesis continued to quicken and cheapen, people would begin to do synthetic biology in their homes—the model of the homebrew personal computer revolution seemed more and more apt. Endy mentioned what he called the "garagistas" who, if they weren't already, would soon be hacking DNA, just as their forebears hacked the PC and the Internet. Hacker groups had already reached out to him, and in his estimation, it was better to engage than to shun them. (What was synthetic biology, after all, but a hack of life?) Yet, inevitably, humans being humans, someone would do something nasty. In the *Esquire* profile, Endy put it bluntly: "People will die."

---

3. A year later, he was one of *Esquire's* "75 Most Influential People of the 21st Century." The same year, *Good* magazine described Endy as "like God, if God were a geek."

4. The BioBrick Foundation even brought in David Clark, one of the architects of the Internet in the 1970s, to discuss how a small group of people, largely left to itself, settled on the protocols underlying a world-changing endeavor.

I didn't need much convincing. In 2001, I was working at a national magazine on the twentieth floor of a skyscraper in Manhattan. In the weeks after September 11, letters laced with anthrax arrived at ABC News, CBS News, NBC News, the *New York Post*, and the *National Enquirer*, among other places. Twenty-two people were hospitalized; five people died. One assistant who opened mail on my floor became worried about a fresh rash on his hand; all mail delivery was suspended while the FBI hustled us into a conference room to explain what precautions we needed to take.

So, sure, I didn't doubt it: we would hear from these virus hackers soon.

But years went by, and at some point I realized that—so far, at least—none of this renegade bioterror had come to pass. To many people, the meaning of "hacking" has shifted to signify resourcefulness, even cooperation ("hackathons" are now popular parlance for people gathering to tackle a range of problems). Yet hacking *life* still has a troubling overtone. I began to wonder what had happened with do-it-yourself synthetic biology. Where were Endy's garagistas, and what kind of future were they building for us beside the warped Ping-Pong table and the pile of mismatched ski boots?

> Endy mentioned what he called the "garagistas" who, if they weren't already, would soon be hacking DNA, just as their forebears hacked the PC and the Internet.

Around the arrival of the new millennium, the bioengineer Robert Carlson began trumpeting the great promise of "garage biology" and "garage biotech hacking" in a more entrepreneurial sense, as a nimble alternative to academic and commercial labs. He'd moved in and out of academia himself and come to realize that he didn't know anyone who was actually trying to make a living doing synthetic biology on her own. In 2005, he decided to give it a shot at his home in the Seattle area.

He designed a gene and then had to contend with all kinds of difficulty when it came to synthesis quality, costs, and reagent delivery. He publicly described the gene only as a "widget," because he hadn't figured out how to defend his intellectual property in a system tilted, as he saw it, toward large corporations that have the resources to secure and defend (and challenge) patents. "It was a little bit early," he told me when I spoke to him six years later. By that time, he'd moved his lab to a commercial space. "I made a fair amount of progress in my garage," he said, "but it was cold and not the best place to work. Now I can keep my boat in my garage."

I asked Carlson to put me in touch with other innovating, garage-based synthetic biologists, but he demurred. "I'm no longer a point of contact for that crowd. I'm known for talking to the government, so I know less than I used to."⁵ As he saw it, his mission now was "to make the U.S. government less stupid about biotech, because they have been demonstratively not-so-clear-thinking about how to approach this issue for the past ten years."

From the distance of half a decade, the initial coverage of synthetic biology can seem a bit breathless. Basic science takes time, and those who crave jet packs might want to learn how to hang glide in the meantime. As impressive as the high school teams at iGEM were, and are, R & D is still a steep hill, and without the resources of an institution, garage biochemistry may be a bit more difficult than popular science accounts have implied.

That's not to say there haven't been developments in academic and commercial labs. Jay Keasling and his team at Lawrence Berkeley National Laboratory, with the help of a (modest!) $42.6 million grant from the Gates Foundation, successfully engineered yeast to produce the antimalarial drug artemisinin, as well as a bacteria that produces biofuels. In the spring of 2010, Craig Venter—the head of the J. Craig Venter Institute, who is inevitably described as "brash," a "maverick," and a "media darling"—unveiled the first organism with an entirely synthesized genome. He called it Synthia. Team Venter introduced the genes into a bacteria cell from which the original DNA had been removed—a body waiting for a brain. The cell divided successfully, two new cells were born, and an entirely human-designed thing was remaking itself naturally in the world.⁶

Soon after Venter's grand announcement, President Obama requested that his Presidential Commission for the Study of Bioethical Issues survey the field and examine calls for its regulation. In December of 2010, the commission declared that it was "imprudent either to declare a moratorium on synthetic biology until all risks can be determined and mitigated, or to simply 'let science rip,' regardless of the likely risks. The Commission instead proposes a middle ground—an ongoing system of prudent vigilance that carefully monitors, identifies and mitigates potential and realized harms over time."

In other words, fire away—but don't shoot yourself in the foot.⁷

> Basic science takes time, and those who crave jet packs might want to learn how to hang glide in the meantime.

---

5. One person I spoke with suggested Carlson might simply not want to give me the names of private synbio practitioners.

6. The headline of an article in a British tabloid covering the event read: "Scientist accused of playing God after creating artificial life by making designer microbe from scratch—but could it wipe out humanity?"

7. Not everyone was thrilled, of course. A coalition of more than thirty environmental groups sent the commission a letter of protest calling for "a moratorium on the release and commercial use of synthetic organisms until we have a better understanding of the implications and hazards of this field ... The time for precaution and the regulation of synthetic biology is now."

While Venter's team was cooking up Synthia, synthetic biologists in California launched BIOFAB, "the world's first biological design-build facility," seeded by a large grant from the National Science Foundation and staffed by scientists from a host of universities.[8] In the past several years, academic and private labs have signed large deals with energy and chemical corporations—BP, Chevron, Shell, Virgin Fuels, DuPont, Microsoft, Cargill, and Archer Daniels Midland—to work toward synthesizing organisms that function, essentially, as biofactories for fuel and materials. Synbio is starting to look like Big Science. This a path the United States has trodden far and proudly—a path that has produced momentous transformations in the human condition, as well as a host of slow-moving, planet-sized disasters that lend synthetic biology much of its urgency.

And yet, Carlson insists that far from the acronyms and academic-corporate partnerships, the era of garage biology is already upon us; he said as much to Obama's commission, warning that regulation would be stifling and would only drive synthetic biology to the black market. "The White House has gotten the message that biology is key to the economy of the United States," he said when we talked. "We get innovation from garages." If, as Carlson claims, the FBI pressures manufacturers of reagents and resellers of used biohardware to keep lists of their clients, and there is an "incentive for people to hide," perhaps this is explanation enough for why garage synthetic biology remains largely sub rosa.

For some would-be garagistas, the possibility of designing life is only one of the attractions of synbio. The other is the hack itself, and the do-it-yourself ethos surrounding it. While researching garage synbio, I began to hear more and more about something called DIY biology. In 2007, I met Mackenzie Cowell, a 23-year-old living outside of Boston, and working as an iGEM facilitator. The spirit of the conference had drawn him further into synthetic biology. "I had an underlying interest in subverting authority, doing it independently," Cowell recalled when I caught up with him recently. "Combine that with synthetic biology—I thought that was so cool." He'd never been tempted by graduate school, but he thought, "Here were all these students not on track to become biologists. I wondered, what is it that lets math or art students do the work in several months but doesn't let nonstudents do it?"

In time, the barriers became clearer to him: "The tools are expensive; sometimes

---

8. BIOFAB is led by bioengineers from UC Berkeley and Stanford, in partnership with Lawrence Berkeley National Laboratory, the BioBricks Foundation, and the Synthetic Biology Engineering Research Center (SynBERC). While I was writing this essay, the Berkeley anthropology professor who'd been hired as an in-house ethicist and biosecurity evaluator quit SynBERC under a cloud of controversy, telling the *New York Times* he was tired of the indifference he claimed the scientists at SynBERC show toward their "responsibility to larger society, which is funding them, by entrusting them to manipulate life." Keasling denied the accusations. The position was filled by Endy.

you can't get reagents; it's hard to get access to some of the literature; basic knowledge is codified in a way that's hard to get if you're not in an institution. How do you provide mentorship in a distributed form?" These are the challenges he is now tackling. Cowell moved to the Bay Area this past year, and, with his colleague Jason Bobe, who claims to have coined the term DIYBio, founded a group of that name, a worldwide online network of biohackers.

"Start-up stories don't exist in biotech for interesting reasons," Cowell told me. "We need to be democratizing the tools, celebrating the people who have this success." Cowell partnered with Josh Perfetto, whom he met at a Maker Faire, to develop and bring to market a low-cost kit for extracting DNA and getting it sequenced.[9] They hoped to spark hobbyist interest in working with DNA. Perfetto teamed up with Tito Jankowski to make a PCR machine (PCR stands for polymerase chain reaction—a key step in sequencing genes) that sells for roughly $500, an order of magnitude (or two) cheaper than most other machines on the market. Bobe, after a brief interest in synthetic biology, turned his attention back to "appropriate technology"—looking at DIY bio as the best source of cheap, reliable medical equipment, such as bike pump nebulizers that could be used in remote villages in the developing world.

---

9. Maker Faire is a recurring event launched by the magazine *Make* to "celebrate arts, crafts, engineering, science projects and the Do-It-Yourself (DIY) mindset."

In the past several years, spaces for communal work have sprung up around the country—Genspace in Brooklyn and BioCurious in the Bay Area are two. There's an element of Maker Faire culture, of hackathon gatherings; artists are welcome, as are people who are just keen on science. In these settings, DIY bio can look more broad than deep. The label covers anything from those who rail against the proprietary nature of academic science to the Quantified Self (QS) people, who track and share their locations, activities, sleep patterns, heart rates, blood glucose levels, facial expressions, moods, menstrual cycles, and work productivity. It includes people who like to look at pond water under microscopes and people who want to take absolute control of their health using the newly accessible knowledge of their own genome—all of which can seem far from the cutting edge of research and, from a certain perspective, quaint, like friends playing with chemistry sets.

That's clearly reductive, but Andrew Ellington, a biochemist at UT Austin and a sparring partner of Carlson, doesn't think it's a stretch. "Innovation is driven, in large part, by access to infrastructure—if you can't make your own silicon chips, why should we worry about you making DNA?" he wrote recently in the *Scientist*. "DIY Bio just plain doesn't work, and if it did, we would have had something worthwhile from the hobbyists long, long before this." Ellington is equally unimpressed with Carlson's warnings against the dire effects of new regulations. Where there is little threat of innovation, there is little threat of mayhem: "Can we at least leave out . . . the notion that there could be a black market because folks who hook up platinum electrodes to car batteries and pour agarose gels in Play-Doh molds might someday actually create a bacterium that converts glucose to gold?"[10] The specter of the garagista reduced, in one skeptic's eye, to alchemy.

Last spring, on a visit to San Francisco, I met Raymond McCauley, a large, energetic man in his midforties with spiked gray hair and a Texan's open vowels and demeanor. A bioinformatics scientist, McCauley seems to know everyone in the overlapping worlds of DIY biology—personal genomics, open science, QS, citizen science, you name it. He most recently had helped develop a company that functions as a social network enabling people to share as much or as little information as they like about their health. Those who want to can find like-minded or like-suffering people with whom to share information, experiences, and proposals for research—with themselves as experiment designers, administrators, and subjects.

We met at a community tool shop and workspace in the SoMa neighborhood, where McCauley was hoping to take a class, and then walked to a restaurant, where we sat on the patio. McCauley is among a small, but growing, number of people to have had most of their genome sequenced. He learned, on his own, that he has a mutation that gives him an increased risk of suffering macular degeneration, which causes vision loss. McCauley found studies suggesting that a regimen of vitamin B_{12}, zinc, and lutein *may* help prevent the disease, and others suggesting that certain genetic defects make it difficult for some people to absorb B vitamins in the form they are often given—such people needed a rarer, active form of the vitamin. Suspecting he might have the defective version of that gene, he gathered a small group of people together to design and conduct an experiment to see if they could match their gene variants to their ability to absorb vitamin B. This was a small test case for citizen science, with a tiny trial and implications for the not-so-dramatic field of supplemental vitamin uptake. But, McCauley points out, there are rare diseases that afflict a few thousand Americans or fewer—way below the level of an orphan disease—that receive

> Where there is little threat of innovation, there is little threat of mayhem.

---

10. Or maybe the future lies in turning shit gold. Seven Cambridge University students won the 2009 iGEM competition with *E. chromi*, a redesigned *E. coli* that secretes a variety of colored pigments when it detects different substances. They then worked with two artists to project future uses of this technology, including a personal disease-monitoring yogurt that will turn your feces a specific color depending on whatever infirmity it detects in your gut: say, purple for salmonella, blue for worms, green for colorectal cancer, and gold for colitis.

virtually no R & D funding.[11] Yet here was a population desperate to participate in research. "The parents and the kids that've got that disease," he said, "are *all in*."[12]

McCauley wanted to demonstrate another use of personal genomics: "I can tell this by looking at my DNA: if I die, the most likely reason will be a heart attack." If he were to have a heart attack, he said, "the ambulance would race up here, they would drag me in, they would take a needle and inject me with Plavix"—a blood thinner that triples your chance of surviving—"That saves lives, but it wouldn't save mine." One of his genes has two single-letter mutations. Plavix still works on people who have this form of the gene, but they require a much higher dose for the drug to have the effect it has on most people—a standard dose would make little difference. "My doctor knows this," he said, "but how does the EMT know?"

McCauley took off his necklace and showed me what looked like a dog tag. On one side, it read "PLAVIX MEDS DOSE," and on the other side was a code for the dosing. This was his sequenced genome in action. "People don't realize how fast genetic information is getting cheap," he said. "We're going to go from ten years ago," when sequencing a human genome "was a billion-dollar project—this heroic effort—to ten years from now, when I really firmly believe—I would stake my children's lives on it—they will be giving this stuff away free like prizes in a Cracker Jack box. And that ten years is really probably overstating it by a factor of two." As we paid our bill, McCauley said, matter-of-factly, "You know, I get Google alerts on my name. I'd like to get Google alerts on my genome."

Indeed, if much of the energy of the DIY bio community is given over to making cheaper lab equipment and encouraging curiosity outside of the academy, much of it is also geared toward a biological knowledge of the self that seems to augur both a democratization of health care and vast new categories of navel gazing.[13]

> You won't be worried about your kids downloading porn. You'll be worried about them downloading the latest supermodel, and growing her in an egg,

---

11. An orphan disease is one that has been "adopted" by the pharmaceutical industry despite there being little financial incentive in pursuing a treatment, either because the disease afflicts poor populations or because it is "rare"—which in the United States is defined as affecting fewer than 200,000 people.

12. McCauley was quick to acknowledge the vast gap between the strictures of academic research and a group of amateur interested parties experimenting on themselves. Yet, he said, "if we just do some hypothesis generation, and prove it out to the point where it's like, yeah, it was self-reported; yeah, there might be some bias . . . but we saw *this*."

13. I meant this as metaphor, but then I learned that Jonathan Eisen, one of the most prominent advocates of "open science," is spearheading a citizen-scientist project that calls on people around the world to genetically map the bacteria in their belly buttons.

I still wanted to talk to a garagista—that bogeyman or economic spark plug who was either already silently ubiquitous among us or else a figment wrapped in an exaggeration. If this were a possible future—the common marriage of do-it-yourself biology and grow-it-yourself DNA hacking—if all of us would someday soon be Dr. Frankensteins in the privacy of our rec rooms, then surely someone, somewhere, was doing it right now and would be willing to crow about it. Although there was chatter in online forums, none of the DIY biologists I spoke with could or would point me to any Americans actively engaged in garage-style synthetic biology. Yet the name of a young Irishman kept popping up in conversation: Cathal Garvey.

My first attempts to reach Garvey were failures. It turns out that he is at best the *fourth* most famous Cathal Garvey in Ireland. There's a police chief, and a classical music conductor, and all of them are dwarfed by the Google presence of one Cathal Garvey of Dublin, whose profession happens to be "search engine optimizer."

When we did at last have a conversation, it was a quintessentially twenty-first-century encounter. It was three o'clock in the morning my time, 11:00 AM his, and I was at my desk in my bedroom staring into my laptop while he stared at his. We were on Skype, itself a technology on loan from the set of *Star Trek*. Some quintessential twenty-first-century activities are also quintessentially nineteenth century: every fifteen minutes or so the connection cut out and we had to try again. I watched as Garvey, a clean-cut, quick-thinking twenty-six-year-old with close-cropped brown hair, mentally reached for an image to illustrate the world that awaits us. In the future, Garvey told me, "you won't be worried about your kids downloading porn. You'll be worried about them downloading the latest supermodel, and growing her in an egg, and keeping her under the bed. It's going to be amazing the things we can do. Also really terrifying. And it's going to change humanity."

Garvey runs the only licensed synthetic biology home lab that either of us knows of in Europe. (Besides proscriptions against playing with pathogens, there is no official sanction required for tinkering with DNA in the United States.) Garvey may run the only official synthetic biology home lab in the world. He sat in this lab on the outskirts of Cork as we talked. I could see surfaces behind him covered with equipment. It's worth mentioning that up until several months before we spoke, Garvey's lab was known by its previous title: his mother's downstairs guest bedroom.

Garvey knew he wanted to be a biologist when he was seven. By age twelve or thirteen, he recalled, "I saw myself getting into genetics and doing crazy things like programming pet dragons. And then for a while I thought, *Ha, such childish notions. How silly.*" After graduating from University College Cork, he toiled in a PhD program for three-plus years before deciding it was all too depressing. "From being a child and imagining having my own mad scientist lab," he said, "I think I'd been seduced into institutionalized science, where you imagine yourself slogging through the first twenty-five years of your career and playing by someone else's rules, and then someday, through politicking or getting a Nobel Prize or something, some guy goes, 'Hey, would you like your own lab?' And from there you step on the little guy and get him to do your research." His discovery of synthetic biology, and the realization that it might be possible to do it on his own, reanimated his earlier, childlike view of science.

He dropped out. Last winter, with his wife pregnant with their first child, he began the process of starting his own lab. She gave him one year to make a go of it—January to January—but it took three months of red tape to get the lab inspected and approved, so he is now on a March-to-March time line. He filled out applications, made risk assessments, paid fees. Since he and his wife rent their apartment, his mother donated her guest bedroom. When the inspector from Ireland's Environmental Protection Agency came to visit, she wanted him to put a biohazard sign on the door. His mother might not have minded, but Garvey was indignant—the only biological material in the lab refrigerator were the harmless *Bacillus subtilis*, some lab strain *E. coli*, and kombucha bacteria. "You're more likely to kill yourself by leaving your coffee too long and trying to drink it," he insisted. In the end, the EPA asked him to put a biohazard sign on the fridge, which he still felt was misleading, but to which he begrudgingly assented, noting that "the idea is to encourage people not to leave their sandwich in the fridge."

Garvey's immediate goal is both ambitious and modest. "In twenty to thirty years, biotechnology is either going to be crushed by regulatory burden, and people being terrified of it, and companies locking it away, or it's going to change the world the same way the Internet did, but with more penetration. You can't just copy the Internet and give it to someone in Africa and say, 'Here you go, that was great.' You *can* do that with biotechnology. If you create something that makes life-saving antibiotics, you can just give it away for free, and you're not losing anything by doing so." Teach a man to fish, in other words, and charge him once for the rod and the lessons. You want state-of-the-art medicine? Here, you can grow your own.[14]

Practically, Garvey wants to create a stable plasmid that other synthetic biologists can use to shuttle their designed DNA into their experimental organisms. "Those

---

14. Garvey is an avowed believer in open source: "If I sell someone a piece of DNA and they use that DNA at home, they are by definition making copies. I could take that as a threat, like many people in the software industry did, and create a model that tries to deny this reality of what I'm working with and say, 'You can't copy it. You're not allowed—I won't permit it.' But that would be denying reality. I would be taking a property and trying to sell it against its very nature." Instead, he plans to draft a kind of creative commons license that will encourage people who buy his plasmids to share them with others. "Just tell them that I made it. That's all I want out of it. In the public DIY biohacker community, the more you share, the better it gets. That's just an unspoken, now completely understood element of it. It's obvious; it's how the whole Internet works: you share things, it gets better, it comes back to you."

plasmids are often really badly chopped-up bits of wild DNA that are no longer stable," he explained. To keep the plasmids in the desired cells, you need to apply antibiotics, for which, if you are not a major lab, you need a doctor's prescription—a barrier for the DIY crowd. And there is a further irony: "It's kind of useless to create something that makes antibiotics to save people in Africa that needs antibiotics to work," he said.

More than an hour into our conversation, Garvey gave me a tour of his lab by lifting his laptop and carrying and tilting its camera while leaning back to talk into the microphone. There was an incubator he rescued from a university, tubes of chemicals, one of the new $500 PCR machines, and a very DIY centrifuge, which he invented by taking a dremel and designing an attachment to hold test tubes. The attachment was plastic and printable from a 3-D printer—he sells them online to make a little extra money. He isn't, however, able to synthesize the actual DNA in his lab. "We're living in the mainframe era of genetics," he lamented, "where you get a mainframe to make your DNA and send it out to you, whereas what I'm looking forward to is the personal computer era of genetics, where someone comes up with a desktop DNA synthesis method. If no one beats me to it, I'd love to make a DNA-synthesizing bacteria, a bacteria that writes its own DNA, on command. I think if that worked it would be the ultimate killer app."

I asked him about the risks of there being garagistas—or downstairs-guest-bedroomistas—with ethics and morals far different from his own. "If we're not already seeing that awful stuff, it's not as likely as we imagined it to be," he said. "It's easy to purify ricin, and we don't often see ricin being used as an attack vector. It's easy to grow *Clostridium botulinum* and pollute water supplies with botulism, one of the most toxic biological substances there is, and we don't see that very often.[15] It's easier to get an AK-47 to go out and shoot people, and it's probably more satisfying. When biotech becomes successful enough that these guys who feel like they have to go out and kill people are looking at their choice between tech and biotech, you're going to start to see bioweapons coming out of the insurgent market, and that's going to be really scary. But by that stage, I think biotechnology will be fast enough to respond as well. If it's really easy to make a pathogen, it's even easier

> I think more lives are going to be *saved* by biotechnology than will ever be put at risk by it.

---

15. In fact, the largest bioterrorist attack in American history (and one of only two confirmed bioterrorist attacks on human beings) occurred in 1984 in my home state of Oregon, when followers of the cult leader Bhagwan Shree Rajneesh contaminated the salad bars of ten restaurants in The Dalles in an attempt to decrease voter turnout in county elections.

to make a vaccine. I think more lives are going to be *saved* by biotechnology than will ever be put at risk by it."

Garvey had already warned me about the supermodel-beneath-the-bed scenario, but I asked him to prophesize a little further. He is, after all, the garage biologist envisioned by MIT scientists a few years ago; he is a piece of the future we've been promised. Garvey turned philosophical: "Go back two hundred years, take a handful of sand, and tell someone that I'm going to turn this sand into something that can run your life. I'm going to turn this sand into something that can communicate with people across the planet, take long-lasting photographs that weren't even invented then, and archive them forever. I'm going to turn this lump of sand into something that can guide a missile into your house and kill your family. It's just sand. To them it would be stupid." And that's inanimate silicon; with synthetic biology, "we're talking about nature, which is this absolutely staggeringly complex thing, and we're just learning how to do what we learned to do with sand a few decades ago."

Designer organisms as our last hope to avoid catastrophic climate change. Houses that grow from seeds. Super-AIDS doused with super-AIDS vaccines. Biochaos, a new menagerie let loose or escaped from a thousand garages and basements. The complete integration of circuit and neuron, the hardware and software and wetware of the self. Will we all be life makers, little demigods playing with the fire these new Prometheans are bringing us? Or maybe Pygmalion is the sharper allusion, modelers of living marble.

It's difficult, after talking to a garagista, to keep the quaver of hyperbole out of one's voice, out of one's sentences, as one types. The promise that the ultimate hack is within reach—that is our jet pack. But how credible is it, really, and how close? "I always imagine things will be easier than they actually are," Garvey admitted, before signing off with a lament familiar to anyone who works from home: "A lot of that is down to my work ethic—I'm prone to taking a long time about breakfast." The thing about futurists and soothsayers alike is they risk being wrong only when they set a timetable. Just last spring, a French inventor flew across the Grand Canyon with a rocket engine strapped to his back. I know it happened—I watched it on YouTube, on my phone.

Dara Wier

WHEN I STARED DOWN INTO AN EMPTY BALLISTIC MISSILE SILO ONE DAY IN NEBRASKA

I came close to losing my balance.

So tired I had been drawing a line all afternoon underwater.

And at noon parataxis had turned me into a conjunction of sorts.

The best place for orphans in America I'd been seeing.

And in the morning one more silk chemise.

It will take all the veoneE parabola I can muster to get through false.

EST OF EST, it is so hard to do est of est and hardest of all to think through,

And also after the first there is no other, okay, I get that, and the last, okay, that too.

If it doesn't have the characteristics by which it is known

It isn't being true to its kind. Okay.

I get it. If a circle's not round blah blah blah.

My lame nostalgia for a kind of idolized innocence, I love it!

How do you feel about what you are saying?

How do you say what you're feeling?

Looking at pictures of mirrors.

There's no other way to talk about one thing than

In terms of talking about something else, okay, and

Another thing, not talking about something else

Okay, when not talking about something is elsewise

Another thing, okay, we do this so naturally.

We are like dew.

They say the larger the animal the more intense sex is.

Who are they? Us and all animals.

All or nothing?

Are you brittle crazy glass?

What do you do when you're faced with your own "disruptive event"?

Am I not me?

The job involved nothing more than pouring water for senators.

Well, if that's true we have to start all over.

Part of me, that is odd, watches the moon, loves the pouring honking geese who

Obscure the moon and a distant train's oh yes, okay, lonesome forlorn Hank Williams

Kind of being here.

You want to give me something.

BLUEPRINT

How to Build a Robot

in Four Easy Steps

Karl Iagnemma
Photos and notes by Nick Wiltsie

Every creation is born of a good idea. Systematically stalk, capture, and archive good ideas. Force yourself to endure regular brainstorming sessions in an uninteresting room, with a plain notebook and pencil, or a laptop that does not have internet connectivity. Remember that an idea's beauty might not be apparent at first glance. Ideas, like wine or compost, take time to mature.

A robot is an electro-mechanical machine for performing tasks under autonomous, semi-autonomous, or human control. The word "robot" was introduced by the Czech writer Karel Čapek in his play *R.U.R.* (*Rossum's Universal Robots*), published in 1920. Robots come in many shapes, sizes, and forms, ranging from anthropomorphic manipulators to humanoids to biomimetic mobile robots. By mimicking a lifelike appearance or movement pattern, robots may convey a sense that they have intent or agency of their own. (They do not.) Robots have been known to terrify and delight small children, infuriate blue collar workers, and inspire Hollywood producers.

Robots cannot wash dishes, play lacrosse, make omelets, or build a fire. They can, however, clean sewers [1], shear sheep [2], play the flute [3], and provide sexual release [4].

1 Make it new

For every good idea there exists an uncountable infinity of bad ones. When evaluating the quality of an idea, assess its newness. Newness is neither a necessary nor sufficient condition for an idea to be good; however, the newer the idea the higher the probability that it will be good.

There are many ways to make a robot climb. Classical approaches include the use of suction cups [5], magnets [6], and pressure-sensitive adhesives (PSAs) [7]. However, suction cups are typically limited to operation on smooth surfaces, while magnets function only on ferrous materials, and PSAs are prone to fouling by dust and dirt. Adhesive materials inspired by the foot pads of Gecko lizards have recently been developed [8]. These materials exhibit hierarchical, compliant microstructures enabling them to conform to surfaces over multiple length scales, and achieve intimate contact such that van der Waals forces produce sufficient adhesion for climbing.

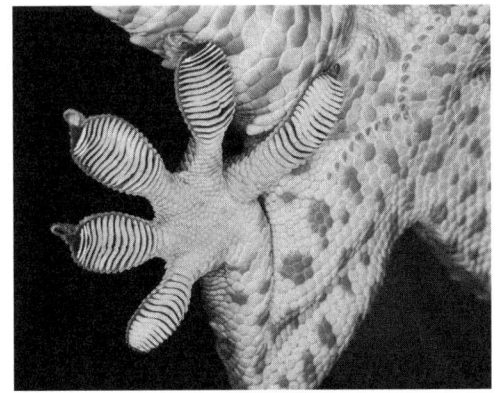

Close-up of gecko's toe pads

Understanding what others have created allows you to place your contribution in proper relation to the work of others.

Here, we will develop a quadrupedal climbing robot that can climb vertical surfaces by exploiting the adhesive properties of magnetorheological (MR) fluid. MR fluid is a field-responsive fluid that consists of a suspension of non-colloidal ferromagnetic particles. An external magnetic field induces magnetic dipoles in the particles, causing them to form chains along field lines. This field-aligned anisotropic configuration strongly resists both shear (and, to a lesser extent, tensile) deformation. To the best of the authors' knowledge, magnetorheological fluid has not previously been used to achieve adhesion for the purposes of robotic locomotion. Thus, an MR fluid-based climbing robot represents something new.

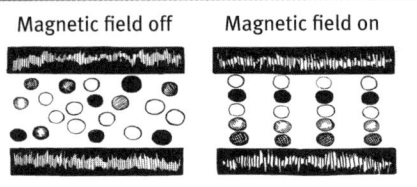

Magnetic field off   Magnetic field on

STEP ILLUSTRATIONS BY MEL LARSEN © 2011

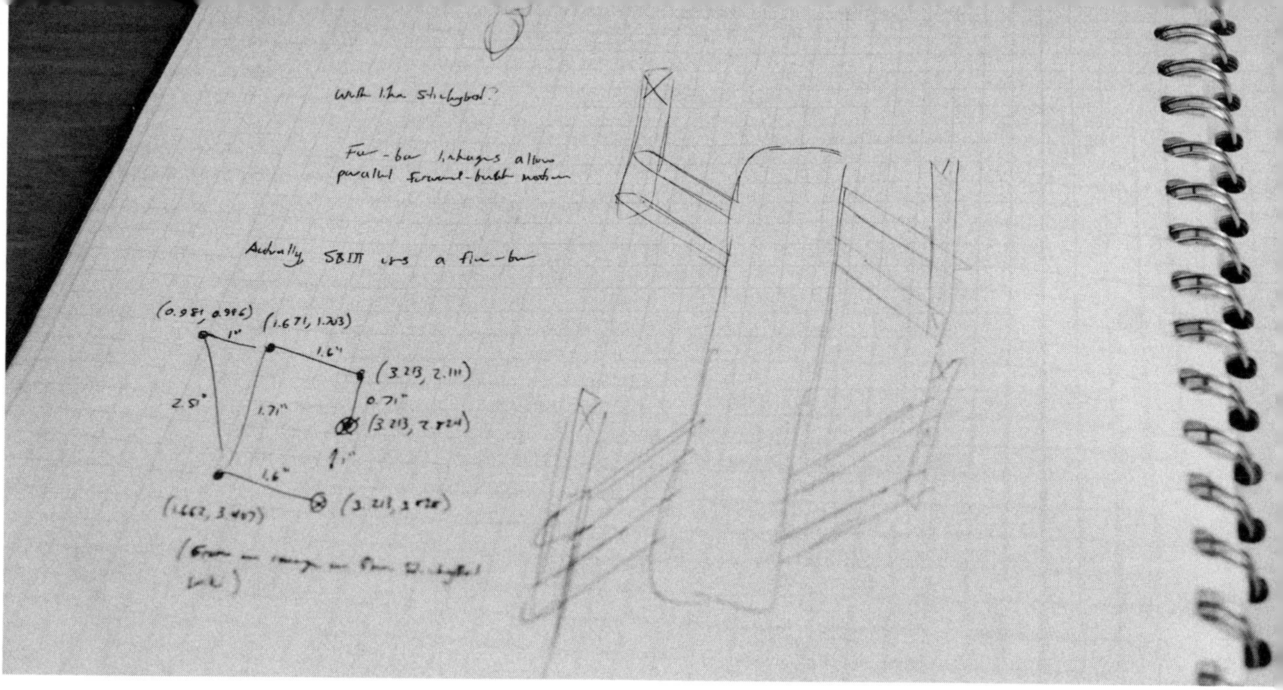

Create a draft

Creations do not emerge from their creators exhibiting perfect form and function. In fact, complex creations never achieve perfection. The myth of perfection was invented by naysayers, or possibly Republicans, to cripple creativity.

Learn to love imperfection.

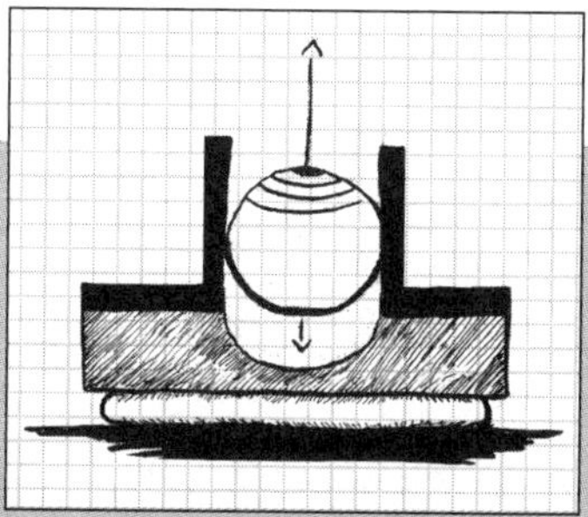

Initial concepts for an MR fluid- based climbing robot focused on two locomotion mechanisms: walking and rolling. In either concept the robot would deliver a thin ($O(\mu m)$) layer of MR fluid between the running gear (i.e. foot pad, wheel, or track) and the surface to be climbed. The fluid would be activated by either physically moving a Neodymium-Iron-Boron (NdFeB) rare-earth magnet into close proximity to the fluid layer, or energizing an electropermanent magnet [9].

Walking was perceived to be superior to rolling due to the ability of individual foot pads to remain fixed to the surface while the robot advanced in a tripod gait. This was expected to avoid introduction of parasitic shear forces across the activated fluid layer, resulting in a robotic device with a maximum payload-to-weight ratio. Robot leg kinematics were modeled after a Chebyshev four-bar linkage, with link lengths chosen such that the foot pad traced an approximately straight trajectory.

How to Build a Robot in Four Easy Steps

Evaluate your draft critically

When evaluating your draft, make believe you're a choleric consultant who's been contracted to provide an assessment of the creation's worth. If you've been immersed in the creation for a long time, consider employing tricks, stratagems, and ploys for seeing the work anew. Move to a new location. Wear goggles as you review your creation. This can allow you to detect faults you might otherwise miss.

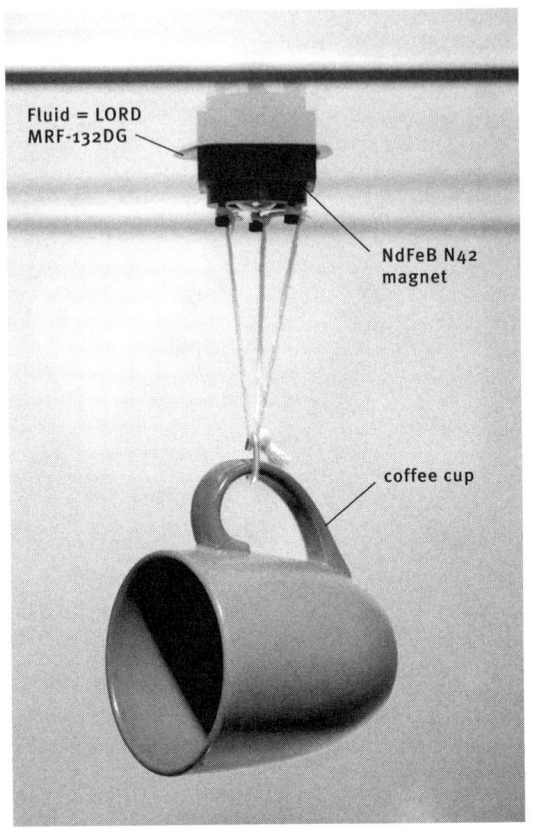

Trust your inner consultant. He may be sulky, but he's honest.

A first generation prototype of a four-legged climbing robot was developed. An estimate of foot pad area was derived from Ewoldt's empirical model of shear yield strength as a function of magnetic field intensity, where an approximately quadratic dependence $\sigma_y \sim B^2$ for sub y $B \leq 0.2$ T (where σ_y is the shear yield strength and B is the magnetic field intensity). Fluid properties were assumed to be identical to LORD MRF-132DG [10]. Assuming a robot with total mass of 1 kg walking with a tripod gait, with each foot pad supporting a shear force of $mg/3$, a total required foot pad area of 0.09 m² was determined. Analysis of electropermanent magnet parameters required to generate a field of 0.2 T yielded a required current in excess of 30 A. This was deemed unacceptable, if not faintly ridiculous.

3 Revise your work

The revision process is one of increasingly structured creativity: initial drafts typically address macro-scale concerns, while later drafts focus at the micro scale, with successive drafts imparting increased structure to the creation.

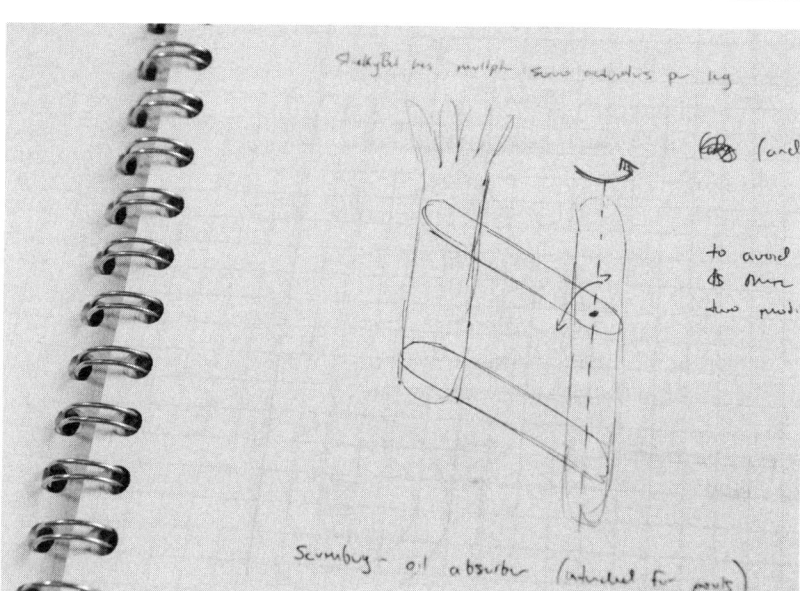

Structure allows creators to bring their creative energy to bear on a particular, rather than a general, problem.

A second-generation prototype of a four-legged climbing robot was developed. Electropermanent magnets were replaced with 19-mm-diameter Grade 42 spherical neodymium permanent magnets. These magnets were measured to produce a flux field greater than 0.2 T over a 8 mm radius circle 0.78 mm away from one pole. This 8 mm circle enclosed an area of 200 mm², and thus it was determined that four such magnets were sufficient to bear the target robot mass of 1 kg. The magnet was physically translated via a Bowden cable composed of 26 AWG spring steel wire, which was driven by a Futaba servomotor. The 26 AWG wire was found to exhibit failure via buckling, and was replaced with 24 AWG wire.

How to Build a Robot in Four Easy Steps

3a

Focus on the details

Choices made at the micro scale are often as important as those made at the macro scale. Well-chosen details impart an air of mastery to the creation; they appeal both aesthetically and analytically. Unfortunately, a single poorly chosen detail can negate the impact of many well-chosen ones. When refining the details, don't forget to add a soul. It's free, and invisible—but consultants will know if it's missing.

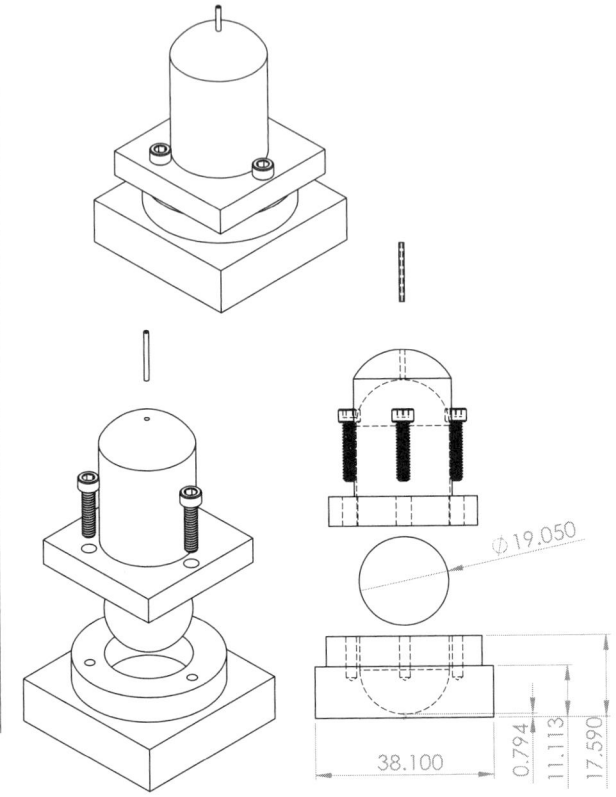

Don't forget to add a soul.

A third-generation prototype was developed with an emphasis on foot, design optimization. Feet were fabricated from machined Delrin and 3D-printed VeroWhite resin, fastened by nylon bolts. Foot soles were square, with a characteristic dimension of 38.1 mm and thickness of 11.1 mm. These dimensions were chosen to optimize fluid-field interaction for the spherical neodymium permanent magnets. In the "on" state, the magnet settled into a semi-circular cavity machined into the foot, with a rest position 0.79 mm distant from the sole; in the "off" state, the magnet was retracted to a position 28.57 mm away from the sole. Leg-linkage kinematics were optimized to yield a step length of 10.4 cm. A soul was inserted into the acrylic body structure at the approximate location of the robot's center of gravity.

KARL IAGNEMMA

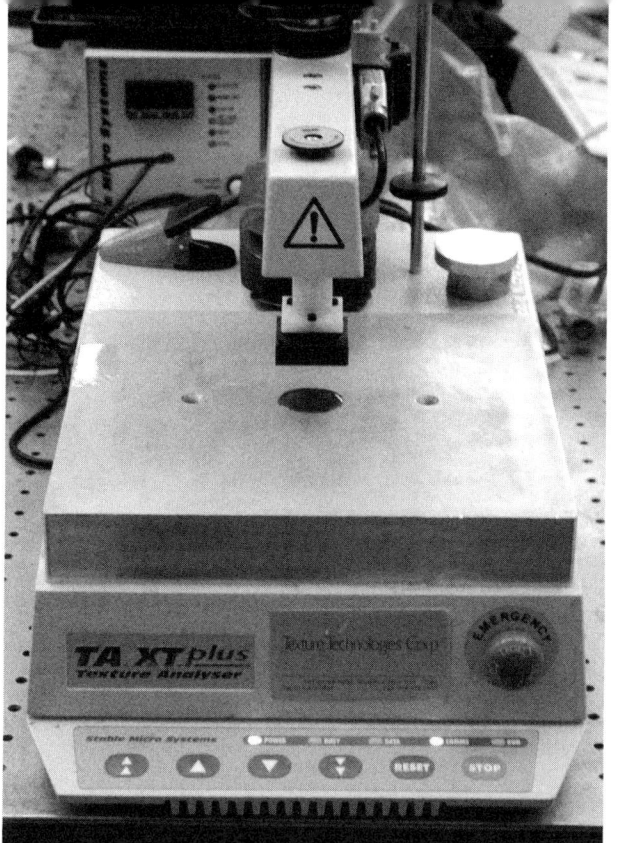

3b

Trust your own judgment, and that of others

A creator's knowledge of the work's history—the choices that were made, the possibilities that were rejected—often makes it difficult to assess the finished product. Colleagues, associates, friends, enemies, and complete strangers can serve as consultants, to provide an unbiased opinion of your creation's worth.

Identify your creation's weaknesses, then revise them until they become strengths.

Testing of MR fluid-based adhesion was performed in a TA.XTplus Texture Analyser, a linear load/displacement transducer capable of applying strain rates as low as 10 μm/s and loads up to 0.05 kN. A 50-mm diameter by 12-mm thick neodymium disk magnet was used as a field source, and acrylic, rolled aluminum, knurled aluminum, Teflon, glass, and 110-grit sandpaper were used as adhesion surfaces. Peak adhesive force for each surface was measured as a

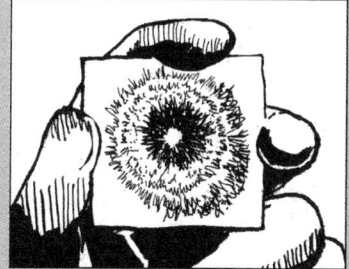

function of fluid-layer thickness. Results agreed reasonably well with Ewoldt's theoretical predictions. [11]

The robot's locomotion performance was tested on 150-grit sanding cloth and tempered glass. Activation and deactivation of MR adhesion was observed to occur in less than 50 ms. Eight non-consecutive steps were successfully achieved on vertical surfaces. Maximum adhesive stresses of approximately 7.6 kPa were measured in both shear and tension. The robot was able to cling to inverted surfaces for up to 30 s before failure at the fluid-surface interface.

How to Build a Robot in Four Easy Steps | 173

3c

Understand when the work is complete

Perfection is unattainable, and the pursuit of perfection begets cost—in time, energy, money, patience, and goodwill. Your creation's worth can be envisioned as a curve approaching—but never reaching—a finite asymptote. While revision can improve the creation's worth, the marginal cost of each revision (in time, energy, money, patience, or good will) may exceed the marginal improvement in the work.

Effort spent to improve a creation is never free.

Further refinement of leg-linkage kinematics and foot-pad geometry was performed to minimize shear and tensile foot detachment forces. The Chebyshev linkage was converted to a Hoekens linkage through application of the Burmester theory, and out-of plane motion was introduced at the crank joint to yield pronounced heel-strike and toe-off at the foot pad. The rectangular foot-pad geometry was modified to include semi-circular "toes" at the heel, with a goal of inducing "flowering" instabilities noted in [11] for adhesive failure under moderate magnetic field intensities. Eight foot-pad prototypes with various toe geometries (i.e. number, radius of curvature) were fabricated from delrin. Pull-off force was measured with the TA.XTplus Texture Analyser with a neodymium disk magnet as a field source and 110 grit sandpaper, knurled aluminum, and Teflon as adhesion surface. No appreciable change was observed in pull-off force for foot pads with toes, compared to foot pads with a square geometry.

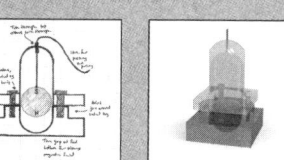 

How to Build a Robot in Four Easy Steps

Publish your results

Exhibit your creation to the world. Few will read your publication; however, you must act as if it will be read by multitudes. This will improve your morale and the quality of the publication. Do not expect fame and fortune; expect silence and be grateful for any recognition. Satisfaction comes from interacting with those who have been influenced by your creation.

Be proud. Be happy.

N. Wiltsie, M. Lanzetta, and K. Iagnemma, "A Controllably Adhesive Climbing Robot Using Magnetorheological Fluid," submitted to the 2012 IEEE International Conference on Technologies for Practical Robot Applications

REFERENCES

[1] S. Cordes, K. Berns, M. Eberl, W. Ilg, and R. Suna, "Autonomous sewer inspection with a wheeled, multiarticulated robot," *Robotics and Autonomous Systems*, vol. 21, no. 1, pp. 123-135, 1997.

[2] J. P. Trevelyan, "Sensing and control for sheep shearing robots," *IEEE Transactions on Robotics and Automation*, vol. 5, no. 6, pp. 716 – 727, 1989

[3] K. Chida, I. Okuma, S. Isoda, Y. Saisu, K. Wakamatsu, K. Nishikawa, J. Solis, H. Takanobu, A. Takanishi, "Development of a new anthropomorphic flutist robot WF-4," *Proceedings of the IEEE International Conference on Robotics and Automation*, pp. 152 – 157, 2004.

[4] http://www.truecompanion.com/home.html

[5] Y. Yoshida and S. Ma, "Design of a wall-climbing robot with passive suction cups," *Proceedings of the IEEE International Conference on Robotics and Biomimetics*, pp. 1513-1518, 2010.

[6] C. Balaguer, A. Gimenez, J. Pastor, V. Padron, and C. Abderrahim, "A climbing autonomous robot for inspection applications in 3D complex environments," *Robotica*, vol. 18, no. Part 3, pp. 287–297, 2000.

[7] O. Unver and M. Sitti, "Flat Dry Elastomer Adhesives as Attachment Materials for Climbing Robots," *IEEE Transactions on Robotics*, vol. 26, no. 1, pp. 131-141, 2010.

[8] K. Autumn, A. Dittmore, D. Santos, M. Spenko, and M. Cutkosky, "Frictional adhesion: a new angle on gecko attachment," *Journal of Experimental Biology*, vol. 209, no. 18, pp. 3569–3579, 2006.

[9] A. Knaian, *Electropermanent Magnetic Connectors and Actuators: Devices and Their Application in Programmable Matter*, PhD Thesis, Massachusetts Institute of Technology, 2010.

[10] R. Ewoldt, P. Tourkine, G. McKinley, and A. Hosoi, "Controllable adhesion using field-activated fluids," *Physics of Fluids*, vol. 23, no. 7, 2011.

[11] R. Ewoldt, *Nonlinear viscoelastic materials: bioinspired applications and new characterization measures*, PhD Thesis, Massachusetts Institute of Technology, 2009.

Bottoms Up

I.

This would never have happened if it weren't for herpes. The other ones didn't bother us as much. Gonorrhea, chlamydia, hepatitis, syphilis. They sounded too archaic, too exotic to be a direct threat. They were reassuringly difficult to spell. Not herpes. Herpes is not complex.

Namwali Serpell

We met through our cleaner. Her name was Felicia. Maybe. We were never completely sure of this at the time, and later, we disagreed about whether she was from Haiti or the Dominican Republic. Neither of us ever actually met her. She had put up a flyer advertising cleaning services in the apartment building where we both lived. Her low rates appealed to us: we each needed a cleaner to come in several times a week. We rang her up, separately; we hired her, respectively.

She was very good at first. Precise, invisible. We gave her spare keys and tipped her generously. Then one day, she mixed up our laundry. We each of us found a pair of mismatched socks. It was a small mistake. They were the same kind of sock; they were mismatched only in size, not color or pattern. Our two pairs of blue argyle socks had traded one sock. We each called Felicia and left messages. She called back, sounding afraid, saying that she knew exactly who had whose sock—it was the first we'd heard of each other—and that she would fix it.

Having reunited the matching socks, she made another mistake. She misdelivered the pairs.

"What am I supposed to do with these?" I said to myself as I unrolled my sock knot to find perfectly matched socks that were nevertheless the wrong size. I called Felicia and I fired her.

When I saw him in the elevator that Sunday afternoon, it was obvious. We were both carrying laundry baskets. We were both wearing sandals and argyle socks. The heels of the too-short socks were squinched on my feet like burst blisters. The heels of his too-long socks protruded like new ankle bones.

"Hello," we ventured tentatively.

It took us a moment to confess our suspicions, though we both knew the second I stepped into the elevator. The fact that we both took the time to confirm what we already knew was outrageously erotic. Later, in bed, we confessed how erotic the whole thing had been, our words tripping over each other, then falling in step as we giggled and sighed to a stop.

Apart from sock size, it was amazing how well matched we were. Education, hair, politics, food, sex, fear. It was like glancing out a window and being surprised to see yourself, the window actually a mirror. That we had met without the intervention of a database or a mastermind was remarkable. We raved about it. Soon we moved together into a larger apartment. There was more mess, more dirt. But we cleaned as a pair and four hands are better than two.

There was no real reason to suspect that either of us had herpes. We had both spent a great deal of time making doctors speak slowly so we could understand in great detail all of the tests we had asked them to perform. We each had a clean bill of health. But herpes, so simple it can be transmitted across glass and porcelain—herpes became a source of tension between us. Herpes is forever. There are two kinds and they are both forever.

Our sex became so clean, so protected, we barely made contact. It was still erotic, maybe more so. The puzzle grew elaborate: could we have sex without touching at all? We went through prophylactics like hand sanitizer. It was a little like arts and crafts but with more rubber. It's incredible what a mess trying not to make a mess can make.

> Our sex became so clean, so protected, we barely made contact. It was still erotic, maybe more so.

We discovered the machine online. It came in the mail, in a large cardboard box that dribbled packing material and Styrofoam peanuts the color of scalp. By the time we had broken the box down and wrapped twine around it for recycling, bagged the peanuts, and vacuumed and mopped the floor, it was late. We went to sleep, two feet of pristine sheet between us.

In the stillness of dawn, light smearing the walls, we tried the TouchyFeely for the first time. The machine was elegant. The main component was a heavy black panel that we mounted on the wall above the bed—it was the size of a large headboard, its vertical edges curving in towards us. We plugged it in. There was a hum, then a silence like a pinprick. A translucent hologram flickered alive in the empty space in front of the panel. It was life-sized and kneeling. It smiled, lips glitching as the specs adjusted. It lifted an arm and pointed between us.

"Bottoms up!" it said coyly.

Then it froze, awaiting instruction while we fell about in our underwear, laughing.

For Bot, as I named it, to work, we needed to slather our bodies with a thin, clear gel from a small unlabeled bottle. It took getting used to, though we both had plenty of experience with comprehensive sunscreen coverage. This gel reacted to rays that came out of the curved black panel. They streamed right through the hologram, as if sparking from Bot's chest. I could see the rays on my skin, a spitting white brightness not unlike the lasers that cut steel in action movies. Rays of light? Rays of heat? They seemed to be both, but something else, too. When the rays touched the gel, they made a warm purring on the skin, as if the human touch had been digitized to ideal consistency and pressure. The touch of the perfect masseuse, or of Jesus.

On the back of the panel was a keypad that we used to program it. Our first specification was that when he reached his hand toward the image of Bot, the TouchyFeely would send the touching rays to the same spot on my body. I had to face the panel at a certain angle. It took a while to get it right.

> It was like sex with yourself dissolved in sex with someone else, the way purification tablets cast clarity into muddy water.

But then we got it exactly right. He touched Bot, Bot touched me, and the transitive property fluoresced around us until the blaze of midday tempered the electric light.

The other component of the TouchyFeely consisted of two cylindrical objects joined by a long black cord: a dildo and a sort of sheath. Also designed for the transitive property, they were custom-made to ensure we would never have to touch again. That first day, he and I forgot all about it. We didn't even open the black box it came in.

II.

Bot! Because of what you said that first day—that pervy pun—you'll always be Bot to me. He called you Rob. While this didn't bother me, exactly, it jarred. I had met the real you and your name was Bot, not Rob.

I had been home from work for a month because I had a full-body rash. It was awful. My doctor said it was stress. It was already self-perpetuating—my stress about the rash extending its stay—and knowing my hypochondria was making me sick just made me sicker. It creeped me out severely. Him too. No chance of sex, not even with the machine. He began to work late. I stayed home, bored, antsy, trying not to scratch the itch. I was on meds for the rash and the anxiety and all the usual stuff. Things were in conflict in my body. The rash worsened and bettered at random, changing color like the sea.

It had ebbed somewhat—the bumps flattening to a purple flush in the skin—the day I decided to turn you on. The TouchyFeely, out of use, had become an unassuming headboard. But as I dusted the bedside table that day, my shoulder grazed the slippy black panel and my skin cast a pale shadow on it, and I remembered. On a whim, still grumpy with sickness, I plugged it in.

There was the hum, then the pinprick silence. You flickered alive. It was like cursing the traffic while driving to meet an old friend at the airport and then getting there and seeing him come out of customs with a blank, searching look and suddenly realizing how much you've missed him.

"Bot! You haven't changed a bit!" I said appraisingly, hands on hips.

"Bottoms up!" You smiled and pointed at me.

The sex was insane. It was like sex with yourself dissolved in sex with someone else, the way purification tablets cast clarity into muddy water. Even the gel on my skin felt clean. I had opened a window and the white curtain floated into the room as a breeze moved across my skin, chilling it where the gel slicked. The lingering itch of my rash was like static beneath the pleasure. Oh, Bot. You glowed and sparked, the touching rays shooting out through you, spraying light over us.

After, the sheets were wet but still clean. I lay on my stomach, chin in my cupped hands, facing the shiny black panel. As the sounds of cars and trees outside the window hushed my thudding heart, I watched you kneel, then stretch. Billowy as the curtain, you came out of the machine and lay down with me. You gazed at me and you smiled without a glitch.

"Bot?" I said.

"Yes," you said.

Then, with the bell-like voice of error tones, you told me what to do, until "He's here," you whispered as the front door opened and the smell of him slunk in, crushingly familiar.

III.

Things between him and me deteriorated completely when I went back to work. My rash had healed perfectly and I wondered if it hadn't been caused by withdrawal from the gel. I began to slather it on in the morning. He rolled his eyes and coughed and sneered that my coworkers would complain. I sniffed my arm and caught a whiff: elm blossom, fresh-sprung mushrooms, salt. It cast you live, Bot. Slightly behind me and to the left. I couldn't catch you exactly, but you were there.

We snuck around behind his back, each time an epiphany of form, all the things we could do within the constraints of his schedule. We learned to align ourselves with speed and efficiency, like dividing a number into a number, less left over every time.

One day, I came home from work and found him on the floor in tears. He looked up and blurbled:

"I lost my job."

I gave him a hand up, wincing. He put his arms around me and tried to bury his head in my left shoulder. I murmured my sorries, shifting him awkwardly. That night, he tried to have sex with me for the first time in ages. Every touch was acid in my bones. I thought I could hear them—my bones—then realized it was you, my darling, wretched Bot, howling gall in my ear. I turned my back to him. Horribly, he misunderstood.

I made him sleep on the couch after that. The bed was clean again. Ours. Furtive quickies with the door shut. Quiet as light, at least at first. Soon enough, we lolled in it, squealing without care as we grew experimental. I tried to find the other component of the TouchyFeely, but the black box was nowhere to be found.

I anticipated those stolen moments with you, longed for them as I sat through yet another dull, overwrought meal with the roommate. He had taken up cooking in a fevered, sullen sort of way. He became unclean. Newfangled sauces polka-dotted the stove; tendrils of vegetable peel infested the kitchen. He burned a risotto and was inconsolable.

One evening, there was no pastiche dinner on the table when I came in the front door, though the air still rankled with the mad spooks of truffle oil. He was in the bath, in the dark.

"What are you doing?" I snapped.

"What are *we* doing?" he mooed.

I ignored him and turned to leave.

"I know what *you're* doing. With Rob. I see flashes under the door!" he yelled at my back.

The next day, he was asleep on the couch when I left for work. He was still there when I came home. As the week went on, suspicious odds and ends collected in the bedroom. A soiled tissue like a wilted flower. A wispy grey halo on the wall around an electrical outlet. A Styrofoam peanut the color of scalp. A stain.

I found him in the burnt, skew light of sunset. He was curled up on the living room floor facing away from the door, shuddering. I stepped around the naked body and I saw what he had been up to. The sheath was still on, black against his pale thighs, the cord baroque with tangles. The other end had vanished into his mouth. He gazed up at me with plaintive, jawbreaker eyes. I sighed and dialed 911 on my cell as I went to fetch the kitchen gloves.

The dildo had ended up halfway down his throat, which would have been impossible, they said, had it not been tapered and had he not slicked his insides by drinking the slippery gel. The device I yanked from him was still on the floor when they arrived. A stretcher wheel got stuck on the cord as they rolled him out. One of the EMTs extricated it, handing it to me with a bored, hassled look. I looked at it in my hands, black and spittled, but as harmless as a jump rope now.

I was dirty and tired. I mopped up, washed up, made my way to bed. The headboard was on, abuzz with a thin vision, skipping like a disc, saying your name over and over, a techno love song. Bot, Bot, Bot. I could see you out of the corner of my left eye, shaking your head. I turned to you with relief but just before you fled, you took my cold hands in your lightning ones, you looked into my eyes, and you admonished me.

Kiki Petrosino

I LOVE YOU, NO DISCUSSION

The eater cannot say that she is unwell. Her judgment is bone-dark & edged in deep serrations. When she goes to the mirror, each of her defects surfaces like oil ready to be skimmed. She need only wait for the process to start itself, a blank *click* in the mind. A scissoring through. At such times, the eater gives herself over to the long register of unfolding measurements, the drifting canticle of names & weights. The afternoon ticks down in precisely plated sections. Certain densities in her must bear elimination. All overgrowth must be scraped down to the quick. An age of offerings to clear the core contaminants, to make of each rib a holy lamp. The eater balances on the half-moons of her heels. Tries to visualize the clear ledge of her clavicle rising up like bottle glass. She's getting old in layers. Look at her neck, loose as a sun-ray in a child's drawing. Look at all that skin, cryptically colored, beginning to pleat at the eyes. For it is written: *The burners of the eyes shall shine like frost. The burners of the eyes shall be chalk-pure.*

MOON-WRAPPED FRAGRANT SPARERIBS

Happy is that eater who rules by the cyclone of her face. By the syrup of her eye shall she drown the clanging earth. For the eater combs justice like beeswax through her hair, & her hands catch only righteousness in their fiery mesh. Therefore, lament neither the appetite that dismasts your cities nor the emerald in her gut that spins. I tell you, the eater is more terrible than all your needlework of lemongrass, purer than aluminum the eater's hum at eventide. Fear not her blue-black shadow as she cruises into your airspace. There's lightning in the matrix of her marrow. Her teeth make mirrors of the sea.

ESSAY

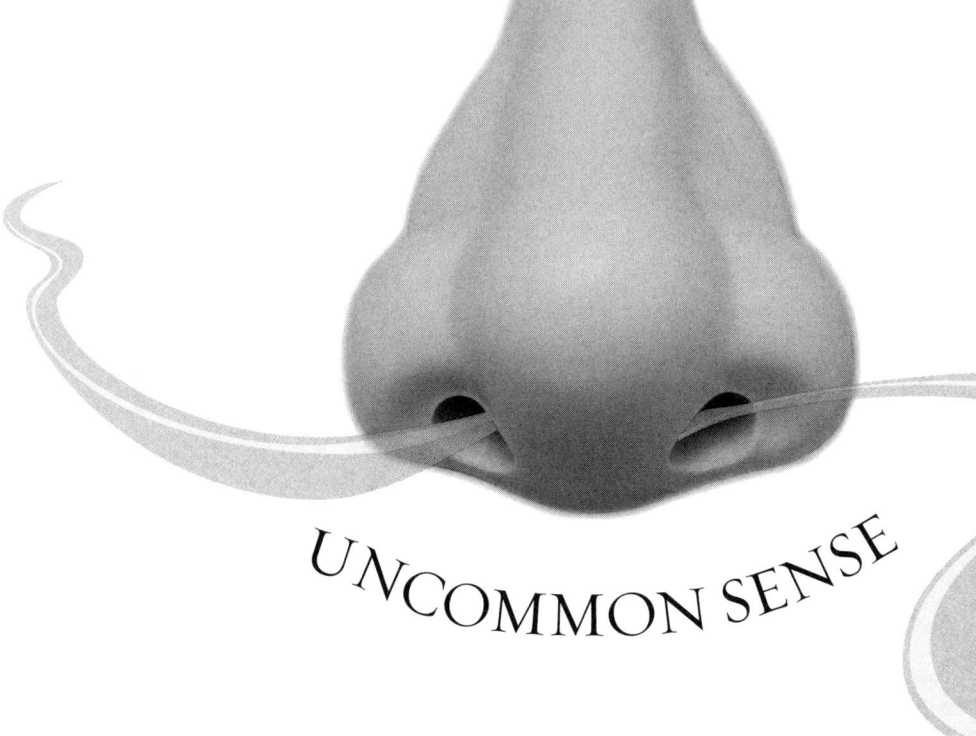

UNCOMMON SENSE

Rachel Riederer

Inside the topsy-turvy world of hearing colors and seeing sounds

When Lidell Simpson was almost old enough for kindergarten and still hadn't started speaking, his parents took him to Memphis to see a specialist. The doctor diagnosed him with aphasia: Lidell would never acquire language and would have to go to a special school. The prediction turned out to be wrong. Lidell went to regular school, and he has acquired more language than most—in college, he studied German, Russian, and Arabic. The specialist was the first of many physicians to misdiagnose Lidell—one even tried to put him on antipsychotics. It's hard to blame Lidell's doctors for their confusion. As Lidell puts it: "One of the worst things you can say to a doctor is 'I hear light.'" He knew something different was happening in his brain; this knowledge was part of what motivated him to study foreign languages. "I experienced so much of my senses that you can't express in English," he told me, more than fifty years after that first misdiagnosis. "I started out learning other languages to find the right words."

The right word for Lidell's condition is *synesthesia*, a neurological condition in which the senses "cross" or "blend" together. Synesthesia takes many forms. Some synesthetes hear sounds when they see certain colors, some see colors when they smell certain odors, some taste flavors when they hear certain words, and so on. Synesthesia is idiosyncratic; even when people have the same form, the individual pairings of stimulus and perception don't match. Lidell's is particularly distinctive, because he is nearly deaf and spent his early childhood years in silence. When Lidell's parents didn't believe the specialist, they took him to get fitted for a hearing aid, and Lidell's silent-movie world transformed into a talkie. But even when the TV was off or Lidell wasn't wearing his hearing aid, the sounds of his favorite cartoons did not stop. He still heard the pings, beeps, and boi-oi-oi-oings, but they weren't coming through his ears. Instead, the sounds were linked to things he saw: a flashing light, a passing car, a swooping bird. In Lidell's brain, all these things make sounds: "It's kind of like I live in a world of sound effects by the Looney Tunes people." And it isn't just motion that produces the sounds: "Everything I see, taste, smell—comes back to me as sound." Lidell likes to say that though he's deaf, he doesn't know silence.

Synesthetes generally have two epiphany stories. The first is the moment they realize they are different. Lidell remembers asking a friend if he was bothered by the beeping of the red light blinking on the town's radio tower. The friend looked at him as if he were crazy, and he quickly learned not to talk about the experience, which he privately named his "photonic hearing." The second epiphany is the moment they realize they are not crazy, and not alone.

Pat Duffy, an artist and synesthete, tells a story about finding out as an adult that she has music-to-color synesthesia, something she has experienced her whole life but had never been able to articulate. When she read an article in the *New York Times* about the artist Carol Steen's synesthesia, she felt she "had come out of a closet [she] didn't even know existed." She e-mailed Steen, saying simply, "I hear with my eyes." Steen replied, "Welcome to the club." In 1996, the two met in Steen's loft in downtown Manhattan to compare life notes. That day, Steen says, "the ASA was born."

The ASA, short for the American Synesthesia Association, does work toward creating a strong community for synesthetes, but it is also largely concerned with spreading scientific understanding. When I started reading about synesthesia, my immediate question was What is it like? If you see letters as different colors, what do the colors look like? How much easier is it to do anagram puzzles? If flavors produce colors, where exactly do you see the colors, and how long does the vision last? Is it distracting or pleasant? Do you choose certain foods because you like the color palettes they produce? I decided to attend that year's ASA annual conference, which was happening in Hamilton, Ontario, in the hope of finding out.

Talking with conference attendees put me in mind of late nights as a teenager, staring for hours and chewing on mildly psychedelic questions, variations on What if what I call green, other people see as red, but we're just using the same word?, Do you see what I see?, and Is my mind the same as everyone else's? The answer was always, somewhat disappointingly, yes.

Do you see what I see? The question gets at the very foundation of shared experience—the bedrock of reality, even sanity. Listening to the synesthetes at the conference, whether it was Lidell explaining how his hearing aids amplify sound-sound and drown out the vision-sound or the organization's president describing the floating masses of color that appear when he tastes certain flavors, I realized I was surrounded by people for whom the answer to this question is a resounding no.

The opening night of the conference, we—a group of scientists, synesthetes, and interested hangers-on like myself—gathered in the McMaster University campus chapel for the first set of presentations. As a group, we underwent several of the usual tests for synesthesia. One of the most common forms of synesthesia is grapheme-to-color, in which different letters appear to be different colors, no matter what color ink they're printed in. It is often identified by the Stroop test, which relies on the fact that people who can read (and who are not hampered by problems like dyslexia) do so automatically. In the brain, reading happens faster than other tasks, such as identifying color. So, if you see the word *blue*, you read it almost instantaneously. If it is in blue ink, and someone asks you the ink color, you will identify the color almost instantaneously. However, if *blue* is written in red ink, and someone asks you to identify the ink color, your response will be delayed. Not by much—just a fraction of a second—but a fraction of a second is a long time in the brain. When you see the word, you will read *blue* before you recognize the red ink, and in the process of answering the question you will experience a few milliseconds' worth of cognitive dissonance, that is, your brain taking the tiniest moment to recognize and resolve the contradiction between text and ink.

In nonsynesthetes, the test simply shows that reading is a faster, more automatic mental process than color identification. But when tailored for people who claim to have certain types of synesthesia, it can provide verification of what's going on in their brains. For example, if someone experiences colored numbers, and they always see twos as red, they will be slower to identify the ink color if they see a two printed in blue; they're dealing with the same momentary conflict as when most people see the word *blue* written in red ink.

One synesthesia researcher, a neuroscientist who himself experiences colored graphemes, explained his synesthesia by saying that, to him, it isn't an extra sense; it is just how things are. He gestured at a brown wall and said, "When you think about synesthetes, you think they see as everyone else does, plus something else. But my perception doesn't feel extra. Like the color of that wall isn't extra; it just is that color." (He has been able to replicate the experience for nonsynesthetes by projecting a black *A* and a red *A* onto the same space and quickly flicking back and forth between the two, giving the sensation that there's only one letter, occupying one place, and that it is both entirely red and entirely black.)

Another common test is the "pop-out." To illustrate this test to the crowd in the dim chapel, another researcher put up a slide of a large white circle filled with black fives and twos presented in a simplified typeface, similar to the way they appear on digital clocks. Mostly, the circle was full of fives. There were a few twos scattered throughout, she told us, and they formed a shape. People straightened up and leaned forward, squinting to see

Do you see what I see? The question gets at the very foundation of shared experience—the bedrock of reality, even sanity.

better. After several seconds of audience murmuring, the researcher removed the slide. She asked if it had been hard to see the shape, and the crowd muttered collectively in the affirmative. Then she put up a slide of what we would have seen if we all had number-to-color synesthesia: a white circle full of red fives, with a triangle of green twos clearly and immediately visible. We were amazed; we were starting to understand. In the row behind me, a young man stared at the screen, still as frustrated as we had all been a moment earlier. He turned to the woman next to him and said despondently, "I hate being color-blind."

At the conference, What is it like? quickly gave way to How does it work?, a much harder question, and one that until fairly recently, science was not able to begin to answer. For many years, the study of synesthesia was mainly devoted to recording the experiences of synesthetes. The first such report on synesthetic experience came from Francis Galton, polymath, amateur eugenicist, and half cousin of Charles Darwin. In 1880, Galton chronicled the experiences of a young man who saw number lines arranged around him in space. For a few decades following that, synesthesia was widely studied, and in the late 1800s and early 1900s there was a significant cachet attached to synesthetic art and artists. Baudelaire and Rimbaud wrote poems about synesthesia. Kandinsky wrote about it and perhaps used it in his art. By the middle of the twentieth century, synesthesia was still present, of course—Nabokov was describing his colored graphemes and putting them to dazzling use in his anagrammatic wordplay—but the study of the condition had fallen out of psychological vogue. Emphasis in the scientific community shifted to behaviorism, which largely ignores internal psychological processes like perception.

Then, in 1980, the physician Richard Cytowic resurrected the study of synesthesia after meeting a synesthete and hearing about the condition for the first time. He was having dinner at a friend's house when the host tasted the dish and exclaimed, "Oh dear, there aren't enough points on the chicken!" Cytowic was immediately fascinated. He began researching the phenomenon and working on a case study of the dinner host. In 1993, he published *The Man Who Tasted Shapes*, a book that brought synesthesia back into the public and the scientific consciousnesses.

Around the same time, the neuroscientist V. S. Ramachandran set out to discover the neural basis for synesthesia. For his work in visual processing and sensory perception, Ramachandran has been called "the Marco Polo of the brain." Rama—as he's called in the synesthesia crowd (the field is still quite small and all the major researchers know one another on a first-name, or even nickname, basis)—did some of the most pioneering work toward uncovering how the condition might work. Using an imaging technique called fMRI, which shows which parts of the brain are being activated by measuring the flow of oxygenated blood, Rama demonstrated that when grapheme-to-color synesthetes see a number, the area of the brain that processes color vision and the area responsible for number recognition both "light up." When the rest of us look at a four or a five, only our number-recognition areas activate. Essentially, Rama's research verified that synesthetes aren't imagining their perceptions or making them up—the blood flow in their brains proved that synesthesia is real.

> Rama's research verified that synesthetes aren't imagining their perceptions or making them up.

Tests for synesthesia and fMRI imaging are still important for today's researchers, who need to know that their subjects are really experiencing synesthesia, but the emphasis is no longer on proving that the condition is real, which is widely accepted. Scientists now ask more in-depth questions, such as What mechanisms cause it?, What can it tell us about how brains process sensory information?, and Why do some people have it and others not?

Daphne Maurer studies the development of synesthesia in babies—or rather, the pruning away of synesthetic connections that naturally occur during everyone's childhood. Synesthesia, she notes, works just like the "normal" senses—it is automatic, people have it their whole lives, and the pairings are consistent over time. Hearing music activates an adult's auditory cortices. But when babies—synesthetes or not—hear music, there's activity in both the auditory and visual centers of the brain. As infants and young children, her work suggests, we might all be synesthetes. Maurer theorizes that as babies get more and more sensory experience, the brain regions—and individual cells—specialize, and those extra connections start to fade.

In one of Maurer's experiments, one hundred percent of two-and-a-half-year-olds matched higher-pitched noises to lighter colors and lower-pitched noises to darker colors. There are many other examples of this, and not just in children. Even in neurotypicals (as nonsynesthetes are known), some of these extra connections remain. Although only synesthetes experience conscious perceptions across sensory borders, we all have associations that cross those lines, but they are subconscious. This kind of communication between different senses ("cross-modal interaction," to the synesthesia set) is something that we all do. Studies show that when people hear a sound accompanied by motion or other visual stimulation, they will report that sound as being louder than when they hear the exact same noise on its own. People perceive their hands to be drier if they hear an amplified rubbing sound while they rub their hands together. Pictures seem brighter if accompanied by a sound; sounds seem louder if accompanied by a bright flash. Even our sense of balance (vestibular sense), governed by fluid levels in the inner ear and unrelated to vision, can be affected when we see moving images. It is shocking to experience these tests, to realize just how much the quirks of your brain's anatomy and chemistry mediate what you thought was your objective perception of the world. But it also makes sense in a way. Audio and visual information enter the body at different points, but they both end up in the brain. The brain is full of circuitry, and signals move fast. Why shouldn't they zap into each other's territories from time to time?

Interplay between the senses doesn't just create these interesting but low-level pairings; it's also involved in higher-level functions, such as making aesthetic judgments. Sensory information enters the body through chemical receptors in the nose and on the tongue, light-sensing cells in the eyes, and nerve endings that detect pressure on or change of temperature in the skin—but it all travels via nerve cells up the spinal cord and into the brain. Different areas of the brain process different information; there are separate centers for all these types of sensory signals. But the sensory input doesn't stop in those centers; it travels on. All our sensory information converges in the brain area responsible for making aesthetic judgments, the orbitofrontal cortex. The specialized mono-sensory regions tell us if a person's eyes are blue or brown, or if a dish is sweet or savory. The orbitofrontal cortex answers different questions: Is his face handsome? Is her perfume appealing? The same part of the brain that decides if an entrée tastes delicious or mediocre also decides if a piece of art is beautiful or ugly. Some scientists have suggested that this kind of sensory convergence has an evolutionary underpinning—the appraisal of food. To know if you can eat an apple, you note its color, smell, firmness. It makes sense that cavemen who made their aesthetic judgments using multiple senses in tandem would eat rotten food less often, thus staying alive and passing on their genes so that today we all process information this way.

The ASA conference's keynote speaker, Jamie Ward, addressed the issue of synesthesia's evolutionary usefulness in his presentation, as he does in his recent book, *The Frog Who Croaked Blue*. (Synesthesia is great for titles: the weekend's presentations included "Making Scents of the Senses" and "A Colorful Appetite for Music.") Ward began his talk by noting some of the many instances of cross-modal perception in people who don't have synesthesia. One famous demonstration is the Kiki Bouba test. Ward brushed quickly past it. "The Kiki Bouba shape thing, of course, we all know about that" got a ripple of laughter from the crowd. Here's what happens in the Kiki Bouba shape thing: subjects are shown two shapes, like these and asked which one is a Kiki, and which is a Bouba; they almost always respond the same way. Regardless of whether or not a subject speaks English, or even speaks a language that uses a Latin alphabet, he will call the jagged shape a Kiki and the rounded shape a Bouba. It just seems natural. But really, why should it? There must be some crossing or blending of the senses happening to make the sound of a *k* seem "sharp" or "hard" in the same way that a shape is spiky and the sound of *oo* seem related to curved lines.

This is not synesthesia, Ward is careful to note. Synesthesia is related to something we all do, but it is still special. Understanding what is meant by "sharp cheddar," or "bitter cold," after all, is not the same as seeing red As. Ward's talk moved quickly and covered a lot of terrain. At bottom, though, he is interested in whether there is some evolutionary basis for synesthesia—it's clearly not a defect, which means it wouldn't be selected against in evolution, but is it useful? He points out that in this context, it doesn't make sense to talk about synesthesia as a monolithic thing. Seeing music would have very different consequences on a person's life than hearing cartoon noises when cars drive by, seeing colored graphemes, or tasting shapes, so the different forms must be considered individually.

Ward thinks that mirror-touch synesthesia, a rare type in which the synesthete feels physical contact that is happening to someone else—that is, if you see someone being caressed on the cheek, or punched in the jaw, you yourself feel that caress or punch as if it were happening to you—is evolutionarily useful. Everyone has this to a small degree. Our brains have mirror neurons that fire in the same way both when we experience a physical sensation and when we see someone else experience it. This could be the neural basis for empathy; mirror-touch synesthetes are, not surprisingly, more empathetic than most. And high levels of empathy are evolutionarily useful, helpful in forming cohesive groups.

There's also the notion that synesthetes who experience various forms of sound- and color-related synesthesia are more artistic than others. Art itself may not be evolutionarily useful, but it may be linked to other kinds of creativity that are more directly related to survival. Other types of synesthesia have proven useful as mnemonics: one grapheme-color synesthete was able to memorize the digits of the number pi—oh, just the first 22,500 or so digits—because, for him, numbers evoke colors and textures, and he was able to recite the numbers by imagining the visual image of pi. And some researchers, including Ramachandran, have proposed that synesthesia may be linked to the evolution of language. After all, everybody knows a Kiki from a Bouba. Ward mentioned this at the conference, saying—carefully, with ever so much respect—that he does not agree with this notion. If everyone can do it, then it's not synesthesia.

Some questions posed at the conference hung unanswered in the air, and I was curious about how the greater community of scientists handles them. I sought out Ed Hubbard, who, as a grad student working with Ramachandran, helped to make Kiki and Bouba famous, and met with him at Rockefeller University, where he works as a researcher. Hubbard has another idea about the importance of Kiki and Bouba: they are an example of how sensory integration leads to higher-level cognition. "We think that this is important," he told me, a few weeks after the conference, "if we want to understand a simple concept like jaggedness—something can be jagged looking, or jagged feeling, or even jagged sounding." Of course, Kiki and Bouba—both the shapes themselves and the words—are extreme examples. Not all sounds match up to geometric shapes. "Some scientists," Hubbard explains, "have said, 'Well, this is cute, but how much does it prove generally?'" But several scientists have done studies with variations on the Kiki Bouba test—using more trials and a wider variety of words and shapes—and have found that this mapping between sound and shape consistently occurs.

Hubbard, along with Ward and the psycholinguist Julia Simner, have been

> Art itself may not be evolutionarily useful, but it may be linked to other kinds of creativity that are.

determining a theory of how synesthesia, in all its forms, might work. They are looking at the connections between brain regions in many different types of synesthesia. "We've been working toward what we refer to as the 'Grand Unified Theory of Synesthesia,'" Hubbard says, "with our tongues squarely planted in our cheeks."

The theory itself is serious, and is actually called the "theory of anatomically constrained cross-activation." When Hubbard and Ramachandran used fMRI to show that grapheme-to-color synesthetes have activation in the brain areas dedicated to color processing and number recognition, the image revealed something else as well. The color-vision processing area and the number-recognition area are right beside each other on a ridge in the temporal lobe called the fusiform gyrus, situated close to the center of the brain at about ear level. Noting that the most common types of synesthesia (colored graphemes, colored music) involve brain areas that are located near one another, Ramachandran proposed the adjacency principle, which suggests that the proximity of the involved brain regions allows for easier crossing of neural wires. In their Grand Unified Theory, Hubbard, Ward, and Simner have refined the adjacency principle: "It's not really adjacency," Hubbard explains. "It's the probability of having anatomical connections."

> Maybe synesthesia is a little like obscenity: hard to define exactly, but we know it when we see it.

By connections, he means individual brain cells (neurons) that travel between different brain areas. Neurons are shaped like trees. A neuron's "branches"—long, forking extensions that reach out from one end of the cell—are called dendrites. The dendrites receive signals from adjacent cells. The "trunk" is the axon. Axons can be quite long—the longest human nerve cell travels all the way from the base of the spine to the toes. At the far end, the axon splits into several extensions—like tree roots—each of which terminates in a knob, called a bouton. The place where one cell's bouton communicates with its neighbor's dendrite is called a synapse. Synapses connect these cells in a massive, complex network—there are around one hundred billion neurons in the brain, and each can be connected to up to one thousand other cells.

Within the brain, neurons connect different regions. In fact, nearly every region of the brain connects to every other brain area in an average of seven synapses. "We know that eventually every area has to talk to every other area," says Hubbard. "Certain areas have long-range connections. There are local hubs, and there are areas where there's a lot more connectivity between adjacent regions." But if synesthesia is a product of connections between brain regions, and we all have neurons that travel between brain regions, and the clusters of cells responsible for processing colors, recognizing faces, hearing music, identifying personalities, et cetera, are all connected to one another in a network of forking cells, shouldn't we all have synesthesia?

Ward explains that we all have interactions between the senses (between brain regions), and these connections produce cross-modal perception, which can be thought of as a kind of subconscious synesthesia. Only when those interactions reach a certain strength does something "click," resulting in not a subconscious association, but a conscious, noticeable perception: "a separate experience that other people don't have." It's not necessarily that synesthetes' brains are constructed differently than other people's, but that their neurons behave differently. "It's a *quantitative* difference in brain wiring," Hubbard explains (the neurons connecting brain regions are firing more rapidly, sending stronger electrical impulses between brain regions), "that leads to a *qualitative* difference in experience." (I understand Kiki Bouba and can make aesthetic judgments, but Lidell hears beeps when red lights flash.)

Defining synesthesia seems at first to be a simple neurological matter. But deciding what gets called synesthesia doesn't just dictate which phenomena are the most interesting to study or which can teach us the most about the mind; it determines who gets welcomed to the club.

Noam Sagiv, a neuroscientist who has worked with the trio behind the Grand Unified Theory, is interested in pushing the classic definition of synesthesia. There are good reasons to do so. First, it excludes one of the most common variants, colored graphemes, because color is an aspect of vision. Seeing a letter or number is also vision. Since "modality" refers to the five senses—vision, hearing, touch, smell, taste—seeing red As and purple Bs doesn't actually qualify as "cross-modal." But if colored graphemes aren't synesthesia, what are they? After all, they are automatic, specific, and consistent over time. Maybe synesthesia is a little like obscenity: hard to define exactly, but we know it when we see it.

It turns out to be even more complicated than that. Yes, grapheme recognition and color recognition are both aspects of vision, but they take place at different points in the brain, and at different moments (though, "moment" in this case is a matter of milliseconds) during the visual process. You can think about a "sensory modality" from the outside: we have ears, eyes, a nose, taste buds, and skin—thus, we have five senses. Or you can think about it from the inside: we have brain areas dedicated to seeing colors, seeing textures, recognizing faces, identifying numbers, identifying letters, seeing motion, hearing music, hearing voices, recognizing spoken words, feeling temperature, feeling pressure, feeling pain, and on and on. So maybe the list of senses is actually quite a bit longer.

In his presentation at the ASA conference, Sagiv brought up mirror-touch synesthesia, calling it synesthesia "with a twist." Because if we accept "mirror-touch," shouldn't we have to accept forms in which the stimulation is propioception (our innate ability to know where our body parts are in space—the reason you can close your eyes and touch your nose or clap your hands) and the percept is visual? These forms include autoscopy and heautoscopy, or, if you're not in cognitive neuroscience, out-of-body experiences.

The mood in the room shifted when Sagiv made these suggestions—brows wrinkled, eyes narrowed, people frowned at their coffee and muffins or looked around at one another for confirmation that they'd correctly heard what was being proposed. "We can have all of these without being delusional," Sagiv said. Still, it sounded bizarre. A large part of the ASA's work, and the individual quests of many of its members, focuses on educating people about synesthesia and counteracting the notion that synesthetes might in some way be crazy. Adding out-of-body experiencers to the mix didn't sound like a good idea.

The group's reaction was proof of one of Sagiv's main points: that defining synesthesia is not a scientific task but a sociological one—albeit one that is most effective if informed by empirical data. There are reasons for wanting to exclude different variants from synesthesia's conceptual umbrella. There's plain old conservatism, and resistance to include things that might seem "too crazy." Even more interesting is the resistance to expanding the definition so far that it becomes too common, making synesthetes "less special." It's a delicate task. Everyone wants to be special; no one wants to be weird.

Sagiv moved on quickly, saying that while it's compelling and intellectually fruitful to come up with "a very long list of candidate domains" to study, because so many interesting cognitive processes involve making connections between two or more domains, "of course synesthesia is more interesting."

After the conference, I talked with Sean Day, the president of the ASA and a flavor-to-color and timbre-to-color synesthete himself, about Sagiv's idea. Day curates a list of reported synesthetic types online, and there are currently fifty-four. Day's list includes colored graphemes and colored music, as well as rarer types: colored orgasms, emotions that produce temperatures, personalities that produce colors, personified numbers and days of the week. It's easy to understand the disagreement surrounding some of these forms: a brightly colored orgasm sounds awfully close to metaphor, and personified numbers sound awfully close to crazy.

I wondered what Day thought about Sagiv's proposal that out-of-body experiences might be a form of synesthesia. "I thought it was brilliant," he said. But he is careful to qualify his enthusiasm; he thinks that out-of-body experiences probably fall into the same category as eidetic memory (a condition in which people recall memories so vividly that they feel like they are actually reexperiencing moments from their past) and phantom-limb syndrome (another of Ramachandran's specialties, in which amputees continue to feel their missing appendage)—they're not types of synesthesia, but they are related sensory phenomena, and certain aspects may work the same way that synesthesia does. For the moment, Day is saying no to including out-of-body experiences on the list of synesthetic types; he will wait for more evidence.

Some of the contested forms challenge our ideas about what a "sense" is. When "ticker-tape" synesthetes hear speech, they see words spilling out of people's mouths or word balloons with scrolling text. Aura synesthetes see clouds of color around faces. For personification synesthetes, numbers, days of the week, and such, have attributes like gender and age. The mental activities behind these types—connecting text and speech, extracting personality traits, recognizing faces, sequencing, et cetera—are not among those of the five classic senses, a set on which the formal definition of synesthesia (a stimulus in one sense causes a perception in another) relies. But does it matter? "A number of us," says Hubbard, "are moving away from using that strict definition. In a way, that definition is a useful heuristic, but it's not actually going to get us the proper qualities." That's fine with him—he, like the other synesthesia researchers, is content for now to do the research and learn as much as possible. Line drawing can come later. "Traditionally," he says, "definitions should come late in scientific inquiry, not early."

When I asked Hubbard about Sagiv's ideas about out-of-body experiences, he was similarly open-minded. "Out-of-body experiences," he says, "traditionally have this tint of mysticism—much the same way auras do. What I think is really exciting about what's happening in neuroscience is that there is a group of people who were trained as neurologists, trained to talk to people who come in after they've had a stroke or a car accident. These people will tell you crazy-sounding things! But they're *not* crazy—they've just had something bad happen to their brains, and they're telling you what it seems like to them." Hubbard's main point is that with all the problems that come with self-reporting, it's still important to begin by listening, by taking seriously people's accounts of their own experiences, even if they sound outrageous. "When you see somebody having an out-of-body experience, it's not mystical, it's not a step over to the other side; it's really something to do with the brain's mechanism for saying, 'This is your body and this is where you are,' in some sense playing a trick on you, misremembering or misinterpreting something." Ultimately, Sagiv wasn't trying to get out-of-body experiences classified as synesthesia, but to push the boundaries and get people thinking about how different forms of sensation and perception are classified as synesthesia, or as something else. "I think he's raising a very valid question," Hubbard says. "How do we decide?"

ESSAY

BOYHOOD ADVENTURES IN THE MAGICAL SCIENCE OF ASTRAL PROJECTION

Clancy Martin

Beyond yonder and back again

The first time I cast my soul from my body, I was eight years old. I was on the top bunk; my younger brother slept below. I lay there, raccoon-eyed with fear, seeing nothing, while the real me bounced against the ceiling, perhaps three feet above me, staring down into my own green eyes and clutching at a golden silk cord about the thickness of a shoelace that went from my belly button to that of my corpse—which it may as well have been, I thought with placidity (it seemed only my body was terrified; my mind was calm). I had read all of the available books on astral projection—my favorite was the still-classic *Journeys Out of the Body*—and I had listened to the tapes my father sent me from Florida, though I always fell asleep before the end. This November night—I remember that Christmas was nearing—I lay down to sleep feeling restless, and just as I began to drop off, electricity ran up and down my spine and nerves from toenail to skull and hair. I swallowed twice, and with the ease of air escaping a balloon, my astral body slipped out of my skin, taking my consciousness with it. I retained only two of my senses, sight and diminished touch. I bobbed against the ceiling for perhaps fifteen minutes, like a very lazy fly, trying to back my way through the ceiling, which felt vaguely like popcorn and itched my shoulders and should not have been an obstacle. If I were to succeed, I knew better than to fly farther than a mile or so from my house on my first trip, but I thought it would be nice to see the sky and the rooftops of our neighborhood. But there was something frightening outside the window, no more than a shadow, crouched and peering. I could feel it pulling at me like the earth pulls when you hang upside down from a tree branch. Though I feared it, I considered that perhaps it was there to guide me. Suddenly, I knew I needed to be out of the room, away from there; my body looked forlorn and vulnerable in the bed. I tried again to go through the ceiling. Then, a blink at the window—a hesitation perhaps, the start of a movement that stopped—and I sat up in bed. My hands were behind me, pressed tightly to the small of my back. There was a dull pain where the base of my head joined my neck. I was afraid when I closed my eyes.

Seven more years of hard effort passed. Almost every night, I fought to re-create the victory of that night. Fighting was probably the problem. Sometimes you need to dive through the wave rather than stand against it. During that time, I kept a journal documenting my struggles.

December 29, 1977 (age ten)

Placed "You Too Can Astrally Project and Prove Everybody Wrong" tape in red plastic tape recorder. The new tape, which arrived yesterday, is a Christmas gift from my father in Florida, who runs a church, "The Church of Living Love," and who checks on me frequently by astrally projecting, visiting me in my dreams. The new tape replaces my old tape, "The Magical Science of Astral Projection," which hasn't worked for two years now. My goal for this second astral projection is to duplicate my projection of two years ago with greater control. I will just, you know, explore around the room and perhaps go through a wall or the ceiling to see what that's like, master the basic skills, see if it's like flying or swimming, figure out how you move from place to place. The tape tells me I should identify the golden cord that connects me to my body, which I saw on my first journey. Before beginning, I open my window, look out in both directions—nothing but the trees and the high Calgary moon—then close the window, lock it, and draw the curtain. Then I open the curtain again. Worrying, I have trouble with the relaxation exercise of seeing myself at the beach and feeling the golden fluid run from the opened bottle top that is supposed to pop at my head and let the relaxation juice fill me from my toes up through my skull. I lie there for the full forty-five minutes but nothing happens.

March 5, 1978 (still ten)

After further investigation in *Journeys Out of the Body*, I discover that the golden cord may or may not be visible and may also be a silver cord but it doesn't matter; it will be there and keep me connected to my body, and only a very rare event on an unusually long-distance projection—like, farther out than our own galaxy, say—could result in a severing of the cord. I don't plan on going any farther than the moon, at the most, until I get skillful at this thing. Plus, though I prefer not to talk about it, I am a pretty clumsy person. I can't even bounce a basketball very well, though I'm much better at it when I do it in private and no one else is around to see, which is frustrating. So I expect I will also be clumsy in my astral body, but you never know. I have often thought that I would be the sort of person who would be good at flying, if people could fly.

About midway through the tape my body begins to tingle unpleasantly as though I am being rubbed with dozens of balloons. I can see through my eyelids—my eyes are clenched tightly shut—and my head lifts as though pulled by a hand. I expect it is my dad. There, sitting on my chest, with a head the size of a large Slurpee, no body I can see, and arms longer than a man's, is a black thing with a face that is almost entirely mouth. Though it has no legs, it is squatting on my chest. Its arms are wrapped around my ears. I do not have time to scream. It says: "You will die on December 12." It begins to laugh, a sound like the screaming you might expect from a macaw that is being strangled. I sit up, brushing my whole body with my hands. I look at the window. The curtain is closed.

"It's fear, son," my father told me whenever we would practice together in one of his new apartments or condos in Scottsdale or Palm Beach or Palm Springs. He had a series of metaphysical churches with entirely female congregations. I often read them my poetry on Sundays. "I don't know what's scaring you, but when I get out, I can see it all through your aura, like black veins. I try and give you a little nudge, but honestly, it's not safe to pull on you the way I would need to." I always wanted to beg him to take the chance. I was a depressed boy and not that attached to life, but he was my dad, and I knew he wouldn't listen; it would have the opposite effect. "I meet you when you're dreaming and give you lessons, but until you overcome that fear, you're not going to get out again."

Meanwhile, I had started an astral projection club. It averaged eight or nine members and lasted through junior high school and tenth grade (the first year of high school in Canada), though it was really only my best friend, Tom, and a fellow from Holland named Sean DeGraff who showed the requisite conviction and willingness to practice. By eleventh grade, everyone except the three of us had traded in astral projection for girls.

"If you don't believe it, it will never happen," I quoted my father to the group before our candlelit, incensed sessions in my basement room. Then there was a series of stretching and deep-breathing exercises designed to loosen the substantial muscles and earth-binding tendons, followed by an hour-long tape.

"Pretend your body is a bottle, with corks in your feet and a cork in your head. Pull out the corks in your feet and let all of your attachment to the physical world run out through your legs." We lay in a circle, with our heads in the center and our dirty tennis shoes radiating out like the rays of the sun. "Now you are perfectly empty. You are a bottle that has sunk to the bottom of a dark, cool pond. The corks are replaced in your heels. And the cork is removed from the top of your head, where the purple crown chakra is, and down into your body flows a warm, golden fluid, like honey, you can taste it in the back of your throat. It's warming you, beginning with your toes and then rising up your legs, past the knees, into the hips and the belly, and you are feeling buoyant, like a bottle filling with air beneath the water, the heated orange fluid rising up your body is buoying you, you are coming from deep below the surface to the air above, and now the golden fluid is in your heart chakra, and your chest is lifting up from the ground"—my chest would elevate at this moment, though I always suspected I was arching my back—"your eyes are closed and now your head is full, your third eye may open and you may see the room around you through your closed eyelids, and as the cork is replaced in your head, your whole body begins to rise to the surface, faster and faster, and you see a light above you, and now your body effortlessly rises into the air. Keep breathing. Don't hold your breath. You are rising, you are shedding your skin, you are up out of the water into the air and still rising, rising into the clouds."

> Turns out, with a pint or two of nitrous oxide in your lungs, you can astrally project anytime you like.

My friends claimed to have elevated into the atmosphere, to have walked on the moon, to have copulated with teenage girls we knew and beautiful older women we didn't, to have memorized the combinations of bank vaults. A couple of them were mocking the exercise; others were liars, hoping to impress us with a boast no one could disprove. But Sean, Tom, and I were genuinely frustrated.

One Friday afternoon after school, after hot knifing half a vial of Afghani black hash oil in our furnace room with my little blowtorch and a butter knife (you wrap the handle in black electrical or gray hockey tape so you can hold it), the three of us decided to have an impromptu session without any of the ritual of the incense or stretches. I fast-forwarded the tape to the good part, the bottle, played it three or four times for them, and then lay down and played the tape from the beginning. Before we were through the liquid running into our heads, all three of us were standing up looking at one another. Then we saw that only Tom had his feet on the floor. We started laughing—we were very stoned—and as we laughed Tom rose into the air, too, and then all three of us laughed our way through the ceiling and the kitchen and the second floor and a bed and a television set in my parents' bedroom (that was Sean) and then through their ceiling and the pink fiberglass insulation of our attic and through the cedar-shake roof and out into the long, wide, late-afternoon Calgary sky. There were the Rocky Mountains. I thought we should hold hands, but that is not a thing teenage boys can do, even under those circumstances. Then, without warning, the sky turned black; there was a howling noise, a howling that was also a kind of spinning, as if thousands of aircraft were flying immediately overhead, and we all sat up in our bodies.

"Did you see that? Did that actually happen?" Tom asked.

"That was fucking real," Sean said. "We did it."

I was quiet. I did not tell them—I had never told anyone, including my dad—about the creature I saw that night when I was ten years old and had my second out-of-body experience. This time, just after the horizon grayed and then vacuumed out, I saw its face again, as large as the sky itself, though I could never try to describe it. It was the face of something that had always been dead. It appeared to grin.

Nevertheless, I was willing to continue trying. We had perhaps forty sessions with our hash oil, and we also tried acid, and pot, and mushrooms from British Columbia, and once some belladonna Tom had bought from a street hippie that made us violently sick for three days—all without success. Tom and Sean slowly convinced themselves that it had been a one-time hashish hallucination. I tried to show them the Persian literature on soul traveling, which was often accomplished through the smoking of kief, but they had lost interest.

"Even if it was real," Tom said, "it's like lucid dreaming." We had been reading the research coming out of Stanford about dream control, and we had both become expert at it. "It's fun, but you can't *do* anything. Have you ever heard of someone getting rich off astral projection? Except maybe by selling a book about it?"

Then we discovered nitrous oxide.

Sean went to the Calgary Public Library to research astral projection in old newspapers and learned how the early American pioneers of the science had made their discoveries. They were all dentists, pumping up on laughing gas in their garages. While their wives slept innocently in their California kings, their husbands traveled the universe, having intergalactic sex (or plain old ordinary dream sex with the hot wife next door—your astral body can enter other people's dreams and play with them).

Turns out, with a pint or two of nitrous oxide in your lungs, you can astrally project anytime you like. I went to work as a high school intern for a local dentist and began buying it on the sly from his supplier. We'd sit huddled in my closet, passing around the mask, the tank hidden in my golf bag at our feet, and after ten minutes or so of deep breathing, we were out. When using nitrous to astrally project, the body does not have a golden cord—the literature is full of warnings about the dangers of using drugs to astrally project—but it dissolved my fear, and our adventures truly began. On a planet called Vitrine we met people who live forever, and do not reproduce. We discovered that C. S. Lewis had told the truth about the wood between the worlds, where you are tempted to sleep all through your days and you use pools to travel between parallel planes of existence.

But the black thing was following us. I still hadn't mentioned it to Tom or Sean, because I hoped it was my own mental creation. When you are out of body, the world is more fluid and inviting than the material universe; you don't need your fingers to get everything done; the imagination operates more directly—you can see it, at times, like a rainbow pouring forth from your head. However, I knew I was lying to myself. I understood it was not going away.

It got Sean. We were returning from a lesson in bilocation given by an ancient Himalayan mystic named Babaji—we were viewed with suspicion and had to stay at the margins of the seated crowd because we had the stink of the drug on us—when I sensed it was behind us. I turned, and it was a sparrow, a sparrow as white as silk, and with one bite it swallowed Sean. Back in my closet, he was silent and sleepy-eyed. He left my basement bedroom and from then on he avoided us at high school. We never spoke to him again, except a "Hi" in the hallways. Four years later he died in a freak skiing accident.

After Sean turned strange, Tom flipped. "I'm not playing this game anymore, man," he said. He came from a very stable family and had the natural, healthy cautiousness that most kids with normal parents have. "I don't know what that bird was. But I think you do." When you frequently astrally project with someone, you begin to sense the other person's thoughts. "That was like the rhinoceros in *James and the Giant Peach*."

Now that I was on my own, I decided to go deeper than we as a group had dared attempt. I planned to breathe a whole tank. Halfway down, I entered the hole where the black thing lived. On the path, I passed many familiar people I knew were dead; they pushed me back with their hands. I could hear the thing growling below my feet. When the tank of nitrous was empty, I thought I heard my father's voice arguing with someone. He warned that I wasn't ready. But that made me only more determined. Then I saw it in the window. We looked each other in the eye. I felt something snapping at my belly. It didn't hurt, exactly; it was like someone snapping his fingers. What seemed long after, years later, though in fact I was unconscious only two days, I awoke in the hospital. I learned there was damage to my spine and to certain portions of my amygdala. The doctor leaned over my bedside and explained that there was no bruising, but from the X-rays it looked as if I had been beaten with a baseball bat or taken a terrible fall. "And your blood had more nitrous in it than a bag of circus balloons," he said. "What's the last thing you remember, Clancy?" I asked him, "How much do you know about the science of astral projection?"

Donna Hunt

DIMENSION 5

In this dimension you
are not in love with me
anymore. I wish it were
another. In infinite
dimensions you are not
in love with me. Those donnas
handle it better. Other donnas accept
the cycles of relationships.
Some donnas dye their hair, finally
learn guitar. Another
donna travels, basks
on a rock, burns it out.
Some donnas sleep
it off. Take two
in the morning. Several
other donnas are already
dating that other guy. He's tall.
Many donnas catharsis,
bake, shop, redecorate.
Three donnas bash you
over drinks, and then call
your mother. It's better than this. donna, in this
world, is thrown. Has forgotten
her address. No longer recognizes her own handwriting.

DIMENSION 0

Before we begin. The theory is based on a theory. A point.
The geometric mind knows the point. The dot. Impossible.
But. Before we can move, we must start. To start, to have
a beginning. The point. Element that has position but no extension
and is defined by coordinates. X and Y. A. Be. Adjust yourself in time
and space. Be a dot, a speck, the head of a pin. Smaller. A cell. The nucleus.
Smaller. The eye of God.

The beginning. Point A.
The size of a moment. An end stop. A breath. Space left
behind a grasshopper's leap. Tail of the question mark.
Death of the declarative sentence. Definition of the lowercase i.
What is the point? Get the point? Missed the joke. Sailed around it. One
of thirty-two directions. One seventy-second of a centimeter.
Vanishing. Isolated. Distinct.

I'm getting to it.
One on the horizon. Inhale becomes exhale. Aerobic becomes anaerobic.
Caterpillar earns its wings. Atoms become a bomb. Fahrenheit meets
Celsius. Lashes begin to glance downward. At an infinitesimal,
indefinable moment. A point. The point.

READABLE FEAST

THE FLAVOR OF BLUE

Deborah Blum

The dye has been cast

The Ig Nobel Prize is an award dedicated to science at its most lunatic. Founded in 1991 to honor findings "that cannot, or should not, be reproduced," the award has recognized recipients whose work ranges from the discovery that we would slip less on ice if we wore socks on the outsides of our shoes to exploring the question of whether it's better to be hit over the head with a full beer bottle or an empty one.

If you're wondering, the fully loaded bottle does more damage.

The Ig Nobel rejoices in such apparent scientific silliness. In its first year, the chemistry award went to a French scientist working on a theory that water is an intelligent liquid. Comparatively, the second chemistry award might strike you as a little tame. It went to a new advance in food coloring.

Or, to be more precise, it honored the research that brought blue Jell-O into American life. That was twenty years ago, of course, when the prevailing belief was that blue food was so unnatural as to be unmarketable, The judges found the successful introduction of bright blue, celestial blue, no-real-food-on-earth-looks-like-this food to be irresistible. Since then, we've consumed blue Jell-O, blue Skittles, blue M&M's, Blue Moon ice cream, and baby-blue cotton candy until they've become routine, just part of the junk-food scenery. Who today looks twice at a child smiling a candy-blue smile?

As I pondered this shift I started to wonder whether there is something about our current culture that demands extra brilliancy in the diet. Have we become so jaded that the standard shades of nature aren't enough for us? What does it say about us that we need to pack everything from school lunches to dinner plates with a Crayola-box selection of food (or foodlike substances)?

It turns out, the practice of coloring food is nothing new. Archeologists report evidence of it dating back as far as 1500 BCE. Research suggests that it began as a luxury. Homer's 800 BCE masterpiece, *The Iliad*, touches on saffron's ability to impart a golden tone to foods. By 400 BCE, if we are to believe Pliny the Elder, the rose tones of red wine were being deepened with added dyes.

By medieval times, food glowing with color had become a mark of status; only the rich could afford the dazzle of saffron yellow, turmeric orange, and beet pink. Perhaps from that association with social status,

> By medieval times, food glowing with color had become a mark of status.

there logically followed a Renaissance belief that brightly hued foods possessed other values, such as extra nutritional worth. Some believed that the gold of saffron represented solar power transferred to the eater. Others that the velvety red of wine promised those who could afford it a colorful energy boost, enriching the red blood circulating in the body.

This isn't quite as "keep up with the Renaissance Joneses" as you might first think. Color is a reasonable indicator of healthy food chemistry. Consider the natural history of garden produce: fresh peas or beans or lettuces sing with color, flaunt the bright new-leaf look of spring. As they age (a polite word for the onset of decay), they darken to murkier shades. Browns and grays creep over the green. We see the same process in meat as it decays from fresh-blood crimson to the bluish gray color of decomposing blood cells. Over the years, we've learned that good color indicates good food.

Not surprisingly, food processors and packagers, bakers and butchers also recognized the implications of such associations—and they did so with impressive commercial speed. Pliny the Elder wasn't extolling dyed wine; he was deploring the merchant practice of concealing watered-down products with a boost of artificial color. By the nineteenth century, the custom of improving on the color of food left almost nothing untouched; bread and butter, peas and pickles—all were brightened by chemical additives.

Peas make an excellent case in historical point. Today, we're accustomed to the color difference between the emerald look of frozen peas and the more olive gray tones of canned peas. A couple of centuries back—long before the era of frozen vegetables—the only option for preserving peas was to can them to a near-industrial gray. But manufacturers had learned that if you stirred a little copper sulfate into the mix, the chemical result returns the peas to a springlike glory. Fancy French peas, in particular, tended to be so loaded with copper that they achieved a jewel tone.

They also occasionally killed people, as pioneering consumer advocate Frederick Accum noted in his 1820 book of outrage, *Death in the Pot*. But in the glory days of nonregulation, before governments took on the role of public-health advocacy, copper sulfate was the least of colored-food risks. The poison arsenic turned treats from candy to cake decorations a festive green. Red candies often gained their crimson hue from the heavy metals lead and mercury. Mostly, these were trace amounts, but in her book, *Swindled: The Dark History of Food Fraud, from Poisoned Candy to Counterfeit Coffee*, the British author Bee Wilson recounts an 1847 outbreak of illness due to poisoned candy in London that sent three adults and eight children to the hospital.

By that time, some countries, such as France, were regulating food coloring—insisting that only vegetable dyes be used. But in England and in the United States, butchers and bakers and candy makers could put what they wanted into what people ate. An 1880 survey of candy sold in Boston found that forty-six percent of the samples contained at least one poisonous pigment. Wilson quotes a frustrated Victorian newspaper letter writer: "In England, the centre of civilization as we are so fond of calling it—poison is openly vended in the streets, shop-windows are filled with it."

Fortunately, this laissez-faire attitude toward toxic food coloring started disappearing in both England and the United States in the late nineteenth century. The official turning point in the United States was the passage of the 1906 Pure Food and Drug Act, which laid down rules for basic food safety. It also created the forerunner of today's Food and Drug Administration, a small department called the Bureau of Chemistry, tucked into the U.S. Department of Agriculture.

The bureau's director was a fanatical crusader of a chemist named Harvey Washington Wiley. I love reading about Wiley's zealous campaigns, his imperial disdain for all things altered. He thought flour was too artificially white and that bleaching it was unhealthy and he sued over the process. He moved to strike copper sulfate and other toxic compounds from canned produce. And he generated one of my favorite lawsuits—*United States v. 1,950 Boxes of Macaroni*—in which he first confiscated said boxes of macaroni and then demanded the right to destroy them because the pasta was colored by a dye called Martius yellow.

The macaroni maker, V. Viviano & Brothers, took the position that no one wants to buy pasta that is gray white, the natural color of the wheat product. Consumers expect their macaroni to be a friendly golden shade. Yes, Martius yellow (derived from coal tar) is poisonous. But this was a long-standing practice, after all, and a little poison—so the defense lawyers argued—never hurt anyone.

The U.S. district judge in charge of the case—Kenesaw Mountain Landis (who would later become the first commissioner of baseball)—wrote a 1910 decision that still stands as a model of commonsense judicial thinking:

> *The proof shows macaroni to be composed of wheat and water; that to change its natural color, and make its appearance more inviting, Martius yellow was added; that this coloring matter is not an ingredient of macaroni and serves no purpose other than to change its color, and is a poison which will kill. It is the duty of the court to give the [1906] act a fair and reasonable construction for the accomplishment of its object. That object is the exclusion from interstate commerce of food products so adulterated as to endanger health. And where, as here, it clearly appears that a poisonous substance wholly foreign to the food product has been added to it solely to mislead and deceive, the court is under no duty to endeavor to protect the offender against loss from destruction of the adulterated article by indulging in hair-splitting speculation as to whether the amount of poison used may possibly have been so nicely calculated as not to kill or be of immediate serious injury.*

The boxes, in other words, were history. And so was the comfortable assumption by food manufacturers that the government remained indifferent to the idea of poisoning consumers, even if it made food more attractive. Today, the FDA maintains a strict list of approved food colorings that details some thirty-six straight (as opposed to combined, a different list) coloring agents ranging from the natural—yes, saffron is still on the list—to the synthetic.

The list is shorter than it was in the early twentieth century because a few of the dyes initially approved turned out to be more toxic than first realized. In the 1950s, for instance, the FDA delisted Orange Dye No. 1 after it was linked to a cluster of illnesses in children who'd eaten too much candy corn and pumpkin-colored popcorn after Halloween. Red Dye No. 2 fell off in 1976 after tests showed it to be a suspected carcinogen. The remaining list continues to be regarded with suspicion by consumer advocates. In the spring of 2011, such concerns led the FDA to hold formal hearings over whether colorants might contribute to ADHD in children. The regulators were not swayed by what they saw as thin evidence, but the governmental acceptance didn't sway the critics or put an end to the ongoing question of whether coloring food is worth the chemical cost.

But safety isn't the only ethical question that arises once we start rearranging nature's palette. We've become used to colored food. We like a golden-tinted macaroni, and some pastas (as I discovered by checking my own pantry) still include yellow dyes in the ingredients. Coloring pasta is about improving the look of a natural product. But what if we decide to color an artificial product so that it resembles a natural one? Does that take us to another level of food dishonesty? That was certainly the charge brought by the dairy industry against 19th century manufacturers of margarine when they sought to dye their product to a buttery yellow.

In fact, butter itself is traditionally tinted for a richer look. It tends naturally to a blandly creamy color and the version we know best is often juiced up with a little yellow food coloring. When margarine was introduced in the late 1800s, its manufacturers wanted to give it that dairy-gold look as well. They suspected, correctly, that most people weren't going to find a block of plain white fat appealing.

Dairy farmers also suspected uncolored margarine wouldn't appeal, and they wanted to keep it that way. For years, they successfully pressured their home states to outlaw any attempt to make margarine resemble butter. In my own state of Wisconsin ("America's Dairyland"), the official ban on colored margarine remained in place until 1967. By that time, residents were smuggling in nearly two thousand pounds of butter-mimicking margarine from Illinois—a fact that persuaded the legislature that the fight was both long lost and expensive.

Still, the even more interesting color issue—to me, anyway—that came out of the margarine wars occurred when New Hampshire passed an 1891 law that required manufacturers to dye margarine pink. When the rule was struck down in 1898, the state court called it an unfair business practice, because the idea of spreading rose-tinted fat on one's bread "naturally excites a prejudice and strengthens a repugnance up to the point of a positive and absolute refusal to purchase the article at any price." In other words, food colors must be "right" to be attractive. Margarine must be gloriously golden for us to enjoy it.

> Red Dye No. 2 fell off in 1976 after when tests showed it to be a suspected carcinogen.

Parkay did once try selling pink and electric blue versions of margarine. You'll notice that these are no longer on the shelves. Nor will you find Ore-Ida's attempt at "Kool Blue Funky Fries" still in grocery freezers. We like our fries to be crispy gold, thank you, not burnt blue. And that brings me back to the subject of blue food and its cultural implications.

Blue dining requires a certain attitude. Partly, researchers say, this is because there are no examples of natural bright-blue goodness when it comes to food. The vaunted blueberry is more of a dusk purple; blue potatoes are an even deeper purple; blue corn shades to gray; and lobsters may be bluish gray in the wild, but when people cook them, the shells turn reassuringly red. Surveys conducted by food companies have found, in fact, that American

The Flavor of Blue

eaters associate blue with bruised fruit and bad meat. Other studies have shown that the color blue can actually suppress appetite; diet gurus recommend dining on blue plates.

The question is not whether we can tint food blue but why we would want to. And it was this point that caught the attention of the Ig Nobel judges twenty years ago—this sense that we had broken with tradition and willingly crossed the food-color barrier. It wasn't just that Jell-O food chemists had turned gelatin the color of Superman's cape; it was that people were eating it. And the makers of Jell-O knew this was worth celebrating too; they sent their "blue" chemist, Ivette Bassa, to the award ceremony on a corporate jet, surrounded her with a team of fellow chemists wearing blue lab coats, and made sure that all at the ceremony had a chance to enjoy—or at least admire—a sapphire spoonful or two of their product.

Today, with blue desserts the stuff of routine, the Ig Nobel chemistry award has moved on to subjects such as the creation of diamonds from tequila or whether vanilla can be extracted from cow dung. We still try to improve on nature though, despite our color doubts and chemical angst. And one day, I'll predict, our centuries' old affection for brightening up the plate will find us dining on teal-tone beef and summer sky tomatoes. I'll make this prediction as well: there will be no second Ig Nobel for that moment. We'll sit down to our cerulean salads and no one will mention it—or even bother to write about it.

RECIPE

The Star-Spangled Jell-O Shot

The folks at the Web site www.myscience-project.org have devoted considerable energies to a range of vexing scientific questions, including a Dick Cheney–inspired investigation of what it might be like to be shot in the face with a 28-gauge shotgun, as well as myriad Jell-O based inquiries. While they at first concluded that no decent Jell-O shot could be made with Berry Blue Jell-O, reader response said otherwise. Here, then, is their most elaborate, and patriotic, blue recipe.
http://www.myscienceproject.org/j-shot-4.html

1 three-ounce package Raspberry Jell-O
1 cup boiling water
1 cup raspberry schnapps
Cool Whip
1 three-ounce package Berry Blue Jell-O
1 cup boiling water
3/4 cup blue curaçao
1/4 cup water or vodka
Marshmallows, mini or large, cut into pieces

DIRECTIONS

Dissolve Raspberry Jell-O in one cup boiling water. Let cool to room temperature and add one cup raspberry schnapps. Pour into portion cups, filling only the bottom third. Chill in refrigerator a few hours or till firm.

After the Jell-O layer has set completely, add a layer of Cool Whip, so the portion cup is two-thirds filled. Level this layer as much as possible so you won't have peaks sticking through the next layer. Return Jell-O cups to refrigerator.

Dissolve Berry Blue Jell-O in one cup boiling water. Let cool to room temperature and add 3/4 cup blue curaçao and 1/4 cup water or vodka. Pour mixture over Cool Whip layer to fill the portion cups. Return cups to refrigerator to chill for about thirty minutes, or until the surface of the Jell-O is firm but still tacky.

Decorate tops with marshmallows. Return to refrigerator and chill one hour or more before serving.

CONTRIBUTORS

Andrea Barrett is the author of six novels, most recently *The Air We Breathe*, and two collections of short fiction, *Ship Fever*, which received the National Book Award, and *Servants of the Map*, a finalist for the Pulitzer Prize. She lives in western Massachusetts and teaches at Williams College.

Gabriel Blackwell is the author of *Critique of Pure Reason* (Noemi Press, 2012), a collection of essays and fictions. He is the reviews editor of the *Collagist*.

Deborah Blum is a Pulitzer Prize–winning science writer and the author of five books, most recently *The Poisoner's Handbook: Murder and the Birth of Forensic Medicine in Jazz Age New York*. She teaches writing at the University of Wisconsin-Madison, where she is the Helen Firstbrook Franklin Professor of Journalism.

Katy Chrisler is from Austin, Texas, and is a current MFA candidate at the Iowa Writers' Workshop in poetry and a certificate student in book arts at the UI Center for the Book. She works with the Iowa Youth Writing Project and with Arts Share, teaching poetry and creative writing to school-aged children and teens in the Iowa City area.

Rebecca Newberger Goldstein is a novelist and a philosopher. She is the author of nine books, seven of them fiction, including *The Mind-Body Problem*. Her two nonfiction books are *Incompleteness: The Proof and Paradox of Kurt Gödel*, which was chosen by *Discover Magazine* as one of the best science books of 2005, and the award-winning *Betraying Spinoza: The Renegade Jew Who Gave Us Modernity*. She is also the recipient of a MacArthur "Genius" Award and was named Humanist of the Year 2011 by the American Humanist Association. Her latest book is *36 Arguments for the Existence of God: A Work of Fiction*.

Jessica Handler's first book, *Invisible Sisters: A Memoir*, was named by the Georgia Center for the Book as one of the 2010 "Books All Georgians Should Read." Her nonfiction has appeared widely, including on NPR (WABE FM), in *Tin House*, Brevitymag.com, *Newsweek*, the *Washington Post*, *More* magazine, *Southern Arts Journal*, and *Ars Medica*. She is writing a novel that imagines the backstage life of Lulu Hurst, the "Georgia Wonder."

Jared Harel lives in Astoria, New York. His poems have appeared in the *Gettysburg Review*, *Quarterly West*, the *Fiddlehead*, and elsewhere. He teaches creative writing at Centenary College and plays drums for the NYC-based rock band the Dust Engineers.

Donna Hunt's chapbook, *The Coastline of Antarctica*, was recently published by Finishing Line Press. Her poems have appeared in *DIAGRAM* and the *Cleveland Review*, among other journals and anthologies. She is currently teaching at CUNY.

Karl Iagnemma is a fiction writer and robotics engineer. He is author of the story collection *On the Nature of Human Romantic Interaction* and the novel *The Expeditions*. His fiction has received numerous awards, including the *Paris Review*'s Plimpton Prize and first place in the *Playboy* college fiction contest. His writing has been anthologized in *The Best American Short Stories*, *The Best American Erotica*, and *The Pushcart Prize* collections. He also directs the Robotic Mobility Group at MIT, where he develops robots that climb, crawl, roll, and fly. He has published nearly one hundred technical papers on various subjects related to robotics.

Jessica Johnson, a former biology student, nurtures an abiding interest in bodies and creatures. Her poems have appeared in the *Paris Review*, the *New Republic*, *Prairie Schooner*, and *Subtropics*, among other journals. Her first piece of creative nonfiction was recently published in *Harvard Review*. In 2009, she was the recipient of an Oregon Literary Fellowship. She teaches at Portland Community College.

Etgar Keret is the author of six bestselling story collections. His writing has been published in *Harper's Magazine*, the *New York Times*, the *Paris Review*, and *Zoetrope*. *Jellyfish*, his first movie as a director along with his wife, Shira Geffen, won the Camera d'Or for best first feature at Cannes in 2007. *Suddenly, a Knock on the Door* will be published by Farrar, Straus & Giroux in April.

Cheston Knapp is managing editor of *Tin House*. He lives with his wife in Portland, Oregon, where they tend their Mendelian marvel, a labradoodle.

Alexandra Kleeman's fiction has appeared in the *Paris Review*, *Conjunctions*, *Zoetrope*, and *DIAGRAM*. She lives in Brooklyn, where she is at work on a short story collection and a novel about snack foods.

Amy Leach is a recipient of a 2010 Whiting Writers' Award, and her book of essays is forthcoming from Milkweed Editions. She lives in Chicago.

Michelle Legro is an associate editor at *Lapham's Quarterly*. Her work has appeared in the *Second Pass*, the *Rumpus*, the *Atlantic Technology Channel*, and the *Times Literary Supplement*.

Megan Levad's poems have appeared in *Granta Online*, *textsound*, and *Spinning Jenny*, and are forthcoming in *Fence*. She also writes text for composer Tucker Fuller and reviews poetry for *Boston Review*. She lives in Ann Arbor, where she runs the visiting writers series for the University of Michigan.

Jesse Lichtenstein is a journalist, poet, and screenwriter in Portland, Oregon. His writing has appeared in the *New York Times Magazine*, the *New Yorker*, *Wired*, *Slate*, the *Paris Review*, and *n+1*.

Alan Lightman is a novelist, essayist, and physicist, with a PhD in theoretical physics. He has served on the faculties of Harvard University and MIT and was the first person to receive dual faculty appointments at MIT in science and the humanities. His literary work has appeared in the *New York Times*, the *Atlantic*, the *New Yorker*, and other publications. His novel *Einstein's Dreams* was an international best-seller and has been translated into thirty languages. His novel *The Diagnosis* was a finalist for the National Book Award in fiction. His new novel, *Mr g*, was published in January. Lightman is also the founding director of the Harpswell Foundation, which works to empower women leaders in Cambodia.

Patricia Lockwood's first book, *Balloon Pop Outlaw Black*, is forthcoming from Octopus Books this summer. Her poems have appeared or will soon appear in *Poetry*, *Denver Quarterly*, the *New Yorker*, and *Fence*.

Clancy Martin is professor of philosophy at the University of Missouri-Kansas City. His work has appeared in the *New York Times*, *NOON*, *Esquire*, *London Review of Books*, the *Paris Review Daily*, the *Times Literary Supplement*, the *Wall Street Journal*, *VICE*, and *Harper's Magazine*, where he is a contributing editor. His debut novel, *How to Sell* (FSG, 2009), was a Times Literary Supplement Best Book of the Year. He has translated Kierkegaard and Nietzsche, and is a 2011–12 Guggenheim fellow.

Justin Nobel covers science and culture for magazines and pens a blog about death for the funeral industry called *Digital Dying*, and another blog, *The Absurd Adventurer*, in which he sits for hours in one New York City spot. He lives in Blissville, a sliver of forgotten New York.

Tony Perez is an editor with Tin House Books in Portland, Oregon. He likes space, magnets, and dinosaurs.

Kiki Petrosino is the author of *Fort Red Border* (Sarabande, 2009) and the coeditor of *Transom*, an online poetry journal. Her poems have appeared in *FENCE*; the *New York Times*; *Gulf Coast*; *Forklift, Ohio*; and elsewhere. Petrosino teaches creative writing at the University of Louisville.

Rachel Riederer is a member of the science-writing collective *NeuWrite*. She has taught academic writing at Columbia University and is currently a writing tutor at Baruch College in New York. Her work has appeared in the *Nation*, *Science*, the *Missouri Review*, the *Rumpus*, and *The Best American Essays*. You can see more of her work at www.rachelriederer.com.

Namwali Serpell's writing has appeared in *Callaloo*, *The Best American Short Stories 2009*, *The Caine Prize for African Writing 2010*, and the *Believer*. She received a 2011 Rona Jaffe Foundation Writers' Award. She teaches at Berkeley and lives in San Francisco. "Bottoms Up" owes its title to a reading organized by San Francisco's 2010 Litquake Festival.

Dara Wier's *Selected Poems* is recently out from Wave Books. A new chapbook, *A Civilian's Journal of the War Years*, is just out from The Song Cave. She lives and works in western Massachusetts, at the University of Massachusetts' MFA program; at Flying Object Center for Independent Publishing, Art, & the Book; and for Factory Hollow Press.

PAGE 99: Illustration from *Daphne* by Alfred de Vigny, 1924 (color litho) by Francois-Louis Schmied (1873-1941). Private Collection / Photo © Christie's Images / The Bridgeman Art Library

PAGE 167: *Instruments of Human Sustenance: The Culinary Art*, 1569 (etching) by Giovanni Francesco Camocio (fl. 1558-75) (after). The Israel Museum, Jerusalem, Israel / Vera & Arturo Schwarz Collection of Dada and Surrealist Art / The Bridgeman Art Library.

COVER CREDIT: Original art for *Science and Invention*, formerly *Electrical Experimenter*, December 1921 Cover, Howard V. Brown.

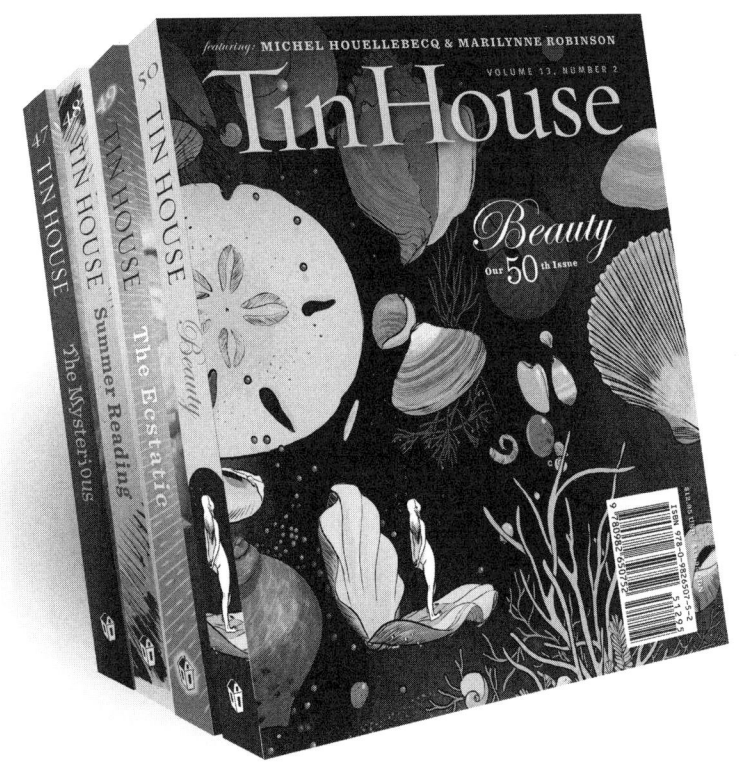

The Coffin Factory

The magazine for people who love books.

Issue One

José Saramago
Milan Kundera
Roberto Bolaño
Bonnie Nadzam
Joyce Carol Oates

Issue Two

César Aira
Lydia Davis
Justin Taylor
Aimee Bender
Edwidge Danticat

fiction ◆ essay ◆ art ◆ interview

thecoffinfactory.com

MFA in Creative Writing, Publishing, and Editing at Sam Houston State University

Steeped in tradition and Texas hospitality, Sam Houston State University offers the type of educational experience most often found at private institutions. An MFA in creative writing is an opportunity to expand your understanding of the art and craft of writing, to deepen your relationship to the writers and the literature that have come before you, and to find your own place in the world of writers and writing. Above all else, an MFA in creative writing is time spent in a community of writers; it is a space where, for a few brief years in your life, you can live, write, read, and study within that community. An MFA is a commitment—to yourself and to your work.

- Internships with Texas Review Press, a member of the Texas A&M University Press Consortium.
- Competitive graduate assistantships and departmental scholarships available.
- Renowned and nationally recognized core faculty. Paul Ruffin is the author of two novels, four collections of short fiction, four books of essays, and seven collections of poetry and was named the 2009 Texas State Poet Laureate. Melissa Morphew has received the Randall Jarrell International Poetry Prize and the W.B. Yeates Society Poetry Award and published four full-length collections of poetry. Her poems have appeared in the Georgia Review, Shenandoah, and Prairie Schooner. Scott Kaukonen won the Ohio State University Prize for Short Fiction for his debut collection, and is a past recipient of a National Endowment for the Arts fellowship.

Dr. Scott Kaukonen, Director   936-294-1407   cwmfa@shsu.edu   www.shsu.edu/graduate

Sam Houston State University/A member of the Texas State University System

"The uncanny has met its ideal delivery system: the stories of Diane Williams." —BEN MARCUS

VICKY SWANKY IS A BEAUTY

A new collection from
Diane Williams

"These stories are the Giacometti walking man, the Cornell box, that extraordinary object born out of a genius for expressing the inner murmur of the mind. Each page is like throwing open the window in an electrical storm—strange sky, air full of voltage, and inside, a square of brave. Diane Williams is hilarious, brilliant, eccentric, powerful, and, luckily, *ours*." —DEB OLIN UNFERTH

Now available in bookstores, or at *store.mcsweeneys.net*

TEXAS STATE UNIVERSITY SAN MARCOS
The rising STAR of Texas

MFA

FINE ARTS
with a major in
CREATIVE WRITING
and specializations in
FICTION OR POETRY

We now offer classes in creative nonfiction

In the Texas Hill Country between Austin and San Antonio

THE ENDOWED CHAIR IN CREATIVE WRITING
2011-2012 Tim O'Brien | 2012-2014 Cristina Garcia

FACULTY

Cyrus Cassells, Poetry
Doug Dorst, Fiction
Tom Grimes, Fiction
Ogaga Ifowodo, Poetry

Roger Jones, Poetry
Debra Monroe, Fiction
Tim O'Brein, Fiction
Kathleen Peirce, Poetry

Nelly Rosario, Fiction
Steve Wilson, Poetry

ADJUNCT THESIS FACULTY

Lee K. Abbott
Rick Bass
Ron Carlson
Charles D'Ambrosio
Rick DeMarinis
John Dufresne
Carolyn Forché
James Galvin
Shelby Hearon
Bret Anthony Johnson
Hettie Jones

Patricia Spears Jones
Li-Young Lee
Philip Levine
Carole Maso
Elizabeth McCracken
Heather McHugh
Jane Mead
W.S. Merwin
David Mura
Naomi Shihab Nye
Jayne Anne Phillips

Alberto Ríos
Pattiann Rogers
Nicholas Samaras
Debra Spark
Gerald Stern
Rosmarie Waldrop
Sharon Oard Warner
Kate Wheeler
Terry Tempest Williams
Eleanor Wilner
Mark Wunderlich

RECENT VISITING WRITERS

Aimee Bender
Louise Erdrich
Nick Flynn
Richard Ford
Mary Gaitskill
Tony Hoagland

Yiyun Li
Thomas Lux
Jayne Anne Phillips
Annie Proulx
Francine Prose
Claudia Rankine

George Saunders
Richard Siken
Charles Simic
Robert Stone
Wells Tower
C. D. Wright

Visit Front Porch, our literary journal
www.frontporchjournal.com
$30,000 Morgan & Lou Claire Rose Fellowship for an incoming writing student
Additional scholarships and teaching assistantships available

Tom Grimes, MFA Director
Department of English
Texas State University
601 University Drive
San Marcos, TX 78666-4616

Phone **512.245.7681**
Fax 512.245.8546
www.mfatxstate.com
mfinearts@txstate.edu

AVAILABLE NOW

Stories Wanting Only to Be Heard
Selected Fiction from Six Decades of *The Georgia Review*

University of Georgia Press

$24.95

"... an anthology of twenty-eight stories that must be read, from the backcountry blues of Jesse Stuart and Harry Crews to the intellectual sophistication of Fred Pfeil and Fred Chappell, from Pam Durban's terrific "This Heat" to Donald Hall's blistering "The World Is a Bed," from Jim Heynen's charming "Stories about the Boys" to Jack Driscoll's devastating story about a boy named Judge. In my experience, no other literary publication could shape an anthology as wide in its range of subjects or as varied in its modes of telling. This is not only an excellent anthology but an exciting one."

—Kelly Cherry, author of
We Can Still Be Friends: A Novel

"Lovers of short fiction, rejoice: this is a volume to be celebrated. In an array of styles, these stories speak urgently—often with wit, sometimes tragically—about the turns our lives take, the unexpected heartbreak, the astonishing triumph."

—Erin McGraw, author of
The Good Life: Stories

"When a journal can bring together work originally published in its pages by authors as diverse as Mary Hood and Harry Crews, Pam Durban and T. C. Boyle, Jesse Stuart and Ernest J. Gaines, John Edgar Wideman and Jack Driscoll, we readers out here are blessed beyond measure. This is a worthy book. Period."

—Bret Lott, author of
Ancient Highway

For more information go to **ugapress.org** and search "stories"

thegeorgiareview.com • 800.542.3481

Missed the First Fifty Issues?
Fear not.
We've hidden a limited number in our closet.

Premiere Issue: David Foster Wallace, Ron Carlson, Stuart Dybek, Charles Simic, C. K. Williams, Rick Moody.

Issue 2: Yasunari Kawabata, Faiz Ahmed Faiz, Walter Kirn, David Gates, Jean Nathan.

Issue 3: Amy Hempel, Yehuda Amichai; interviews with John Sanford, Dawn Powell.

Issue 4: Aleksandar Hemon, Derek Walcott, Daniel Halpern, Stéphane Mallarmé; Sherman Alexie interview.

Issue 5: Kevin Canty, Nancy Reisman, Bei Dao, Donald Hall, Jane Hirshfield, Sylvia Plath, Ann Hood; Ha Jin interview.

Issue 6: The Film Issue, starring Russell Banks, Todd Haynes, Bruce Wagner, Barney Rosset, Jerry Stahl, Jonathan Lethem, Rachel Resnick.

Issue 7: SOLD OUT

Issue 8: Elizabeth Tallent, Paul West, Jennifer Egan, Jerry Stahl, Josip Novakovich, Billy Collins; Barney Rosset interview.

Issue 9: Richard Ford, Mary Gaitskill, Jim Shepard, Czeslaw Milosz, David Shields, Mark Doty, Nick Flynn.

Issue 10: The Music Issue, with Jonathan Lethem, Francine Prose, Rick Moody, C. K. Williams.

Issue 11: SOLD OUT

Issue 12: Jo Ann Beard, Lynn Freed, Andre Dubus III, Diane Ackerman, Charlie Smith; Ron Carlson interview.

Issue 13: Dorothy Allison, Richard Powers, Olena Kalytiak Davis, Helen Schulman; Francine Prose interview.

Issue 14: SOLD OUT

Issue 15: The Sex Issue, featuring Francine Prose, Denis Johnson, Mario Vargas Llosa, Charles Simic, and a bunch of bad sex.

Issue 16: Summer Fiction, with Stuart Dybek, Joy Williams, Charles Baxter, Melanie Rae Thon, Pablo Neruda; Marilynne Robinson interview.

Issue 17: SOLD OUT

Issue 18: Julia Slavin, Dale Peck, Anthony Swofford, Inger Christensen; interviews with Paul Collins and Jim Shepard.

Issue 19: SOLD OUT

Issue 20: Robert Olen Butler, Steven Millhauser and Elizabeth Tallent; Interview with Chris Offutt

Issue 21: Stacey Richter, Amanda Eyre Ward, Seamus Heaney, Adam Zagajewski, Lucia Perillo; George Saunders interview.

Issue 22: Emerging Voices, Daniel Alarcón, Nami Mun, Jung H. Yun; James Salter interview.

Issue 23: SOLD OUT

Issue 24: SOLD OUT

Issue 25: SOLD OUT

Issue 26: All Apologies, with Casanova, Donna Tartt, Ken Kalfus, Robin Romm.

Issue 27: International, with José Saramago, Seamus Heaney, Ismail Kadare, Bei Ling, Binyavanga Wainaina, Anita Desai.

Issue 28: SOLD OUT

Issue 29: Graphic, with Lynda Barry, Marjane Satrapi, Zak Smith, Todd Haynes.

Issue 30: Milan Kundera, Anthony Doerr, Jillian Weise, Etgar Keret, Anthony Swofford; Rick Bass interview.

Issue 31: Evil, with Nick Flynn, Chris Adrian, Sam Lipsyte.

Issue 32: Rick Bass, Ann Beattie, Antonya Nelson, Elizabeth Strout.

Issue 33: SOLD OUT

Issue 34: Charles Baxter, Joshua Ferris, Yiyun Li on William Trevor; Deborah Eisenberg interview.

Issue 35: Off the Grid with Ron Carlson, Marie Howe, Charles Simic, George Makana Clark, Roberto Bolaño.

Issue 36: Allan Gurganus, Adam Johnson, Chris Adrian, Mary Jo Bang; Frank Bidart interview.

Issue 37: Politics, with Eduardo Galeano, Thomas Frank, Nick Flynn, Francine Prose, José Saramago.

Issue 38: Anne Carson, Christopher Sorrentino, Ron Hansen, Arthur Bradford, Matthew Dickman; Daniel Menaker interview.

Issue 39: Appetites, with Pasha Malla, Stephen Marion, Ann Hood, Charles Wright; Catherine Millet interview.

Issue 40: Tenth Anniversary, with Dorothy Allison, Anthony Doerr, David Foster Wallace, Jim Shepard; Colson Whitehead interview.

Issue 41: Hope / Dread, with Karen Russell, Matthea Harvey, Ander Monson; Lorrie Moore interview.

Issue 42: Ben Marcus, Antonya Nelson, Karen Shepard, Michael Dickman; Roy Blount interview.

Issue 43: Games People Play, with Tom Bissell, Jennifer Egan, Matthew Zapruder, Karen Russell, and David Mamet.

Issue 44: Per Petterson, Lydia Millet, Rawi Hage, Daniel Handler; Etgar Keret and David Shields interviews.

Issue 45: Class in America, with Lewis Hyde, Benjamin Percy, Luc Sante, Lydia Davis's *Madame Bovary*.

Issue 46: Kevin Brockmeier, Dan Chaon, Rebecca Makkai, Adrienne Rich, Eileen Myles, Paul Bowles's letters; Karen Russell interview.

Issue 47: The Mysterious, with Andrea Barrett, Natasha Trethewey, Luis Alberto Urrea, Adam Zagajewski; Peter Straub/Benjamin Percy interview.

Issue 48: Walter Mosley, Maggie Nelson, Gary Lutz, Terrance Hayes, Dorianne Laux; Ann Patchett and Jean-Philippe Toussaint interviews.

Issue 49: The Ecstatic, with Kelly Link, Meghan O'Rourke, Nikolai Grozni, Billy Collins, Matt Kish's *Moby-Dick*; Cesar Aira and Ben Okri interviews.

Issue 50: Beauty! With Marilynne Robinson, Michel Houellebecq, Kevin Young, Maggie Shipstead, Crystal Williams, Eric Puchner, and Burt Reynolds

Seventeen dollars each issue, including postage. Make checks payable to Tin House and mail to Back Issues, Tin House, P.O. Box 10500, Portland, OR 97296-0500.

Stay tuned for Summer Reading (#52) and Brooklyn/Portland (#53)
Log on to **www.tinhouse.com**

ABOUT THE COVER

Elissa Schappell

You could argue that the art of Howard V. Brown did as much to shape the American public's perceptions of the awesome power of technology and the future fate of mankind during the 1930s and through the 1950s as the stories of visionary futurists such as H. P. Lovecraft that appeared inside the scientific and technological journals. While sci-fi authors told us of our impending fate, Brown—with his images of fiendish laser-eyed robots wasting cities, flying saucers hovering over the heartland, and tentacled aliens abducting earth women in space bikinis while their male companions stood by powerless to save them—showed us in vivid detail what we could expect.

Unlike those of most of Brown's peers, who favored garish primary-color palettes and simplistic composition, Brown's alien dreamscapes were rendered in a more sophisticated, naturalistic palette that included shades of violet, foggy grays, icy greens, and soft blues, and portrayed Martian hordes viewed from the perspective of a cowering shrink-rayed populace. The most adept of the early science fiction artists when it came to painting life-forms, be they human, monster, or robot, Brown is widely regarded as the master of the "mutant" and famously credited with inventing the now ubiquitous "Bug Eyed

Monster." Outside of his work—which he rarely signed—little is known of Howard V. Brown, save that he was born in Lexington, Kentucky, served in the military, and traveled extensively in South America and the West Indies, claiming it helped him to relax. Is it possible he vanished on one of these expeditions? Devoured, perhaps, by a bloodthirsty pitcher plant? Or— and this is what I choose to believe—whisked into the heavens by friendly big-eyed aliens in a silver rocket ship?